Unintended Lies

by

Linda Kendall McLendon

<u>DEDICATION</u>

Dedicated to Catherine Dowling, who was a bright beacon against the grey fog and left her trailing imprints on my life, and to all who supported me in this endeavor. You know who you are and your important role. Now, enjoy turning the pages...

<u>PROLOGUE</u>

Roger stood at the edge of the road, staring down the ravine at the burning car. The emergency and law enforcement vehicles' lights lit up the dark night. Voices drifted up through the trees and underbrush. He pulled his hands from his coat pockets and walked over to a man dressed in black with the letters NSA on his back, illuminated by the nearby headlights. Roger tapped the man on the shoulder, leaned into his ear, and said, "I'm out of here." The man simply nodded as Roger walked the short distance to his car and drove away. No one seemed to notice.

Alone in his vehicle on the dark curving road, Roger knew no one would be any the wiser. It would appear as if James had merely misjudged his speed, missed the curve, or possibly fallen asleep at the wheel. The horrific accident would be completely believable. The body of his best friend, charred beyond recognition, would be removed from the scene. The autopsy would reveal the trauma caused by the horrendous wreck as the vehicle careened down the ravine. The searing flames would have finished him off. No one would have any questions.

Roger knew this was the only way they could stop it. He had kept himself completely disconnected from all of it, except the part about Catherine. Now that James was gone, it would make sense for him to be there for her. In fact, James had made Roger promise that if anything ever happened to him, he would look after her. I couldn't have planned this any better, Roger told himself as he drove into the night.

CHAPTER 1

Catherine DeLong stared at the small black and white photograph. Her first grade picture had been snapped at Jensen Beach Elementary. In the picture, she was five years old, almost six. It revealed children on a cold Florida day; they were dressed in jackets, sweaters, and flannel shirts. Not all of them were focused on the photographer. In fact, five weren't even looking at the camera. Catherine was standing directly in the center with her face scrunched up from the bright sunlight in her plaid jacket zipped all the way up to her throat. She was clearly separate and apart from the others—the same way she had felt her entire life, that is, until she met James. Catherine pushed the photo back into the album and placed it on the empty shelf. A tear slid silently down her cheek. There were too many memories in those old places. This box had been separated from the others and kept in her car; she had not allowed it to go into the moving van and risk being lost. Placing the lid back on, she slid the box against the wall. It would have to wait.

Her emotions vaulted from excited to scared to death, exactly the same way she had felt the day she started school so long ago. Nothing ever turned out the way she planned. She never expected to be living here completely alone. Suddenly, she had nothing to focus on but herself. She didn't have to answer the phone and no one came to the door. Maybe now, she could begin to unravel exactly what happened.

She couldn't believe she was about to begin her new life in Highberry, a small town she discovered just west of Gainesville, Florida. Nothing was familiar anywhere here and certainly not in her life right now. Peering out the kitchen window into the dim morning light, she watched the gray misty fog float across the fields and swirl around the barn. It was beginning to sink in—just what she'd done.

She thought she prepared herself for the move, expecting to feel lonely, isolated. In her old life, her days were packed with meetings, deadlines, fundraisers, parties and, of course, James. She had once thrived on that frantic pace.

Creating The Missing Link Foundation, developing its programs, and carefully selecting the staff had filled her with joy and given her life meaning. Her work there had changed a lot of lives. The Foundation kept families from falling between the cracks by networking with various organizations to link families to the services they so desperately needed. It quickly became sustainable, enabling her to leave without guilt, and giving her the assurance that it would continue as she had dreamed. Hamilton, her stepfather, had generously donated the initial ten thousand dollars she needed for start-up costs. As soon as she knew what she had to do, she transferred control of the non-profit organization to her staff. She accepted the first offer made on the apartment and immediately called a realtor in North Florida. Her actions had been startling to everyone, especially many of her closest friends. She hadn't even told her family. She made one trip to Highberry and bought the farm. She simply wasn't able to pick up the phone and dial the numbers. When she did, she knew her mother would be completely predictable in her response—Catherine could imagine the very words her mother would say. "Catherine, what were you thinking? Why? Why would you do this?" Now, everything that was left of her life was boxed up tidily waiting for her to figure out exactly that—what to do with it.

Catherine hadn't given much thought to buying a rather large two-story house on over a hundred acres. She always wanted a farm and needed a total change, so she just did it. The first night surprised her. She had been busy all day with the moving company. All the boxes of her personal things were finally in the appropriate rooms. Her new furniture was somewhat situated, and suddenly, everyone was gone.

~~~

That first night was amazingly quiet as Catherine retrieved her cooler from the back of her car. She paused to watch the setting sun transform the entire pasture, giving it a strange pink hue. She hadn't stopped all day to eat and ended up with a throbbing headache. The cold soda can felt good as she placed it against her forehead. *"Whose idea was this anyway?"* she asked herself in an almost inaudible whisper. Her purse, retrieved from under the front seat, held some aspirin. The darkness moved in quickly and the back porch light didn't work. It made her feel a little anxious as she rushed back into the house, trying not to feel scared. The air had suddenly turned cold, sending a chill up her spine.

She was grateful for the cheese, crackers, and the nice bottle of wine she'd bought at the last minute. Late in the night, she finally headed upstairs and fell into bed. Now, her tired body was even more grateful for the master
~~~

bedroom and her wonderful new bed. The bedroom suite had a large bathroom, walk-in closet, and sitting area. She pulled a fitted sheet from a box and stretched it over the mattress, found a blanket and her pillow. She was surprised when she didn't fall right to sleep. Eventually, she closed and locked her bedroom door, curled her feather pillow around her head and drifted off.

~~~

As the days ticked off, her life began to hold a completely different rhythm. The chores were hard on her at first. She would fall into bed at night bone-tired, surprised at how quickly the muscles ceased their aching and began to form tough hard knots. Sometimes she'd catch herself in the mirror, flex her arms, and grin. She looked a lot different than in the days of sitting behind a desk. The solitude was a gift—a chance to catch her breath, turn off her thoughts, and just be. It was amazing to hear silence. In the beginning, it was a little eerie, especially the first few nights in the empty house. The only sound was the clock ticking or the whir of the refrigerator. Sometimes she felt like the lack of noise kept her awake. It seemed silly.

Catherine knew if James were still alive, this place wouldn't have happened. There would have never been a farm. Sometimes she felt as if she had betrayed him when she changed her life so drastically. She had to. She couldn't stand the apartment without him bursting through the door. She couldn't stand the city without a place to meet him in it. The last two months felt like a lifetime.

His death had been sudden, unexpected, and devastating. *The violent car crash, late at night, ended in a*
~~~

fire. That's what they had told her. *Had he fallen asleep at the wheel, or because the Pennsylvania Mountains can be tricky at night, driven off into the ravine? By the time they got to him, it was all over.* Their words kept playing over and over in her mind. Whenever thoughts of James crept in, they literally took her breath away and made her feel paralyzed. She had never, for a moment, expected to be called "a widow." When she overheard a friend referring to her that way, she pretended not to hear, but her knees nearly buckled as if she'd been stabbed in the middle of her chest and then someone twisted the knife. The wound wasn't visible, but it would never heal. She shuddered and let out a long sigh. The decision to move came quickly, without any forethought. Everything was completed before she could even turn around. It just happened.

Her heart felt heavy in her chest as she slowly poured a cup of hot water from the kettle bubbling away on the stove. The dark tea with a hint of lemon grass soothed her in the early dimness of the house. A few birds were announcing the coming of the sun as she stepped out onto the back porch. The cold damp air made her shiver as she opened the door wider. There was no need to hurry. Everything waited for her. Meanwhile, the tea was getting cold and so was she. Catherine set the cup on the porch rail and headed down the path to the barn. Today would be the first day of whatever her life was about to become.

Try as she might, her mind was never still. Financially, she didn't have a care in the world. James had seen to that through a sizeable insurance policy provided by his employer. What she found baffling were the government checks. James' best friend from college and his attorney, Roger Halvesord, told her not to worry.

"Just take the money and be grateful," he said

without elaborating.

Something about those checks nagged at her constantly. After talking with her stepfather, Hamilton Wesley Howell, she decided to stash all of that money into a special account, just to be safe. Her conversation with him made her feel like she was doing the right thing.

"I don't understand this at all, not one bit," she had told Hamilton. "If James honestly worked for Robadeaux Pharmaceutical, then why would the government be involved and sending me checks?"

"Good question," her stepfather had replied. "What did Roger say?"

"Roger said not to question it, but anything to do with the federal government worries me, Dad. I feel like I should be cautious."

She and Hamilton had spoken previously concerning his feelings about Roger. There was something overbearing about him. Hamilton told her, "I immensely distrust him. I know the man is supposedly looking out for you and James trusted him, but there's something I can't explain. Trust your gut. It wouldn't hurt to open a separate account until you figure it out. Are you sure you're okay? You would tell me if you needed anything, wouldn't you?"

"I'm doing okay, really. Better than I thought I could, but it is hard. Thank you for asking."

"I can't even imagine. Promise me you will let me help you if you need it."

"I promise. I know you are there for me. Really, I do." She respected and appreciated him so much. It gave her a sense of security knowing he was as close as a phone call. He just couldn't give her any answers. She shrugged her shoulders, telling herself to *let it go* as she headed across her yard.

Walking into the barn on a cool foggy morning was magical. Catherine slid the tall door open to soft nickers and the sweet smell of wood shavings and horses that amazed her every single morning. Four horses' faces peered at her over the stall doors.

The barn was concrete, but the upper stall walls were lined with wide planks of beautiful wood. The bottom half were protected with rubber mats to keep the horses from injuring themselves if they were kicking. The center aisle was wide enough to run a tractor through with sliding doors on either end. She loved it. The first room on the left was the tack room. The one on the right held the feed. On the outside of that room were double doors that could be opened for the feed and hay to be delivered and stacked inside. Four stalls were on each side. Two horses could be groomed at the same time in the aisle on crossties. At the very end of the barn were two wash racks with rubber mats and a drain in the middle. A plastic storage closet held all the bathing and clipping supplies. Hot water was even pumped to the tack room and the wash racks. The former owner had thought of everything.

Other than occasionally riding horses in Central Park with her friends, and recently trying out a few horses she was looking to purchase, Catherine hadn't really ridden that much. As a child growing up in Florida, she had ridden near her house in the savannahs, in either swamp or sand. They had been lucky to have a hose available to rinse the horse after a hot ride through the sugar sand, a far cry from all the amenities she had available here. But those days had been some of her childhood favorites.

Her life now was good and bad all at the same time. *Convoluted,* was the word. Things got into her mind and twisted up her thoughts, making it impossible to be happy in the simplest moments. James' memory tugged at her, making her feel guilty about even smiling. She had been careful not to bring too much of him to the farm. In fact, she had been mindful that her move didn't fall on any date associated with anything special for them. No anniversary of their engagement, no birthdays, no special events. She couldn't risk anything dragging her down, so she had meticulously packed her things. That done, she had run as hard and as fast as she could away from everything she held so dear. The last minutes in the apartment had been difficult. With everything stripped away, she had stood there looking at nothing but bare walls. She silently told herself, *It was only a home because we were in it. It's just walls. It doesn't mean anything anymore. Just go.* It was nearly impossible to get her feet to move. She wanted to blink and have everything back where it belonged.

She had been ruthless in a way, donating almost everything—all the paintings they'd so carefully collected, all their furniture, even their bed. She didn't want a thing that would catch her and trap her in those feelings. She wanted and needed it all to be new and different in the new world she was creating. The only things she allowed herself to pack were her personal things. She had heartbreakingly sat with all the photo albums one night and gone through every one. She never slept. She just moved through them when the strength was there and she could. Then she carefully packed the ones with James in them, and the next day, she sent them to her stepfather with a note.

Dear Hamilton,

Please keep these for me until I ask for them. I know you understand.
I love you, Catherine

It overwhelmed her. *God, just how do you want me to do this? How do I forget him?*

All too often, the thoughts of James and her past life would overtake her. That was why she tried to stay busy. Today, she briskly headed to the feed room to toss flakes of hay to the four horses. They were stalled two on each side so each had a companion and could also see each other across the aisle. She was content with the way she was learning to run the farm. It hadn't been easy. She'd been lucky to get acquainted with Buck Matthews, the owner of the feed store. He had helped her set things up before she began to accumulate her horses.

~~~

It hadn't taken Catherine long to realize she needed a dog. On one of her ventures into town, she made inquiries. A woman in the pet aisle of the grocery store gave her directions to the Alachua County pound.

The woman said, "You'll hate it. It's really tough. They get some bad dogs out there, but there are a lot of them to choose from."

She was right. When Catherine stepped out of the car, she couldn't believe her ears what with all the barking. She could barely believe her eyes when they finally led her through the maze of kennels. They asked quite a few questions as they walked her through. She knew she wanted a large dog. At least she was spared seeing all the dogs since they had them separated by size.

She knew the moment their eyes met. His name was Champ, five years old. "It's hard to place these older dogs," they told her.

His former owner, who had been admitted to a nursing home, had begged them to wait for "just the right
~~~

person." The entire staff was so excited Catherine wanted Champ that they all escorted him to her car. He was a quiet, obedient, typical golden retriever. He would be a fearless gentle leader, who immediately adored her, and soon became her shadow.

Within a week, General arrived. One of the ladies from the pound called her. It was hard to tell what breed he was, but he was a rangy-looking mutt with hair going every which way, quiet, good manners, and a smooth short coat that was dirty brown with darker flecks. He fell right into place as second in command when Champ simply wagged his tail and accepted him. Catherine was relieved.

It was a first step, and she felt like now she would at least belong to someone.

CHAPTER 2

Buck Mathews unlocked the feed store door and threw his keys on the shelf under the counter. As he was turning the "Open" sign around in the front window, he swore he caught a glimpse of Catherine driving by in her truck. It hadn't been that long ago that Deb Albom had introduced him to her. He would be eternally grateful to Deb for not only showing the old Bensen house to Catherine, but insisting they stop by his feed store. Deb had said, "If she's going to live nearby, she might as well know the owner of the best feed store in town," and then patted his arm and batted her fake eyelashes at him. Every time she had a potential buyer, she made sure they got acquainted with him and his "fabulous feed store."

He knew he was lucky. He had recently retired, and on a whim he had driven to warmer weather and Florida. He had been meandering down a country road when he stopped at a coffee shop. Sitting there, looking out the window, he had made a decision. He picked up a newspaper and called a realtor.

The feed store hadn't even been on the market when Buck first started looking for a farm. It belonged to the realtor's brother. Buck just did it, bought a farm, and became the owner of the feed store, without thinking much about it. It turned out to be a lot more involved than he anticipated. The former owner stuck with him until he felt comfortable and transitioned into handling all the orders. He never expected to be doing something like this someday, but it worked like a revolving door. Every week, the same customers showed up or called. All he had to do was keep the shelves and supplies stocked, and on his way home, he'd make the deliveries. So far, it had worked out. The thing he disliked the most was the computer, but it made ordering and keeping track of inventory a snap.

Sometimes he missed what he thought of as his "real life"—the one where he and his best buddy had been "somebodies." They had retired from a lifetime with the CIA and then found themselves going in completely different directions. It happened suddenly. The first time the phone rang and Zane was at the other end, Buck opened a beer, sat down at his kitchen table and filled his buddy in on the cliff he had jumped off by moving to North Florida. He begged Zane to "Come on down. The weather is worth the trip, man. It reminds me of that island we were stuck on that time, kinda like Bermuda, wherever. There's plenty of room for you. You'd practically have your own suite. And you only have to help at the store if you want to."

~~~~

Deb tried everything, but he had a hard time being interested in her. He hated the way she flipped her red hair over her shoulder. In her high pitched voice, she'd screeched at him, "Buckie, honey, you have my number, but here's my card. Call my cell phone and I'll meet you for dinner, okay, sweetie?"

He'd taken Deb's card and waited for her to look away before he flipped it into the trash can under the counter. He couldn't stand her—there wasn't an ounce of chemistry. That's why when she'd come over later with
~~~~

Catherine, he'd given the new woman in town all of his attention. As Catherine turned to leave that day, he'd said, "Goodbye, ma'am; it was real nice to meet you."

He was staring at her ass when she turned around and said, "You too!" He'd felt the flush creeping up his neck as the two walked out.

Then that damn Deb had come back again, sticking her head in the door. "I'll call you later," she said. "Are you okay, honey? Your face is all red?" He'd nodded, all the while pleading silently, *Please, God, make her phone go dead.*

It had been a good thing those gals couldn't read his mind that day because that had to have been the best piece of ass he'd seen in way too long. He knew he'd have to be extra nice to Debbie some day after he and Catherine were a ticket. He'd tell her how she'd been the one to make it happen. How he'd have to keep an eye out for someone special for her just like she'd done for him by bringing Catherine into the store and all. He'd rub it in—and that wouldn't be the only thing he'd be rubbing.

He spit into the cup he kept on the counter. "Yeah, right," he chuckled. "Fat chance anyone I know would be interested in that piece of lard."

Catherine, on the other hand, made him get that lump where it counted. It was sure his lucky day when she'd bought the farm and needed his help.

He appreciated the business Deb brought into the store, but he didn't appreciate Debbie Albom. He'd heard from one of his customers Deb was divorced and had recently decided her biological clock was ticking all too fast. She made it known she wanted to "land a man, before it was too late to have a little baby." She'd also told that woman, "Y'all know women are having babies a lot later in life, but I don't want someone thinking I'm my kid's grandmother, you know!" He was grateful he'd been warned, because he really didn't have time for this crap.

"She thinks you may be the one," old Mrs. Peters told him. "She thinks the two of you would produce a mighty fine looking boy! Imagine," she sighed as she shook her head.

Buck tried to shake those thoughts from his head as he focused on whoever was coming through the door. He nearly gasped as he realized it was Catherine wearing a crisp white western shirt and tight jeans. Her thick dark brown hair swayed as she walked, her gorgeous brown eyes had a twinkle in them, and her too-perfectly-proportioned breasts bounced just enough. She stopped him from breathing, but she didn't stop his mind. *Those tits have got to be real*, he surmised. *I'd like to give those babies a squeeze.* He was so intent on them that he nearly missed what she was saying.

"Yes, yes," he clumsily answered. "I can get you whatever feed you like. I carry several brands." *God, he hoped that's what she'd asked him.*

She made no comment as he fumbled around on the counter attempting to locate some flyers.

"Take these. Look them over. Call if you have any questions, any questions at all," he said as he clumsily pushed the flyers and a business card at her. Too late, he realized the card was smudged with dirt. He felt idiotic.

Catherine nodded as she stuck the card in her back pocket and held out her hand.

Buck shook it way too long, wanting to pull her close and not let her go.

Then the phone rang. Buck answered it as he watched her turn and walk away.

"*God damn it.*" He wanted to talk to her a little longer. He should have let the stupid phone ring. Now it

was too late. He had wanted to ask her to dinner.
Sometimes he was a moron.

21

CHAPTER 3

Zane Wheeler hadn't intended to head south. He'd finally had the opportunity he'd been waiting for—to travel until he found somewhere that felt right. He'd been promising himself that for as long as he could remember. All he wanted was a spot away from everything and everybody—a place where he didn't have to watch his back. Now, as he traveled down the highway, the monotony of driving set in, and his mind began to wander.

His thoughts turned to an event that had happened a long time ago, when he was a junior in high school back in Montana where he and his best friend, Buck Matthews, had grown up. The already parched land was turning to powder from the drought. The livestock, the ranch, everything was suffering. The cattle prices were down farther than anyone could remember. Even the few horses they sold went for less than they expected.

It was all Zane's idea. "Do you really think we are going to do this for the rest of our lives?" he asked. It wasn't the fact that their fathers and grandfathers were ranchers; even their great-grandfathers before them had been ranchers. They came from the heart of the land—the plains where their ancestors roamed. Zane knew very well where he came from. From the moment she pushed him out into the world, his mother had begun to teach him the ways of her people. They had kept it as secretive as they could. Zane's father thought his wife doted too much on the boy, and what he called "such foolishness." He'd bark at her, "Catch up with the times, woman. That hokey pokey stuff doesn't work. Look what happened to your people. How well did it work for them?" She would look at him in her silent quiet way. She tried to love him, or at least parts of him, especially the part that had allowed her to have Zane. If it hadn't been for her son and the ranch, she would have left there years ago.

Zane knew from the beginning he was from the Blackfeet Nation. He knew his mother was Native American and his father was a white man. They just didn't have very many opportunities to practice her ways with his father's strict rules and attitude. He knew his mother loved her people and the reservation, but she had given them up in order to have a different life—the life of a rancher's wife. She didn't often speak of her former home or her past. Now he knew it must have been painful for her to be so separated. She did use some of the rituals of her heritage. She smudged with sweet grass, planted her garden by the cycles of the moon, and believed in following the patterns of Nature, taking only what they really needed. She listened to the voices of the Earth Mother, Father Sun, and Grandmother Moon. It was something Zane had accepted and understood along with her real name, Maggie White Calf.

On the other side, his white father was Foster Thomas Wheeler, descended from a line of wheelwrights— the people who made and repaired wheels—the wheels that had significantly altered the course of the so-called Wild, Wild West. His father was arrogant about his heritage and often boasted, "This territory would have been nothing without my family and what they did for it. None of this would have happened without them." He felt like the West and all the people in it owed him something, and he acted accordingly. Zane's take on the situation was that he was fortunate to have such great people on both sides of his family. He didn't understand why his father couldn't enjoy the ranch, appreciate his mother, and behave like a father should toward his son. Zane hadn't planned on being alone at this point in his life, but at least he didn't have to worry about screwing up someone else's life the way his father had.

Zane's best friend, Buck, didn't pay much attention to his history. He said, "It doesn't make a hill-a-beans for me to know where I came from. All I care about is where I'm going tomorrow." Plus, Buck thought his family was about perfect.

And so, on that summer night when Zane Wheeler asked Buck Mathews the question that would change their lives, the whole scheme of moving on from his native place was born. Zane was all ears when Mr. Hoyatt, a government recruitment agent, came to his high school and spoke about government jobs instead of other careers or colleges. Zane flew through all the testing, and when it was his turn for the interview, he knew exactly what to say. He had done his homework.

"I've done some research, sir," he said, repeating the words he had rehearsed many times, "and I am extremely interested in the intelligence deficiencies in our country. I would like to serve in a capacity other than the traditional. Can you assist me in this specialized training?"

The man had been stunned and took some time to scramble around in his mind before coming up with an answer.

"Well, son, that's very interesting. Let me pull some things together. I'll be back tomorrow and we can speak again then. I'll bring the materials with me. I'm very impressed with you, son. Most of the kids in this area are more interested in agriculture. I've been doing this testing for a lot of years, and I have to tell you, you are a first."

~~~~

Zane could barely wait until the appointment the next day. He knew a lot of people never made it out of this part of Montana. It was a good life, but tough and money was difficult to come by. He was so excited that he practiced the man's name so he would get it right. Walter Hoyatt. He stared at the clock in the classroom as it ticked off the minutes. He hadn't been this excited since the first time he'd gotten his hands on Mary Ellen's breasts under the bleachers that night after the football game. He squirmed in his seat as he remembered what had come later. Damn she had been sweet.

Zane opened the door with a paper sign marked "Interviews" and Walter motioned for him to sit and then moved his own chair around the desk so he was sitting next to Zane. He had some important looking papers with an emblem of an eagle centered at the top. Zane said, "Thank you for doing this for me, Mr. Hoyatt."

Walter began, "Like you, a long time ago a man was deeply concerned with the safety of the American people. At the time, he happened to be the President of the United States. His name was Franklin D. Roosevelt. He was particularly concerned about exactly what you said yesterday—the intelligence deficiencies. That's why I was so taken back by your question. President Roosevelt appointed someone to draft a plan for a new intelligence service. I won't go any further into it right now, but I copied this information for you last night. I'll give this package to you when we are finished. It explains about
~~~~

how the organization began and how it now operates. Anyway, that's how the CIA was eventually established and continues today. I would like you to start with them in your inquiries about your future plans. It's a good beginning for you."

Zane couldn't wait to tell Buck. Together, they had decided that joining the CIA would be their "great escape" as Zane called it. After that, Zane devoured everything he could find about the CIA and how to join it, even enlisting the school librarian and guidance counselor. The two friends wouldn't even consider any other plan, and overtime, things fell into place for them. But while they were planning, the toughest part was keeping it from their families. Maybe that was the very beginning of how they became legends. They pulled it off. They began their devious plans long before the graduation ceremony, and then they simply slipped away that night, leaving letters explaining what they'd done. That's how the adventure and the lifelong partnership began.

Once they left their homes, Zane didn't spend much time thinking about the way they'd taken off, but in weak moments, he did have an inkling of the great pain he'd caused his mother. Zane and Buck had started running and never really stopped until now. He knew it and he also knew that soon enough it would finally be time to go home.

~~~

Zane knew that all the years he and Buck had spent together had made it hard for Buck to accept that Zane wanted no part of Highberry and his new life. Zane knew Buck was hoping he would visit so he could convince him to stay. Hardly realizing what he was doing,
~~~

and against his better judgment, Zane found himself heading south. Traveling around the country wasn't at all what he'd expected. He hadn't even made it through the first year of retirement and he was bored. The roads were busier than he ever remembered and the traffic sometimes moved at a pace that made him feel like his vehicle was standing still.

He was well past the Florida state line in the town of Madison when he stopped to relieve himself. His mind wouldn't let him think too much on one subject for very long. For a man whose life depended on every single detail, it was unnerving. The physician he was referred to prior to his retirement suggested he "might be experiencing a sort of post-traumatic stress disorder." Zane had scoffed at the doctor and waved his hand. "If you'd seen the things I've seen," he took a breath, "and done, you'd understand why that stuff just couldn't bother me now."

The doctor hesitated for a moment and replied, "Don't be so sure. It's insidious. You think you've seen it all and can control it, but it ends up rearing its ugly head later on. It will sneak up and bite you in the ass. You've been at it a long time. I understand it was pretty rough. Ask for help if you need it. Other than that, you're in incredible shape. Enjoy your retirement."

That day, when Zane left the doctor's office, he had walked across the parking lot to his truck. It looked old and dilapidated on the outside, but the engine and the interior were state of the art. Everything was concealed, including a computer. It was a gift from "the guys" that they had "crafted for him," as they put it. "*You covered our backs, so now we get to take care of yours. You get into trouble, just e-mail.*" They were dangling the keys in front of him as he grabbed them and grinned back, "ET phone home!" That was all he said.

As soon as he was released from duty, Zane put the truck in storage in a warehouse in D.C. and headed to the airport to fly to *"wherever the hell he wanted."* He hopped the next flight out and picked up a clean used Ford F-150 in Newark. It would work for the time being. The print-out in his pocket listed every state, and he intended to check them off one at a time on his journey—only forty-two to go—New Jersey, Delaware, Maryland, Virginia, North Carolina, South Carolina, Georgia, and now Florida. Could you count the District of Columbia for something?

Now he was driving south in the Ford F-150, completely disconnected from the loop, wondering why in the hell he was heading to Florida at all. He couldn't come up with a good answer. He reminded himself, *"Go with the flow. Got nowhere to be and no time to get there."* He knew perfectly well where Buck lived. He'd heard it every time he called. Outside of Gainesville, a small town called Highberry. He took Route 90 through Live Oak down toward Lake City. He was tempted to jump on the interstate, but headed south on 441. He would stop soon and call Buck and head on in, but the next thing he knew the signs were saying Ocala. Maybe it was the scenery that mesmerized him, maybe it was his mind forgetting where he was going—giant oaks, rolling hills, green everything, he had zoned out.

He found a place to grab some grub and thought about turning around, but he decided to blame the truck because it kept on going south. It was late afternoon when he left Sebring and headed toward the town of Okeechobee. He'd remembered something about rodeos; as a kid he'd always wanted to see that big lake that showed up like a large hole on the maps of Florida. It was dark when he found a motel, paid for a room, and fell into bed. He didn't even bother to undress.

Zane slept fitfully, awakening abruptly, but he knew immediately where he was. It was his job. A special agent had to be fully aware of his surroundings at all times, even in his sleep. The most recent vivid dreams were always of the last incident of his career—an event that had actually happened here in the United States—where it shouldn't have happened. It had been a simple meeting with an informant that had gone totally wrong. That's when Buck had been shot and nearly died. The scenes played over and over in his mind whether he was awake or asleep. It should have been him. He should have taken the bullet. How had he let it happen?

As young recruits, they had been trained at The FLETC, a consolidated training facility that initially provided agency-specific basic also known as ASB. It lasted two months. Then they moved up into advanced and specialized training that lasted another three months at the Criminal Investigator Training Program or CITP. They were cross-trained in firearms, legal use of force, defensive driving, crime scene management, controlled substances, felony arrests, case management, case development, informant management, and surveillance. After that, they were periodically subjected to regular specialized training in new legal issues, investigative techniques, hand-to-hand defensive tactics, and use of weapons that were less than lethal force or regular firearms. There wasn't much they didn't know or couldn't do.

Zane and Buck's reputation spanned continents. After all, they worked with an organization that had its roots deeply seeded in history. For God's sake, it began all the way back with George Washington. Not since World War II had things been so difficult. It had become more and more troubling for them as technology took over and the enemy became less and less detectable. Still, they had gone out in a blaze of glory, so to speak. Their dual retirement ceremony was packed with dignitaries. They were lauded for their years of unparalleled service. Some jokes were made about their fearless feats and their deep concern for others, while putting themselves in harm's way. When they were in the midst of it, there wasn't anything fun or funny about it. It was a matter of survival. You did what you had to do to make it out alive. Someone had dug up an old picture of the two dressed as women. Someone else said that people who deal with terrorism tend to think of it as doctors do disease with no cure, or as police do crime—as an ill of the human condition to be addressed one case at a time. They continued, "What Buck and Zane did for our country was to protect every individual. These two men of honor never failed."

Failure was not an option, and it has never been easily confessed by the CIA anyway. The performance of the CIA was measured by its ability as an intelligence service to respond quickly and accurately. Zane and Buck had not only worked for the CIA, but they had somehow crossed over and assisted many of the other entities connected with the country's security. The CIA's history is a record of constantly changing offices and lines of authority, usually reflecting shifting priorities in the White House. These two had stepped up to all the changes and the various authorities, and they had never faltered in their only mission—to serve and to protect.

During all those years, they had both buried themselves in the work and nothing else. Their total focus was on being the best at what they did. That's what made them so powerful individually and even more so whenever they were allowed to be a team. They had an uncanny ability to stay one step ahead of everyone else. Plus, they could read situations and people in a nanosecond. Zane knew very well where that ability came from, so he couldn't stop blaming himself for missing the signs and not protecting them both at that fateful ambush. After a while, it was rare that they needed permission from the Supervisor In Charge to work together. It was a given that they'd get it done better if they came as a team.

In the long silent nights, the scenes played around and around in Zane's mind. Awake or asleep, they never left him alone. That's why he had taken to moving around so much. He figured that if he kept moving, maybe one day he would come to a place where he would escape the incessant faces and scenes. He just needed to give it some more time.

~~~

Ranch life prepared the boys for their career choice in many ways. They had started hunting when they were able to hold a gun. Interacting with the ranch hands and the horses had taught them a lot about patience and perseverance. The lessons Zane's mother had taught him helped equip him for the strange world they entered when they ran away from home.

In the beginning, they were constantly in training. They were eager, impatient, restless. The older men tried to tell them the action would come soon enough and it did. As the years passed, the images and happenings began to intermingle until they found themselves confused about the places and the stories. Soon, as they headed toward retirement, it didn't matter. It became just a job instead of the great adventure they once had dreamed about. Toward the end, there were just too many close calls.
~~~

With all the new technology, it never should have happened, but there was a worm in the salad, and they almost ate it. They were ambushed. All Zane knew was that he'd damn near let his best friend get killed.

It couldn't have been any worse. They were told to meet with an informant—one they had worked with several times before. He had critical information about an event that would occur on the same day at various places across the country. It was to take place at airports and other major transportation systems. When they arrived, they found the man face down in the alleyway in a pool of blood. They were checking for a pulse when all hell broke loose. It happened so quickly they broke their own cardinal rule and became separated. In fact, they had taken off in opposite directions dodging the spray of bullets.

Zane carefully and methodically picked off two of the guys and heard a third run off. Then in the eerie silence, for the first time in his life, he felt panic. He called for Buck twice and thought he heard a sound from a darkened doorway across the alley. He ran straight across, ignoring his normal pattern of zig-zagging as he ran. His quick thinking and training saved Buck's life. The shot went across the front of Buck's abdomen and shattered the top of his hip. The deep pressure Zane applied stopped the bleeding. They had both been lucky.

He replayed that damn scene at least a thousand times. He had to get over it. His mother warned him long ago, "One never knows when a spirit will jump into you. Be careful, my son, what you dream for. When it happens and you are chosen, you must follow where it leads you.

Know this; the most powerful people often lead solitary lives with difficult happenings and few rewards. Be careful. Be careful what you wish for." His life had taken that different turn when he discovered the CIA.

Zane felt he understood his mother and what he'd done to her better now. He had been selfish and self-centered when he'd taken off. He never knew what she really thought. They never spoke of it. He had fought looking back for all these years, but now it seemed the memories of the ranch and the lessons of his youth were coming back to him.

On one of the rare occasions when they were together, his grandfather had told him, "When the wind blows strong behind you, listen to the wisdom of the wind. The spirit of the wind will direct you in the way you should go." He wondered whether he had paid any attention to the wind at all. Had he listened?

The true reason he had come to Florida, he realized, was because he intended to tell Buck goodbye before he headed west. West held all the things he hadn't faced. Visiting all the states was kind of a joke. It was good in theory, but he knew he'd never pull it off. For one thing, he didn't give a flying fig about some of those places.

Their lives didn't allow them to set down any roots. He didn't even have any friends except for Buck. He had no real attachments other than to his mother. There was no time to pursue any of the things he'd enjoyed on the ranch. Once in a while, Buck would schedule a hunting trip for them, but it was exotic—hunting for water buffalo, the big cats, and once shooting birds in Mexico. Zane mostly did it for Buck. They needed the diversion. Never, when they took time off, did either of them talk about heading home to Montana. When Zane allowed it, he did wonder exactly how his mother had managed the ranch after his father died. He knew that Parker Iron Crow, who had become the ranch manager, wouldn't let anything happen to her, so he just let it go.

He liked Okeechobee. He'd been in the motel a few days, found his way around town, and driven out around the lake. The ranches were vastly different than the ranches of his youth, but it was nice to be around people who were more down to earth and like-minded. The flyer in the restaurant where he ate breakfast led him to the rodeo arena and the cattle and horse auction. He had absolutely no desire to be anything but a spectator.

<u>Chapter 4</u>

Catherine scribbled the words on the phone pad—*self-involved*. That completely defined her family. She had moved to the farm over five months ago and had not "phoned home." No one even missed her. Obviously, they hadn't tried to call or they would have been referred to her new number. Soon the truth would be out—"Mom, I moved." In her dreams, her family, if you could really call them that, would be surprised, but supportive. In reality, there would be a million questions, all from her mother.

Seriously, she had tried to call her mother, but every time she picked up the phone that little culprit sitting on her shoulder reminded her it might not be pretty. Now it was ridiculous. If she didn't dial the phone soon, her mother would be more than angry, with a great big "R" for seeing red! She was certain she was about to get an earful. Her plan was to call late and use her own exhaustion as an excuse for making the call informative but brief. Her mother answered abruptly.

"Hi, Mom. It's Catherine."

"Oh for God's sake, Catherine, where in the world have you been?"

Catherine smiled. "Actually mother, I've been in Highberry for the last five months."

"Highberry? Where is that, dear? Five months? Oh my God."

"North Florida, Mom. Near Gainesville."

"What in the world are you doing there? For your job?"

"No, Mom. I sold the apartment and moved."

"Oh good Lord, Cath. Oh, you're not thinking clearly. What about your apartment? What about your job? What is your sister going to think? Why, she'll have a fit."

Catherine knew it wasn't her sister who had the problem with fits. Her mother had enough tizzies for all of them combined.

"Mom, listen, I wanted to give you the new phone number, you know, in case of an emergency." Her mother repeated it one number at a time. "I'm really exhausted, so I'll call you again soon, okay? I promise. Tell Hamilton I send my love. Kiki too. Love you."

"Okay. Bye then. Highberry. Highberry. What in the world? Okay, okay, bye."

Catherine didn't have to say anything else because her mother had already hung up the phone. She sighed. That had been easier than she had imagined.

She hadn't given any thought to moving close to her family, but she had known what she wanted. She wanted everything to be different. She wanted to be in a part of Florida that had seasons. She wanted to live in an area that wasn't congested, and she wanted to own a lot of land for her money. She wanted to be away from the coast, and hopefully, the brute force of the hurricanes. She wanted to be close to a small town near a big town that would afford her some of the amenities she'd become accustomed to in New York. She didn't bother to explain any of this to her mother tonight. Elizabeth wouldn't have understood it anyway.

Once Catherine's mother, Elizabeth, had married Hamilton Wesley Howell, he had become her mother's number one priority. Elizabeth had carefully selected her second husband for the lifestyle he could provide her. Hamilton had been good to her two little girls, while completely spoiling his wife. He treated Catherine and Kiki, short for Candace, as if they were his own daughters. Catherine appreciated Hamilton, loved him in her own way, but not like a real father. He, in turn, provided for and guided Catherine as best he could. He respected her and was proud of her accomplishments. She knew James' death was difficult for him, not so much because he cared for James, but because he worried how it would affect her. At the funeral, he had tried to comfort her, but the man was rigid; she knew Hamilton would be there for her, but he didn't know how to give what she needed. Her mother was, well, her mother, and completely committed to Hamilton. Her sister, Kiki, had been a typical little sister. They loved each other, but they didn't keep in touch; they just lived totally different lives. Catherine had to find her comfort in other ways.

~~~

Catherine was certain the next time the dog people called she would tell them two dogs were quite enough, but when the call came, she caved. She hated the name Scuz and told them so, but the dog sounded so pathetic.

"She's totally timid, part greyhound with really long legs," the lady said on the phone, "and a pointy nose."

Catherine didn't like dogs with really pointed noses, but the next thing she knew, she was getting out of the truck in the rescue's parking lot. The dog was sweet, gray with nearly yellow eyes. Catherine didn't want to like her, intended just to keep going, to say, "No, sorry." The dog was sitting there, peering out of the cage, not barking, not
~~~

moving, following Catherine with her eyes. Her eyebrows were up, giving her that wrinkled, worried look. The poor thing was shaking uncontrollably. As soon as the rescue worker snapped on her leash and let her out, she sat at Catherine's feet, staring right into her eyes and putting up her paw. That was it.

A week later at about noon, the phone rang. "So how is Scuz adjusting?" the rescue lady asked. Catherine's heart was beating too fast. She would just say, "No" this time.

"The neighbors hadn't seen him for two days. They found him dead in the bed with the two little dogs curled up beside him. It took several hours to locate his daughter to come and take the dogs so they could remove him from the house."

Did she say "little dogs?" Catherine was on the verge of a panic attack. She knew she was experiencing obsessive compulsive behavior by adopting three dogs in three weeks, especially when she already had two.

She couldn't help it. Peanut and Gem were in a cage together. They were sullen and wary. Peanut was too cute, a little wire-haired grayish terrier thing. They said he was feisty as he curled up his lip and growled. Catherine could see right through his fear. Gem was equally scared, cowering behind Peanut. More a spaniel-type with a beagle face and ears, she was black and white, but small. The rescue didn't even do the normal paperwork or ask her to pay.

"We knew Mr. Baniff for years. He stopped often with bags of food and toys. We will really miss him. We are just happy for you and his dogs."

She was worried as she drove toward the farm. *"Five dogs. Whatever am I thinking?"* She needn't have wasted her time questioning herself. They were hers now.

She was afraid to let the two little dogs loose in the yard, so she took each one in separately, locking Peanut in the mudroom while she went back for Gem. When she slowly opened the mudroom door and put Gem down, there were a few tense moments. The three senior dogs circled and sniffed, Peanut growled and spun around, and that was it. She wondered whether the first dogs might be telling the newcomers, "Don't blow it! We've got to stick together!" Catherine held her hands over her face and groaned, "I must be crazy."

~~~

Catherine sat in her favorite green chair in her office, staring out the window across the pasture. She couldn't get used to being alone. The first time she had met James was at a party at Arianne's apartment. She had reluctantly stopped by along with another coworker on their way home from work. Later, James would tell her he hadn't even known about the party and had been dropping by to visit his old friend. That decision would alter the course of their lives forever. He loved to tell her the story. He would act it out, pretending to ring the bell and be completely surprised when a strange man answered the door. He swore the guy had said, "Enter at your own risk." He told Catherine every single time he should have taken that as a warning.

James and Catherine had "bumped into" each other three months later when Arianne arranged a dinner party. He hadn't stopped thinking about her, but she hadn't honestly given him another thought. The way Arianne told the story, he had been relentless until Arianne had given in and set it all up. She had purposely separated them at the table, but once the guests moved into the living room,
~~~

she knew James would make his move. Everyone swore later that you could have cut the chemistry with a knife. They teased Arianne that she should have regretted it, but that night was the best thing that had ever happened to James. Catherine witnessed him thank Arianne so many times it was ridiculous. The last time they were all together he had asked Arianne, "You do know how much I love you both, don't you?" Catherine knew it was true.

Catherine soon discovered the friendship between Arianne and James was deeper than most people knew. She became uncomfortable one evening listening to a very tipsy Arianne describe the liberties she had often taken with James. Arianne was laughing as she leaned over to James and whispered, "Cat got your whatchamadoodle?" as she began to nibble on his ear. James had quickly pushed Arianne away and smiled sheepishly at Catherine as he mouthed, "She's drunk." He did, in fact, love them both, and it had been his good fortune that they began to act more like sisters than friends. It was silly, but James would pull them both in close any chance he got and say, "You complete me," and he meant it.

When the phone rang that night, Catherine immediately knew something was terribly wrong. After she'd screamed herself through the initial shock, the first thing she did was call Arianne, who tried to stop Catherine from saying anything, because she knew what was coming. Then Catherine said it, "Arianne, James has been killed. The SUV rolled over. There was a fire." Catherine heard Arianne scream as she hung up the phone. Catherine never slept that night, and at first light, she stumbled her way to Arianne's apartment. The doorman let her in with just a nod. When she went to ring the bell, the door opened and she and Arianne simply fell into each other's arms. They cried for hours. There was nothing else they could do.

Now, too late, Catherine realized that the intimacy between James and Arianne had been way more than familiar, and she wished she'd asked James a lot more questions.

~~~

Catherine knew she was already in big trouble, but the last dog had been all Buck's fault. Buck said he found him at the door in a cage one morning. There was no note, nothing, just a dog in a cage. None of his customers recognized the dog or knew anyone who would have done such a thing.

"Damnedest thing. Maybe someone got off the interstate and passed through town. Who knows? You want 'im?"

Catherine walked away and pretended to be looking at something on the shelf. She had just finished writing out her check when the dog let out a low mournful howl. He was sitting up, begging in the cage. His face was so fuzzy you couldn't find his tiny black eyes. He looked like a chow, but was most likely Pomeranian. He was extremely small.

"Okay, okay," she heard herself say. "Put the cage on the front seat before I change my mind, but if anyone shows up looking for him, he's going back to them."

Buck chuckled as he quickly grabbed the cage and shot out the front door.

"You understand, I'm only keeping him until the real owner shows up, Buck."

"How many does this make?" he asked.

"Don't ask. Six. Six. I can't believe it myself."

He shook his head as he shut the truck door.
~~~

"Thanks. I'm not really into tiny little black dogs," he winked. His phone was ringing as he rushed back into the store.

Catherine shook her head as she climbed into the truck's cab and peered into the cage. The little black fuzzy thing was jumping up and down and pawing the side of the cage. "Okay, Friskie. I guess you'll be stuck with that name until someone tells us otherwise." She stuck her fingers through the wires. "You are just too cute." It had all happened so quickly. Her brain knew it was the wrong thing to do, but they were so needy.

These days, two of her dogs always followed her inside the barn, while the other three carried out their new found morning ritual of scurrying about, motivated by the scent of whatever creatures had been present in the darkness of the night. They gave her another reason to get up every morning. Now there would be six.

~~~

After dinner in the quiet, once the dogs had settled in, Catherine found her journal in a basket on the shelf in her office and curled back into her green chair to write:

It is almost midnight. I made it through another month—another day. Sleep won't come tonight even though I am exhausted. A storm is sitting overhead that is shaking the house. The thunder vibrates the boards beneath my feet. I can hear the rain coming in torrents against the window, but it is black outside—black as the deep dark hole that haunts me.

I saw Halle Berry on Oprah a while ago and they were talking about Halle's movie, Their Eyes Were Watching God. *Halle said, "When we finally get it, we are in that box looking straight up."*
~~~

It took me right to that day I stood looking at James. It was him, but it wasn't him. They told me he was burned beyond recognition. And he was, so much so that the casket could not be opened. That's what they said. I demanded it. I had to see for myself. I can't even allow myself to write a single word to describe it. They warned me. I demanded and then their ammonia brought me back to life. No one said a word. They helped me back to my feet, helped me straighten my clothes and held my elbows gently as I staggered into the next room. They softly deposited me on the couch in the room lit with pink lights and quietly backed out and shut the doors. I knew I was not alone. They left someone standing at the doorway leading out. Did they expect hysteria? Did I?

I could not scream. I could not cry. It was too unbelievable, how he looked with his skin burned and melted and fallen off. He had belonged to me. I was glad then that he was gone. In that horrible unbelievable moment I allowed myself to be glad that he was gone. I can only write this now in the dimness of this room behind the pantry where I hear the thunder, see the flashes of jagged light and hear the beating of the rain. This place allows me to scream—scream from the depth of my gut—deep from my very soul—and I remember what I saw and what I do not want to remember ever again. I scream until I have no voice left to scream and yet no sound comes from my mouth. No tears slide down my face. The sound of the storm in the middle of the night and the emptiness suddenly become words on a page, moving me forward from something I simply do not understand.

It has a life of its own, this grief. I chose this place to come to terms with it. Alone. As my emotions begin to ebb, so does the storm.

I ask myself, "Why?" every single day. Why James?

Why this way? Why am I left to figure all this out. There are no answers—Only more questions.

And then I ask: What—What about those checks? Why so much money? I understand from James' insurance, but why from the government? I don't understand. What? Why? There are still no answers. The rain is now a patter against the window, low rumblings in the distance.

Catherine didn't move for a long time. She sat in the dimly lit room, listening to the storm as it moved away. When she finally stirred, she didn't bother to go upstairs. She dream walked into the front room, slid onto the couch, pulled the throw up around her legs, and drifted off.

~~~

The ringing phone woke her. Champ was panting in her face as she tried to figure out where she was. It was just breaking daylight. She made it to the kitchen, grabbed the phone on the fourth ring, and in a throaty voice said, "Hello." The hands on the clock were pointing to exactly six o'clock.

"Cath, have you seen Buck?" The high-pitched squeaky voice on the other end surprised her, especially so early in the morning. She certainly knew who it was.

"Buck? Buck, oh, you mean Buck from the feed store?"

Deb Albom was talking over her, "I've been calling him for days, but I haven't had a chance to go by the store. I was wondering if he's been spending all his time with you?"

A silly grin spread across Catherine's face. Her realtor thought she was seeing the guy from the feed store. She tried to sound serious, "No, he was here Thursday,
~~~

after he closed the store, with my delivery. That's the last time I saw him. Is he missing?"

"Missing? Is he missing?" Deb hissed her s's out like a snake. "Yes, honey, he's missing—from my life. I think he's avoiding me, and he knows how darn crazy I am about him. I wonder where he is?"

Catherine tried not to show her amusement. This woman was clueless. "I have to place an order today. Would you like me to ask him to call you?"

"Oh, well, sure honey. I think I'll just have to go there though. Confront him, you know. Are you sure he hasn't been over there?"

"Deb, I'm not interested in him. You know, it's too soon." She was trying to be kind, but honestly, she had no desire—not for a man or even for a friend like Deb, who was bothering her at six o'clock in the morning. "Deb, please, I'm really not interested in him and I have to go." She quietly placed the phone back on the cradle.

Wow! What a crazy way to start the morning. She rubbed Champ's head and let the dogs out the back door. *What a terrible place for someone to be. Poor Deb.*

Buck was one of the last men she'd be interested in. He was nothing but a player. She knew that by the location of his stares. He wasn't adept at getting a look in without it being obvious. He practically wagged his tail and panted every time she went into the store. Men like that made her queasy. He had sandy blonde hair that stuck to his forehead, a mustache that curled up on the ends, and he wore baggy shirts. He looked like what he was—a guy who worked at a feed store who sweated and grunted a lot. She wasn't being unkind. She was just used to starched shirts, fitted suits, and men who smelled good. She shrugged and hurried out the back door.

By the time she got to the barn, the horses were

eager to be fed and turned out. She wasted no time in accomplishing the chores and leading the four horses to the pastures. The air was fresh, crisp, and amazing. She watched the horses graze; she loved it when they would kick up their heels and charge around the fields. Life was good. All the animals were settled in, and she was certain it would only get better for all of them. Writing in her journal gave her a release she had been missing. She promised herself she would spend more time writing, and she knew exactly what she would do today to begin that long overdue part of her life.

This place offered so much freedom—the tranquility of the wide open spaces, gazing at the stars in the huge dark sky—the awe and wonder she'd been missing. She had given herself the gift of time and a place to feel safe again. The house wrapped its walls around her like loving arms and filled her with a sense of peace and freedom she had never experienced before. There were no boundaries now except the ones she imposed upon herself. She was beginning to feel alive again.

Catherine went straight to her favorite room behind the pantry and began moving furniture. She wanted to create a sacred place to write. The back room was perfect for positioning the desk to face the east window. She would catch the first rays of light, plus the room wouldn't be so hot during the long summer months. She stood back, hands on her hips, surveying her progress. All she needed were a few special things. It didn't take long to move through the house to gather them—the rock she'd fished from the stream in Georgia, the hawk feather she had found the other day while walking with the dogs, the crystal she bought at the little gift shop down the street from her office. The remembrances of another life, they would bring good energy. She placed some on the windowsill and a few on her desk. Perfect!

She missed the discipline of having a schedule. It would be reassuring to find a routine again. She had accomplished a lot with her Foundation, but it had become successful so quickly that it had been a whirlwind. She could only admit to herself now that it was good to let it go.

She had a need to have her own voice. The Missing Link Foundation did that for her as she became heard and respected. Now she had an opportunity in a different way. As a child, she had fantasized about being a writer. She pictured people in various settings with her book in their hands, devouring her words. She had pages here and there—a novel she started about a woman on a cruise—57 pages. A story about three little girls growing up in North Florida—103 pages. Some of her stories about the Foundation were published in local papers. For a short while, she had written the Foundation newsletter until her schedule forced her to delegate it to someone else. Her journals filled a storage box and had traveled with her to this place. They were her secret treasures, brimming with her deepest feelings, emotions, events, and pain. Something always tugged at her soul to run somewhere and write, but life had not given her the chance for that before. Now, she had a splendid opportunity to do anything she wanted. Today she would finish setting up the room, creating ideas and embracing the beginning of this chapter of her life.

All she needed now was a nice cup of tea and a chance to curl up in that lovely chair she had placed facing the window.

<u>CHAPTER 5</u>

Zane pulled into the parking lot at the Okeechobee rodeo arena. He planned to stay at the auction for a while and then drive west to see what the center of the state looked like. He had heard about the Brighton Seminole Reservation and thought it might have some Indian fry bread. He hadn't eaten any in a very long time.

The cattle looked a bit scruffy to him. They were smaller boned, didn't have glossy coats, and were wild compared to the cattle his family raised. The only thing that impressed him was the price. The auctioneer's voice was irritating as he repeated the same sequences over and over. He lacked rhythm. Still, Zane decided to wait to see what a few of the horses brought. When he walked through the holding area, he was surprised at the variety of breeds.

As soon as they announced the horse auction would begin in five minutes, more people moved into the bleachers. Zane returned in time to see the announcer hand the microphone to the auctioneer.

The first bids came rapidly for a pair of draft horses with the gavel finally sounding at $6,000.00. It was a good price for the pair and the crowd applauded. Several more horses were auctioned—a lovely thoroughbred mare, a quarter horse gelding, and a reining horse that brought $8,000. Zane was just about to leave when a rangy looking thin horse was brought in. The horse's chiseled head, large eyes and nostrils, and his tail carriage gave him away. He was probably black, but the sun had bleached him to an ugly brown. The condition of his coat made Zane think he was wormy. He had a wider chest and was taller than most of the Arabian horses Zane had seen. The bidding started very low at $50 and slowly crept up to $200.

The auctioneer was working hard to stir the crowd, "Come on, people; some little kid would love this black beauty. He's registered—I have the papers right here in my hand. He had all his shots and Coggins. Come on, people; what'll you give me?" The poor horse's ribs were excruciatingly defined and his backbone was protruding.

Zane didn't have a bidding card, but he felt bad for the horse. He knew it would end up at slaughter. He'd be fattened up and put in a can. He wasn't normally impulsive, but at the last minute Zane shouted, "I'll give $250, but I don't have a number." Without hesitation, the auctioneer banged the gavel and said, "Sold for $250 to the man in the gray hat. Thank you, sir."

Zane went straight to the office where he told them his story.

"I'm just passing through. I don't have a trailer, so I need to make some arrangements to keep this horse somewhere."

The two ladies smiled as they looked at each other and then Zane. The older woman was full-breasted, had short, curly blonde hair, and was probably about his age. "It won't be a problem at all for you to keep this horse here at the rodeo grounds for a while," she said. "We've done it before many times. You will be responsible to feed, water, and either hand-graze the horse, or set up a temporary paddock."

It was easy and insane. *What the hell was he doing*

buying a horse now, especially a damn Arabian. Shit! He knew his troubles were about to begin.

The other lady was about thirty, thirty-five; she had dyed black hair and a tattoo of a rose right above the opening of her blouse. She talked with a Southern drawl.

"That's a real nice thing you are doin' for that horse, you know. He doesn't deserve to end up, well, like this, you know what I mean." She hadn't even been able to say what they all knew happened to most of these animals. They just did the best they could to get some of them sold to someone who would keep them.

"By the way, I don't know how much you know about horses," the older lady said, "but it's been our experience that you shouldn't paste worm them when they are in this bad a condition. Sometimes, they'll blow a wad of parasites and they will go down with colic. It's sometimes hard to save them then."

"I appreciate the information. It's been a while since I've cared for one and there's got to be a lot of new stuff I just don't know about."

Zane paid the ladies, who assured him they'd keep his horse safe until he got back. "Let us know when you are back and we'll help you set things up."

Then he headed to the nearby feed store to pick up panels to make a corral and the other items he'd need to care for his new acquisition.

~~~

Within a week, Zane had made arrangements for money to be wired and headed to the truck dealership. He had no problem trading up his Ford F-150 pickup. He felt good as he drove away in his brand new F-350 XLT. From there, he headed down the road to the feed mill, where
~~~

he'd seen a stock trailer for sale in the lot. It wasn't perfect, but it would do what he needed. He made one more stop at Joe's Western Store, where he bought a nice used saddle and brand new bridle, saddle pad, and other supplies.

Trouble—the name Zane chose for him—wasn't the only horse staying at the rodeo grounds, but he was the only Arabian. Zane had started him off slowly by feeding him small amounts of grain and hay every few hours to avoid overtaxing the horse's gut and causing him to colic. He'd used the daily pellet wormer the ladies had suggested. The horse had finally started to pick up weight and look a little better.

Today, Zane groomed him in his stall, spent a little time checking him out, and then carefully tacked him up. The horse yielded away from pressure on his nose and both sides. He was more sensitive on the right. He would give his head all the way down to the ground. He switched eyes when Zane passed behind him from side to side. He had lunged him in both directions earlier in the week, and the horse didn't seem bothered by the flapping stirrups.

Zane walked Trouble out to the open field outside the holding pens. He moved around to the off side first, stepped up into the right stirrup, putting weight across the horse's back, then went around and did the same on the left. The horse stood dead still as he swung on up. He let him find his balance for a minute and then took hold of the left rein. He circled him left, making the left hind cross over in front of the right hind. Then he reversed the circle and did the same with the right. He allowed Trouble to walk off on a loose rein. They rode the entire perimeter of the grounds at the walk. The horse never spooked once and moved on at the same steady pace. What Zane hadn't expected was the smoothness of his gait. It felt like you could ride him all day.

They turned around and Zane squeezed Trouble up into a nice jog. The horse stayed steady with rhythmic cadence. He only bumped him once to slow him down. The jog was smooth as glass and honest. He changed directions, and from the walk, clucked twice, squeezed him up, and sent him off in a nice slow lope to the left. He slowed him to a trot and picked up the right lead. When he felt Trouble drop his shoulder a little, he corrected him by instinctively shifting more weight into his outside seat and foot. It worked like a charm. He hadn't ridden in years, but it was easier than remembering how to ride a bicycle. It was something he'd yearned for and you just didn't forget. His body complained a little as he felt the pain of old injuries and age.

~~~

Zane had promised himself he would only stay in Okeechobee two weeks, but it was over a month before he decided to load up his horse and head out. The time with Trouble was well spent because both he and the horse were back in shape and enjoyed what they had created. Trouble seemed more like his dance partner now when Zane rode him. The horse had muscled up and his coat turned a shiny black. Zane pretty much stopped thinking he'd made a huge mistake. People who frequented the rodeo grounds began to look forward to watching the two of them together. The horse seemed to appreciate the audience, even if Zane didn't.

He walked into the office and told the ladies, "I need to settle up with you today because Trouble and I will be leaving in the morning."

"No," they both said simultaneously.
~~~

Frieda, the older woman, frowned. "We sure are gonna miss the two of you. It's been a real pleasure having you stay with us."

Karen, the black-haired, younger gal, made her way around the counter. "Here," she said as she held out her arms. "I sure want to hug you and thank you for saving that horse. He looks wonderful. Please, please keep in touch and let us know what you two are up to." Zane felt a little embarrassed and stiffened up as she wrapped her arms around him.

He settled up his bill and tipped his hat to them. "Thanks for everything."

They didn't waste any time spreading the word. Several people made it a point to stop and tell Zane they were sure going to miss him and his beautiful horse. In fact, old Rusty, the auctioneer, came by to tell him, "I really thought you had kinda lost your marbles when you bought that horse, but I'll admit that I was wrong. Good job, son." Zane shook his hand and thanked him. No one had ever called him son before, and he barely understood the feeling in his throat as he turned and walked away. He knew it was the perfect time for Trouble and him to move on.

~~~

At least, the weather was cooperating. He'd loaded Trouble into his trailer with no problem. He pulled out onto 441 and headed north. He'd pick up the Florida turnpike in Yeehaw Junction. Zane had a hard time understanding why anyone would settle down in Florida anyway. Everyone said they moved south for the weather, but he found it downright dripping with humidity. He'd been hot before, but he'd never sweated so much, and he
~~~

had so much trouble breathing. On top of that, when a so-called cold front would come in, it would be around thirty degrees at daybreak, but by lunchtime, it would be approaching eighty. It was really hard on the horses and the people. Then the damn cold was so damp it chilled you clear to the bone; he'd come out one morning and found Trouble shivering. Plus, it would be blazing sun one minute and pouring rain the next. Nope, he wasn't going to miss this place one bit.

The new truck drove like a dream, but the traffic was unbelievable. He had expected it to be lighter on a Tuesday, but instead of thinning out, the farther north he drove, the worse it became. He barely knew he was pulling a horse trailer. He was happy when he passed Ocala and pulled off in Micanopy to give himself and Trouble a break. He purposely left Okeechobee a little after midnight so it would be easier on his horse. If he kept up this speed, he'd be in Alachua in an hour. He'd either have to wake up his buddy, Buck, or hang out somewhere for a while.

CHAPTER 6

The last day at The Missing Link Foundation had been difficult. Now, alone on the farm, Catherine knew she'd have days that weren't easy, but she was also certain being here would make the worst days bearable. The apartment and New York held too many memories, with painful scenes that triggered thoughts of James. She missed everything about him, but she was slowly realizing things hadn't been exactly perfect. His work had taken him out of town a lot. She knew it was important, but it got in the way. Their plan had always included children, but somehow the years marched on. Before the creation of the Foundation, she'd been the editorial assistant at a magazine. Then one day, James asked her, "Why keep doing something you don't love anymore? Why not do something you really want to do?" The more they discussed it, the more she knew he was right. It was time for a change. She was certain she'd have more time if she ran her own business, and once she stayed home more without the stress, she figured she would get pregnant.

That was the first time she felt afraid, really afraid. She had no clue how to be a successful parent—no barometer at all. She knew what she didn't want to do or be, but the fear overshadowed the desire. Then, on top of it, he was away so much. Why she'd practically be a single parent, although he had assured her he'd only be a phone call away. She couldn't even imagine herself pregnant. She could barely hear the word without feeling uneasy.

That's how the Foundation was formed. Helping someone else's kids would maybe help fill the emptiness she felt. It was designed for those children who were falling between the cracks. It provided networking, temporary emergency funding, and connected people to a broad spectrum of important health-related services. The team included experts in social, psychological, and medical fields. She loved working with a group of people who were interested in what they could give instead of what they could take. She became invigorated and renewed. James watched her from a distance. Then, when everything seemed so right for her, everything went so wrong.

After James' death, she woke up one morning with a sort of resolve. She went into the office and sat quietly at her desk. She couldn't remember how many times she'd been there since the funeral. She didn't know how much money was in the bank accounts. She didn't even know what day or month it was. She had been stumbling forward, simply placing one foot in front of the other until now. But on this day, she suddenly knew what she had to do. She scheduled a staff meeting for first thing the next morning. She asked the staff members to each prepare his or her appropriate reports, and then she went back home.

Early the next morning, she prayed—she prayed there would be enough money to maintain the Foundation and pay all of the staff. She knew exactly who should replace her as director. She had no doubt that Kyra was the most qualified, but would she accept the position? Catherine waited until everyone was seated, and then she entered the room. They all stood and quietly applauded.

The reports were quite remarkable. In two short years, they had accomplished what seemed impossible.

Without fail, every staff member provided good sound news. She'd had no idea that so many people cared, or that so many people would come together, but in the end there was over half a million dollars contributed in James' memory from various entities. Catherine was stunned and felt a little embarrassed. She was surprised someone's death could actually bring that much money—the one thing that had been somewhat difficult to obtain before.

The Foundation's future was secure for now. Once she resigned, it would be up to the staff to keep that momentum going.

She was tearful as she praised them for the many children and families they had touched. She applauded them for securing the services of some of the finest professionals in the New York area. Then she quietly and confidently told them she was leaving and announced that, if she agreed, Kyra Kirkland would be taking over as executive director, "and," Catherine added, "if anyone objects, well, you're fired," she grinned. Everyone laughed and applauded once more. Kyra's tears ran down her face as Catherine pushed a rather large notebook toward her, saying, "I wrote out my job description for you."

Kyra was Catherine's best asset and had fine-tuned the Foundation with ease. There was no doubt that the integrity of Catherine's dream would continue, plus the notebook had actually been created by Kyra for Catherine. All of this made it easier for Catherine to say goodbye. She bid everyone farewell among hugs, kisses, and tears, and then she closed the door on that chapter of her life.

~~~

When a rooster crowed off in the distance, Catherine stirred in the still dark room. She didn't know if
~~~

the sound was real or part of a dream. It seemed like she had been having a good dream, but she woke herself up whimpering, and her face was wet with tears. She missed him—the way he smelled, hearing his footsteps coming down the hall, how he slid into bed and wrapped himself gently around her, his breathing in the night. She loved when he ran his fingers through her hair. A large tear flowed silently down her cheek and landed with a surprising thud right next to her ear on the pillow.

Grief did that to her. It came in waves, knocked her to her knees, and left here there—always alone. It was like the fog on a cool morning that just sits there. You can stir it with your hand and nearly touch it, but you can't quite get your hand around it. Memory is there, like the fog, but it is distant and evasive. It begins to dissipate and moves off leaving you with no satisfaction. Then, when you aren't expecting it, it's back—thicker and more confusing, swirling around you until you can't see a thing but yourself. She wondered what the hell had happened to her life. In an instant, everything had changed.

Catherine and James had spent a long time stacking the cards. Had it suddenly really been twenty years? They built their strong and beautiful home, but an ill, cold wind had blown in suddenly, without warning, and the whole thing had collapsed around her. The pain cut so deep. She tried to compartmentalize it—stick it away bit by bit in pretty little boxes high up on a shelf deep in the closet where she'd forget about it. She tried to push it far, far away, but she knew where it was.

Slowly, she began to forget what his voice sounded like; she had to focus to recall the exact color of his eyes. How could it happen? Her mind played nasty little tricks on her. She was certain he parted his hair on the left—but he didn't part his hair—anymore.

She got out of bed and carefully pulled his shirt from the drawer to bury her face in it, breathing in his scent. She'd kept it, just one shirt, just to remember him. Catherine stared into the mirror with his shirt in her hands, barely recognizing who was looking back at her.

The phone rang; for a moment, she refused to pick it up. Early morning calls scared her. Her heart was pounding. *Please, God, please, no more bad news.* She hesitated a moment longer—*and it better not be that Deb Albom either.*

She knew she'd heard the voice before, but she couldn't quite figure it out until he told her. "Ma'am, I'm sorry to call so early, but I'm in a little dilemma. This is Buck from the feed store."

Catherine was unprepared for what Buck asked her to do, especially so early in the morning.

"My friend's truck broke down not too far from your house. I've loaned out my trailer. He's got a fifth wheel so I can't pull it. Can you just go rescue his horse until we can get him towed?"

She had no idea what he was talking about—fifth wheel? She said, "No, I'm sorry, but I'm not at all good with the horse trailer. Isn't there someone else?"

"I called around, ma'am, but I've had no luck. He's right there at the corner of 232. It wouldn't take you long."

"It's not that. It's 6 A.M. Plus, I really don't want another horse here."

"It's temporary. I just need a little time to get him hauled."

In the end, she gave in. She hurriedly threw on her clothes from the day before, pulled on her muckers, and grabbed a flannel at the back door. "Stay," she told the dogs as she headed out. It wasn't even daylight as she started up the truck.

It was a good thing she had a little practice with the trailer. She backed up, trying to remember what the man had said about lining it up. She sighed when she had the unbelievably good fortune of doing it on the second try. *Damn, I'm good!* The hitch slid down onto the ball as she cranked the wheel up off the ground, slammed the sleeve shut with her foot, pushed in the locking pin, and attached the chains crisscrossed to her bumper hitch. *Who would have ever believed I'd be doing this?* she smiled. She wished she had grabbed gloves because the metal was cold and damp from the dew.

Turning north out of the driveway, she headed toward the crossroads. Not too far up the road, she could see lights blinking off to the right. She pulled in behind his rig, leaving her truck running and the lights on. As she opened the truck door, the morning fog misted her face. Someone was coming around the front of the truck, and as he approached, he said, "Ma'am, am I glad to see you this morning." He had an odd little twang to his voice. He was wearing jeans, boots, and a long-sleeved shirt. He had on a gray cowboy hat. That was about all she could make out in the light from her truck. He lifted up his head as he stuck out his hand and smiled. His handshake was firm and strong.

He walked to the rear of his trailer, opened the gate, and out backed a black horse. Catherine couldn't believe her eyes—it was a gorgeous Arabian.

The horse took her completely by surprise. She expected some old rangy looking cow pony—the kind she'd ridden as a child on endless dusty trails. She was standing there looking at him when the man handed her the lead rope. "I sure appreciate you rescuing my boy here." He started toward his truck.

Catherine's jaw dropped and she quickly blurted

out, "Excuse me, but I think I'll need some help with the ramp and loading him."

He turned, smiling the kind of smile she'd seen in school after one of the kids landed a spitball in her hair. He walked to the rear of her trailer, put down the ramp, and said, "Nice trailer." When she brought the horse around to the ramp, he took the lead from her, flipped it up over the horse's neck, and told him, "Load up." Without a moment's hesitation, the horse walked up the ramp and stood patiently. Zane went around to the left door and tied him. Catherine forgot to turn on the interior trailer lights, but the early morning sun peeping through the trees gave enough light to make sure he used a quick release knot. She doubted she'd need it. The horse was amazingly quiet.

"I'll call you as soon as I know something about my truck. I'll get your number from Buck."

He was so matter-of-fact. She didn't have a chance to say a word before he continued, "He's got some fancy name on his papers, but I just call him Trouble. I picked him up before he was going to slaughter. I don't think he'll be much of a problem. We didn't expect this." He walked with her to her truck door, stopping to inspect the trailer hitch. She was glad to see he was that particular about his horse.

She finally spoke, "I'll take good care of him. I hope you get your truck fixed soon and the two of you can be on your way." She chewed on her lower lip. It came out of her mouth curt, not the way she wanted to say it at all. It sounded harsh. She gulped.

He started to walk away, turned rather quickly on his heels, and said, "Don't worry, ma'am; I'll get him back with me as soon as I can."

Damn it! It's bad enough that he keeps calling me

"Ma'am," but now I've stuck my foot in it because he knows I really don't want his horse at my place. That word—"Ma'am"—grated on Catherine like nails on a chalkboard. It made her feel old and ancestral. The damage was done. She didn't say anything else. She just shut the door and carefully pulled out, heading north. It would be better to take a different route home rather than try to turn around on the narrow road. It still amazed her that you could be out here and not see another soul. *I'm sure not in Kansas anymore, Toto.*

~~~

Catherine was nervous hauling his horse. She was careful not to make any sudden stops and made the turns as slowly and smoothly as possible. She sighed as she pulled into her own driveway and stopped in front of the barn. Her dogs were barking at the porch door, but she didn't dare let them out until she had unloaded the horse and had him safely in the barn. When one of her horses whinnied, Trouble answered with a softer voice than Catherine had expected. He stood patiently looking over his shoulder at her as she let down the ramp. She opened the left escape door, hooked it, and untied his rope. He never even attempted to back up until she undid the butt bar and moved back around to his head. She was scared because she wasn't that experienced. If he bolted back, she might not make it in time to catch the lead—and then all hell would break out with him loose on the farm.

She swallowed as she took hold of the lead and said, "Back," preparing for the worst. He stepped backwards, one foot at a time, allowing her to duck under the chest bar. Once outside, he raised his head and looked all around, but he waited for her to lead him off. He was
~~~

much braver going into the barn than her horses had been. She put him in the last stall on the left, leaving an empty stall between him and the closest horse. She hurriedly gave everyone hay and filled his water bucket. She gave her horses their morning grain, but she had no idea what to feed Trouble. She'd play it safe for now until she heard from Buck or his friend what's-his-name. "Sorry, buddy, you're only getting hay for now." Catherine left the truck and trailer parked where they were at the barn and headed up to the house.

Late that afternoon, heading into evening, she came through the back door in time to grab the ringing phone.

"Hold on a minute; it's Buck. I'll put Zane on." At least she knew the guy's name now, but what she really wanted to know was when he was coming for his horse.

"Ma'am, first off, thank you for rescuing my horse. Buck's trying to get his trailer back tomorrow. Do you mind keeping Trouble overnight?"

The horse had honestly been no problem. She'd let him out in the barn paddock for a while. She reluctantly agreed, "It's fine. He's not really a problem so far, but what do you want me to feed him? I've only given him hay."

"Sweet feed. Just sweet feed, ma'am, about half a pound or so. He's an easy keeper."

"Okay then; I'll wait to hear from you tomorrow."

"Good night, ma'am, and thanks again."

She wanted then to tell him not to call her "ma'am," but it wasn't worth the effort. With any luck, he and his horse would be on their way soon.

All of her chores were done. The dogs were settled in, and for the first time in a long time, Catherine couldn't think of anything she needed to do. The horse hadn't even messed in her trailer, and she only had to back up twice to get it parked back in its spot. All the boxes were unpacked, the house was organized, and the chores that had once worn her completely out were now just a part of every day. She fixed herself a nice cup of lemon tea and headed to her writing room. There had been no time even to think about writing since the day she had set it up. She'd had no clue until she peeked at her journal that six days had already passed.

Forget all the stuff buzzing around in your head; just write about the horses tonight. She listened to that inner voice and picked up a card she found while unpacking. With a beautiful flowing calligraphy pen she copied it onto the page:

Growing means changing,
Rearranging my life,
Seeing the world in new ways.

She changed pens to the one with peacock ink (her favorite childhood color) and began:

I know I've always loved them. In fact, there is a photo of me in diapers pulling on a horse with wheels. I'm trying to get it back from my cousin. Then there's a photo of me on a paint pony when I'm about five years old. They have always been a part of the dream. Does every little girl want a horse? I begged for one every Christmas. It wasn't until my mother married Hamilton that it became possible for her to afford riding lessons for us. I think she soon discovered it was a safe place to leave us while she catered to her new life. It bothered my sister. She felt dumped, mostly because she wasn't passionate about horses, not at all like me. She tolerated them for me. Thank you, Kiki.

I haven't even explored all the property yet. I keep thinking I'll ride one of the horses, take some of the dogs, but I'm afraid. Who would even know I was missing if I fell off, got hurt? No one. It never occurred to me how alone I'd really be. The phone hardly ever rings. I barely even know what day it is. I could be out there somewhere on the hundred acres forever. It's unnerving. I'm not usually such a scaredy cat. Yes I am!

The dogs and the horses have changed my life completely. I enjoy watching them, being with them. I love the way the horses smell. My favorite moment is late at night when I turn off the barn lights and all I can hear is them munching their hay.

My other favorite moment is when the house is quiet like now. The dogs are asleep, the chores are all done and the night is mine. No television. No interruptions—Nothing at all to do. For the first time in my life, there is no pressure. It seems like I'm dreaming. I just wish the dream had a different ending. Maybe I'll have to write a different version. To be continued....

She spent some time looking over a few of her books, took a quick shower, and then settled into her wonderful bed. The pale moonlight illuminated her room just enough to make it feel dreamy. Her feather comforter warmed her like a cocoon. Sleep came more easily this night.

CHAPTER 7

Zane climbed into the tow truck for the ride into town. Once they got his truck and trailer safely delivered, the mechanic would be able to locate the problem. Buck was waiting at the gate at Rick's Auto & Repair. He was glad he would have Zane captive at least for a little while.

The bear hug lasted much longer than Zane's comfort level until he'd twisted himself out of it, saying, "Geez, honey, not now."

Buck felt deeply emotional, choked up actually. He had never thought far enough into the future to have contemplated what would happen when they retired. He had thought they'd end up in some town together, probably back home. Zane hadn't even talked about going to Montana, but Buck just assumed that he would when they parted ways. Zane had become different, more distant. Now they were both headed in opposite directions. Buck was dismayed when Zane decided just to take off.

Zane spoke to the guy behind the counter briefly and told him to reach him at Buck's feed store. The guy nodded, and Zane and Buck headed down the sidewalk. Buck was grinning from ear to ear as he unlocked the door. Zane was impressed with the feed store and the fact that in such a short time Buck had carved out a pretty nice life for himself. Buck was lucky that way, always had been. Things fell into his lap, almost by happenstance— things other people struggled for.

"Well?" Buck asked, sweeping his arms in both directions.

"You did good, you son of a bitch, but then, you always do. Congratulations, man." Zane slapped him on the back.

Yes, they both had their retirement, but that son of a bitch had bought a lottery ticket years ago and hit a really big jackpot. Zane had talked Buck into seeking financial advice, which had worked out very well for him. Buck paid off his parents' ranch, set up an L.L.C., and even got a crew to go in and spruce up the old place. He had offered to do the same for his friend, but Zane had wanted no part of it. "My father would never hear of it anyway. I'd love to help my mother, but he'd just abuse her because of it. Forget it, man."

Buck refused to invest the remainder of the money in the stock market, so he simply put it in a savings account, where it had been compounding interest all these years. It seemed so long ago, but when Buck decided to buy the feed store and the house, his good fortune had made it easy.

"I know you haven't forgotten that money I won, Zane. Well, that's what paid for all this stuff. It's been accumulating you know. Well, anyway, what I want to tell you is when you get ready, you just let me know and I'll help you get yourself set up first-rate. I mean it. No matter where it is, it's yours. Do you understand me?"

Zane was staring out the front window of the store, lost in a whirl of memories.

"Zane, did you hear me?"

Zane's head snapped around, "Yeah, Buck. I heard you, but I can't take your money. I won't take your money."

"I saved it for us, man. We've always been a team,

partners you know. It was never meant for just me. Say when and it's yours. Even if something happens to me, I've made arrangements, you know. You'll get your share. You need to enjoy it now. Don't be a fool. Not after all we've been through."

"I nearly got you killed."

"From where I sit, you saved my life. Figure it out. If you weren't there, my life would have been over, man. Come on. You know I'm right."

Zane looked out the window, fighting back a tear and attempting to push down the lump welling up in his throat. He hadn't expected Buck to be this generous. They had never discussed it again once he'd told him "No" so many years ago.

"You're the one who pushed me to seek financial help; who knows what I might have done if you hadn't. I would have squandered it all away. Yeah, we spent a bunch of it on those hunting trips, parties, but man, it was worth every penny. Because of you, my family's ranch is secure, and look what I've done with the money now—my feed store, a great house, and the farm. I've waited a long time for both of us to get to this point. You have to take what's rightfully yours."

Buck walked over behind Zane and squeezed his shoulder. "You're more like a brother to me. For Christ sake, you're family."

Zane couldn't say a word.

"Listen, man, if you want, I'll cram the fucking dollar bills down your fucking throat, you asshole!" Buck slammed his fist into Zane's arm. They both finally laughed, and Buck squeezed Zane's shoulders again.

The money would make everything easier for Zane, especially the decisions he needed to make. First, he had to solve the truck problems, and then he'd go get his horse. Maybe he would hang out here with Buck for a little while so he would have some time to figure things out.

"Let's see what happens with the truck," he said. He wanted to make no promises.

"Does that mean you might stick around a little while?"

"That means, let's see what happens with the truck."

~~~

The next morning, Zane was awake at the crack of dawn. It was nearly 8 a.m. when Buck found him sitting on the front porch. The screen door slammed shut and Zane jumped.

"Easy there, guy!" Buck laughed

"I was about a million miles away," Zane explained.

"I'm glad to see you're letting go a little. A few months ago if I'd have done that, I'd have been looking at your revolver," Buck chuckled.

"Yeah, but it bothers me. I feel like I've lost my edge."

"You don't need an edge anymore, man. It's over."

"I don't know. Don't you still feel like you gotta watch your back?"

"Yeah, but not really. Not here anyway. In town sometimes, but lately, the faces are all familiar. It's kinda nice you know. You ought to try it for a while."

"I don't think it's for me, Buck, but don't get me wrong; it sure seems to fit you."

"Well, so far so good. How about we get some grub in town; then we can ask about your truck."

Zane picked up his coffee cup and walked down the front porch steps. It was a nice enough farm, quiet, away
~~~

from town. The sun was playing through the old oaks that lined the drive.

"Hey, how come you don't have any cows? Hell, Buck, you don't even own a damn dog." Buck smiled as he pulled his truck keys out of his pocket. He'd get Zane to stay somehow.

~~~

They ate a hearty breakfast at Rachel's Diner. Buck liked the buffet. It was quick, delicious, and Buck seemed to enjoy being teased by the waitress about his "redheaded girlfriend." Zane could see that his best friend was easily fitting into this rinky-dink little town. Being here seemed like stepping back in time with its old buildings and slower-paced people.

"Don't you need to open the store?" Zane asked when he noticed it was already after nine.

"The sign on the door says '10 a.m.—5 p.m.', but I pretty much get there at half past nine. These people have no problem with waiting or coming back later. It's pretty laid back."

The news from the mechanic was grim—"computer component—fried." Words Zane didn't want to hear. "Could be a week." Zane felt stuck. To make the situation even worse, Buck was having trouble locating his own trailer.

Zane wasn't very pleased with the news. It was a brand new truck. Couldn't a dealer nearby just take a component off a new truck on his lot and let him get out of here? No, the world just didn't work like that anymore. Nothing was practical or made sense. No, you had to wait for the factory to send the component. Things had to match up on the computer. It was bullshit.
~~~

"Tell Catherine it's my fault. She seems like a reasonable person," Buck said.

"You didn't hear the tone in her voice, did you?"

"Charm her. You're the one who didn't have to say a word and women fell on top of you."

"Did you happen to notice the one little detail—they were all pretty much drunk at the time?"

Buck threw his keys at Zane. "Here, make yourself useful. I need to fill her order, and I'll tell you how to get there so you can deliver it, check on your horse, and tell her the news. Pull the truck around back and you can help me load it up."

<u>CHAPTER 8</u>

Catherine took a deep breath and led the gelding out of his stall. She'd been so occupied with moving in, learning how to take care of all of this, she hadn't even had time to consider riding. Plus, she was nervous about riding alone. Sundance was a saint, standing still while she groomed and tacked him up, giving her more confidence. She wore a soft crème colored cotton shirt with the sleeves rolled up, a fleece vest, breeches, and paddock boots. The lady at the tack store suggested a lightweight helmet. As a child, Catherine had loved the feeling of the wind in her hair, but the woman convinced her when she said, "No sense taking a chance with a brain injury. The new models are so much better. You'll get used to it in no time." Catherine adjusted the chinstrap, pulled on her gloves, and looked for a spot where she could easily get up on her horse. She tried climbing up on the fence, but she couldn't get Sundance to stand close enough. She finally found a spot in the yard where he was lower and swung on up. She couldn't believe how stiff she felt.

Sundy walked off and Catherine guided him through the open gate. Her three mares and Trouble lifted their heads as she passed along the lane between the fields. She hoped that cowboy called soon. She left four of the dogs in the house and took General and Champ along. They were looking up at her like she'd lost her mind. They'd obviously never seen a person on a horse before.

Champ looked especially worried; he let out a whine and stood on his hind legs.

Catherine laughed at him. "It's okay. I promise. Come on, let's go." She had no intention of doing anything but walk, especially since she didn't know what was at the end of the lane or even where it headed. She felt silly not knowing about her own property, but today was the perfect day to do a little exploring.

When they reached the end of the lane, she came to a tee. She headed east, hugging a tree line. The soft breeze felt wonderful on her skin. The dogs were clingy, but they managed to have enough sense to stay out from under Sundy's feet. The property rolled up into a rocky area, and Catherine was surprised when she discovered a stand of trees with a fence around it. She tried to move Sundy closer, but he was resisting so she stood up in the stirrups to have a better look. It was a deep sinkhole. She'd completely forgotten about such things until now. She was glad to see the wire was closely woven so no animals could easily get in there. Apparently, it had been a problem in the past.

She found a narrow path she thought would lead back toward the house, and when they came out into the sunlight and the open field, Catherine gasped. The view was amazing. She was up behind the house on a fairly elevated hill. The house and barn were in the midst of the oaks and looked like a picture. She could see the paddocks and the way the fields were fenced. It took her breath away.

"I think I did a good thing, guys. This place is gorgeous." Then she spotted the white pickup. It looked like the one the feed store guy drove. "Oh no, that guy's at the house and there's no trailer. This can't be good."

Catherine urged her horse out into the field, having

no problem getting him to pick up the pace. He wanted to trot, but she wasn't ready to go bouncing through the tall grass. Still, she needed to get back to the house as quickly as possible. No telling what was going on with this man. Luckily, the dogs stayed close.

As she entered the yard, the dogs rushed up to the truck to sniff the tires and then Zane. He was sitting on the tailgate. He had on a long-sleeved blue shirt, jeans, a gray western hat, and dark brown boots.

"I brought you your feed order, ma'am."

"Well, thank you very much for waiting." She tried to dismount gracefully, but her legs felt like rubber.

"I guess I didn't expect to see you riding."

She wanted to say something smart like, "I have a horse farm so I can raise cattle," but instead she told the truth. "First time in years and I'm a bit rusty." He wasn't about to tell her that her right stirrup was two holes shorter than her left. He never understood why people rode in those English saddles anyway. He kept his mouth shut and just smiled.

"Did you see your horse?"

"Yes, ma'am. Thank you. He seems to be enjoying himself."

"He's fine. I guess you are coming back later with the trailer?" She looked over his shoulder at her order.

Zane hated it, but he was really stuck at the moment. He ignored the question. "I'll unload this while you un-tack your horse if you point me in the right direction, ma'am."

They finished about the same time and were both standing in the barn aisle.

He decided to fess up. "There's a bit of a situation with the horse trailer. Buck loaned it to this kid who loaned it to another kid, and now the first kid is trying to find the second kid."

"Sounds complicated."

"Yeah, kinda, ma'am. But, if you want Trouble out of here today and wouldn't mind doin' it, you could haul him over to Buck's place. I'll pay you, ma'am."

She made a decision. "I don't have a problem with Trouble staying here for another day, but I do have an issue with you."

"Okay, ma'am?" he said, making it sound like a question as his eyebrows raised a little.

"It's this 'ma'am' thing. I hate it. Do you really have to call me 'ma'am'?"

"Well, no, ma'am; I don't have to call you 'ma'am' if you don't want me to, ma'am." She knew he was playing with her like a schoolboy. "Incidentally, my mother taught me that 'ma'am' is an indication of respect for someone."

She smacked him on the shoulder with her gloves. "Stop it, please. I really do hate it. I hate it like sand on broccoli."

"Sand on broccoli? Now that's an interesting metaphor. That's probably why I hate that stuff."

She didn't feel like keeping up the bantering so she got back to the subject, "I really don't mind your horse at all. He's easy to care for."

"I insist on paying you."

She stopped him before he could use that word again. "Why don't you just clean his stall? How does that sound?" she asked as she walked away toward the house.

~~~

When Catherine returned to the barn to bring the horses in, she found Zane in the stall with his horse. He had a brush in his hand and Trouble had a brush in his
~~~

mouth, happily pushing it against the wall. She didn't say a word.

He was pulling out in the truck when she brought the second mare from the field. He hung out the window and shouted, "I'll be back tomorrow. Gotta take Buck his truck."

"Thank you," she said. He tipped his hat and drove away. She was grateful when she discovered that he actually had cleaned all the stalls.

~~~

Zane headed straight to Rick's Auto. He was more than disappointed with the news. The truck computer was totally fried and the mechanic was attempting to have a new one shipped. The word "attempting" bothered Zane almost as much as the word "computer." These new fangled contraptions were great until they broke; then you found out how crazy our society had become.

"There's no way to repair it," he said. "Just toss out the old and plug in the new." It sounded so glib that it made him nuts. The worst thing was all the old parts found their way to these man-made mountains called landfills. Those Florida mountains looked so damn unnatural, especially when they later planted them with palm trees. It just wasn't right.

~~~

Catherine watched as the white pickup came down the drive. Zane arrived every evening to care for his horse. The horses were already in their stalls, fed their grain, and happily munching on hay. He told her he'd move the horse to Buck's, but Trouble seemed settled, and it wouldn't be for long. The truth was, she enjoyed watching the horse when she worked outside. Something was different about him—he played. Yesterday she had been fascinated when she saw him pick up a stick and run with it in his teeth. Then he stopped and appeared to throw it up in the air. He did it twice so she knew it was no coincidence.

She closed the oven door, washed her hands, and headed out the back door. Some of the dogs were already outside and had eagerly joined Zane in the barn. The rest she left in the house for now. It was nice having a real person around to talk to. He was just coming out of the barn leading his horse.

"Going for a ride?" she called.

"Just a short one tonight; I'm a little bit tired." Zane swung his leg up and settled in the saddle.

She felt impulsive, and yes, maybe a bit lonely; she had not intended to do it, but she said, "When you're finished, why don't you stay for dinner? It's just chicken—nothing fancy."

He hesitated for a moment weighing the consequences of saying, "Yes," but he'd be leaving Highberry soon. It was a meal cooked by a woman for a change. Why not?

She could see him trying to decide. "No need to hurry," she said. "I just put it in the oven. We have an hour."

She was surprised at that small word. "We...." She hoped he hadn't paid any attention to it. It used to refer to her and James. She said it unexpectedly, but now it was messing with her mind. It made her think of all the things she was missing. She wondered whether he ever thought in terms of Zane and someone else.

Over dinner, it began insidiously. She started asking questions, and when the bottle of wine was gone, she offered "something with a little more bite." His answers began to be more specific, more detailed, encyclopedic at times.

"Montana. I grew up in northern Montana on a cattle ranch. I won't even tell you how large, but it was a pretty good spread."

She felt rather silly, but she asked anyway, "Did you have much contact with the Indians? I mean, I guess I should call them Native Americans. Isn't that the correct term now?"

"Yeah, I did." She watched him drift away.

"Zane, are you okay?" she asked softly as she found herself touching his arm.

His head popped around, and he looked at her for a moment like a man who didn't quite know where he was. "Yeah, I'm fine. I didn't know how to answer that."

"We can talk about something else, really; it's okay."

"No, no, I think I just need to borrow your bathroom for a minute. Overflow, you know."

She pointed down the hall as he set down the glass he'd been gripping tightly. "Down the hall on the right."

Catherine cleared away the dishes and cut two slices of carrot cake. She started a pot of coffee. No sense sending him home half asleep.

"The coffee will be ready in a minute." She thought it best to stay sitting at the kitchen table, so she didn't make him feel too comfortable in the living room.

"My mother is Native American, as you put it. Of the Blackfeet Tribe. I don't quite know what to tell you. She's a wonderful person. I wish you could see her beautiful deerskin dress. It has a hundred elk teeth carefully placed and sewn with sinew. She wraps herself in this beautiful red shawl I bought for her. Around her neck, she wears a large turquoise and silver necklace that

John Yellow Dog made for her. It's a shame because Yellow Dog has so much talent and yet he just stays on the ranch. When the ranch hands gave it to her, they told her how much they appreciated her fine cooking, taking care of their laundry, and everything else she did for them. Many nights she's nursed them through an illness or kneeled by their sides when they pulled a calf or saved a foal. Her gentle ways and secrets saved many a man and even more four-leggeds. She is really quite the woman."

She watched his expression change as his thoughts took him away. She was surprised that he'd opened up and told her so much about his mother. She had almost forgotten what she'd asked him. "Blackfeet. I don't think I've ever heard of them."

"They were and are one of the most powerful tribes in the American northwest. Their real name is Siksika. Three separate tribes living in Montana and up into Canada. They are named Blackfeet because of the color of their moccasins, either painted that color or sometimes darkened by the prairie fires."

"So did they always live in Montana?"

"They were migratory. They roamed the planet for over five thousand years. They followed the French traders west because of the animal furs and pelts. The buffalo played a huge role in their survival."

"That's interesting. Did you have buffalo on your ranch?"

"Cattle—cattle and horses." Zane slowly stood up and smoothed his jeans down the front of his legs.

"Buck has no idea what's become of me, ma'am. I'm sure he wrangled a ride home. Thank you very much for the excellent meal and the good company." As he lifted his hat from the back of the chair and moved to the door, Catherine stuck out her hand, taking Zane by surprise.

She took his hand, pulling him closer, and quickly gave him a hug. She felt him stiffen and he seemed a bit flustered as he barely hugged her back.

"Thank you. It was really nice to have someone to cook for and to talk to. The dogs don't talk to me," she said. She watched him as without a word, he turned and stepped out the door, closing it quickly behind him. She was unprepared for what she was trying hard not to feel.

~~~

Catherine knew without a doubt the screeching voice she heard belonged to Deb Albom. It was the first time she had ventured off the ranch for breakfast, and here was Deb at the Blue Owl Café. With any luck at all, she wouldn't see her in the back corner of the "street side addition," as the waitress put it. The tiny restaurant was surprisingly busy. Deb was waiting by the door, chatting with no one in particular, when it happened. The door opened and Buck and Zane walked in. Catherine heard her, along with every other person in the entire building including the cook, as Deb declared, "Well, ain't this just the cat's meow; my perfect morning, running into the love of my life. Hello, Mr. Buck."

Catherine was surprised that Buck hadn't looked through the window before opening the door, but there he was with Deb wrapped around his neck and curling into him. Catherine could barely hear what they were saying as Buck cleared his throat, apparently signaling to Zane. She heard Buck say, "Sorry, Deb, but we're meeting someone about a business deal," as he unwrapped himself and walked toward her. Catherine could see he'd spotted her. He winked at her as he approached and said, "God, I'm so sorry we're late. Thank you for waiting."
~~~

Catherine's view of the antics at the door and the frantic expression on Buck's face gave her a clue about what would happen. The two men pulled out chairs at her table and sat down. Catherine stood and put out her hand toward Deb as she approached, following right behind the men. Deb defiantly folded her arms, refusing to shake Catherine's hand.

"Hi, Deb," Catherine said. "It's so nice to see you again. I'm awfully sorry, but I've got a lot of business questions for these two about the farm. Can we get together some other time?"

Deb stomped her foot, spun on her heels, and stormed out. The three of them and everyone else in the cafe watched as she fled out the front door, slamming it so hard the little bell rang for what seemed like several minutes. Everyone spontaneously burst into applause at her departure, and Buck stood up and took a bow.

Catherine was surprised at the reaction. Buck said, "Small town. Everyone knows everything about everyone. It's the curse of living the slow life. And, thank you very much for your expert rescue."

"It's my pleasure. I've seen mice run from fat cats before, but you two are hysterical."

"Wait a minute; exactly who are you calling fat?" Buck asked.

Catherine giggled, "Oh no, that didn't come out right. I mean I've seen the cat and mouse game before."

"He's teasing you, Catherine." It was the first thing Zane had said since coming into the café.

"Don't they say you only tease people you like?" she teased Buck right back.

Zane frowned. "They say that, but don't trust him. He's really mean."

"Well, I'd love to keep up the bantering, but I've got

to get back to the farm." Catherine was nervous about being away even for a short amount of time.

"We've got the check. It's the least we can do after you saved us from that woman."

"What's this 'we' thing, Buck?" Zane asked. Catherine grabbed the check, waving it as she headed toward the cashier. She swore as she drove back to the farm she'd never do that again. Too much drama! It was hard to believe she now loved isolation and simplicity so much. Life was certainly easier solo. It was a damn shame that humans experienced loneliness. Too bad you couldn't lock yourself into neutral and really enjoy being alone. She drove slowly up the driveway, taking in the view of the house—her house. It seemed so safe.

~~~

Catherine was turning off the lights downstairs when the phone rang. "Hey, Catherine, it's Roger. Are you doing all right?"

Roger was her husband's college roommate and closest friend. He had been the best man at their wedding, thrown James one hell of a bachelor party, and nearly made him late for the ceremony. Catherine had learned to tolerate him because he had also been James' choice for an attorney. He had been handling all of the affairs since the accident. Catherine's life during those first few months was a blur, but she remembered Roger being there from almost the first moment until she had packed up and moved away from New York—and him.

Roger was the opposite of tall, dark, and handsome. He was medium height, with dirty blonde hair that went in every direction, and he had strange facial features. His nose was too small, his chin was too large, and his eyes
~~~

were too close together. He tried to talk softly, but instead, he always sounded like he had a sore throat, which luckily kept you from wanting to get close to him. Plus, he had faint freckles. Catherine assumed they were all over his body, but they were at least all over every part of him you could see.

Catherine flinched at the thought of him as she said, "Hi, Roger. I was about to call it a night."

"So life on the farm is so boring you go to bed at nine?"

And, he asked stupid questions. She didn't feel like chatting at all, especially not with him. "No, it's not boring. The physical stuff wears you out, that's all."

He had been furious when she told him she was moving. He had plans for her and he told her so. He also told her adamantly how she was complicating everything.

"Your accountant sent me your portfolio. James would be pleased. At the moment, the market seems to be working in your favor."

Roger equated everything with the almighty dollar. He had no idea about feelings. He would never know how it felt to lose the love of your life, the person you expected to grow old with. Roger's women were trophies. Once the win diminished, they became disposable. Oh, occasionally, he would recycle someone, but you knew it was only because of what she could do for him financially or in the bedroom. He gave her the creeps, but she had kept James happy putting up with his good old buddy.

"I haven't even looked at my mail. Sorry."

"Catherine, you are far too naïve. You really need to stay on top of things."

In his reality, she was certain he was thinking about being on top of her. He made her feel uneasy. He liked to play these handy little games, which she had allowed herself to play with him. But she was growing tired of his shenanigans. She knew perfectly well what her financial situation was, and as soon as she could, she was going to stop him from skimming off his "share" in so-called legal fees. She needed to tie up a few more loose ends first. She had already talked to her stepfather, Hamilton, about it, and their family friend was ready to take over. Preston Rutledge knew Catherine's situation and she trusted him completely.

She quickly cut Roger off. "I have a terrible headache, Rog; we'll have to talk another time." She didn't even give him a chance to respond before she pushed the button. She wanted no thoughts of him cluttering up her mind at this hour.

She headed up the stairs with Friskie tucked in her arm, giving in to part of the loneliness by allowing the little dog to sleep with her. She knew Champ would sneak in later; he curled up by her bed every night. They were a great comfort.

CHAPTER 9

The porch on Buck's house faced west, offering a spectacular view of the setting sun. The dark clouds hung just above the tree line, giving the appearance of a mountain ridge. The sandwiches they prepared were an easy meal. Buck handed Zane a drink.

"It sure has been an unbelievable ride." When Zane failed to respond, he kept talking. "I never imagined I'd be here at this stage of my life. Now, I figure maybe ten years and I'll be ready to head back home, unless, of course, my parents need me before then. The ranch has been good to them. They are in excellent health for their ages." He sat quietly, waiting, sipping his drink. He might as well be talking to the air. "So what do you think about Catherine? She's quite the fancy snatch, don't you think?"

Zane's reaction was quick and surprised him. "For Christ's sake, Buck; what the hell's the matter with you anymore?" The screen door slammed behind him. It was the second time today that Buck had seen a different side of him. First, Zane had told Catherine that Buck had a mean streak and now this. Buck shrugged and finished his drink. When the night turned cool and the wind picked up, he moved into the quiet house. Zane was already behind the closed guest bedroom door.

Buck was having frequent dreams about Catherine. He would wake up in the night feeling like a schoolboy—and behaving like one too. He couldn't stop the thoughts;

nor did he want to. He just didn't quite know how to maneuver into her life. It pissed him off that Zane had shown up and without any effort at all, fallen right in with her, even getting invited to dinner. It wasn't right.

~~~

In the dark bedroom, Zane lay with his arms folded behind his head, staring at nothing at all. He knew he should have kept going. There was no telling when his truck would be fixed. The only good part about this situation was that his horse was safe and he had a roof over his head. Meanwhile, he was feeling uncomfortable. He didn't remember being so bothered by things before. Had he just been oblivious, or were you just more aware when you weren't driven by an agenda? It was stupid, really, getting upset over a word, but she didn't deserve to be called something like that—"fancy snatch." She was far above the women he and Buck were accustomed to.

~~~

By morning, Zane's demeanor was back to normal. Breakfast was sizzling and the coffee was ready when he stepped out of his room.

"You sure are right on this morning. I guess all that sleep did you good," Buck said.

Zane ignored him, placing his plate on the table as he sat down.

Buck said, "Say, there's something I want to talk to you about. I thought of it last night after you'd gone to bed. Bill Brannan called me right before you got here. They are looking for you. They thought you were driving those wheels they gave you. Where the hell did you dump it?"

"Do you really think I'd be caught dead driving that thing? I put it in storage until I can get rid of it. It has a damn tracking device. It's fully loaded. Besides, I needed the pickup. It makes more sense now that I'm hauling Trouble around with me. Why the hell is Bill Brannan looking for me now?"

"Said he had a little job for you. How did he know you were in Florida?"

"It's not like we're hiding, Buck. He probably figured I'd be here because of you."

"Here's what he told me. The word is that her husband's death was no accident."

"Who are you talking about?" Zane was looking at him like he was confused.

"Catherine, of course. They think her husband may have been dead when the car went off the ravine."

"Does she know they're questioning it?" Zane asked.

"No. That's why they want you. They don't want any trail leading to her."

"Do me a favor. Don't tell me another thing about it. If Bill calls back, tell him you haven't seen me."

"I can't do that."

"Yes, you can, and you will. I'm not getting mixed up in this." Zane wasn't about to do anything that involved Bill Brannan. That man always exuded problems. You simply couldn't trust him. Zane wanted no part of anything to do with him. What part of his being retired were they not getting? "Don't you remember what I told you? If you have to become your enemy to beat him, then what have you really won? That bastard not only became the enemy, he slept with it. Did you forget how he fell into that information warfare shit with that woman? I wouldn't be surprised if he were the one who nearly got us killed.

Buck, I'm telling you, this is trouble."

"Trouble? Don't you mean troubleshooter? She walked that thin line between good and evil. The threats were growing enormously and they needed her. Everything had become more diverse, complex, and what she did was extremely dangerous. She stayed under the radar and provided a lot of information to Bill about the Taliban and Al-Quaeda way before the Cole attack, and she had just begun working on Massoud. When he got involved with her, Bill had no clue she was a Stinger. Besides, he's always been partial to redheads." Buck smiled his shitty grin and chewed on his toothpick.

"I'm not interested in going over this again," Zane replied. "I don't care. That part of my life is over, Buck. Let it be."

CHAPTER 10

Catherine expected to be lonely. She missed meeting friends for tea or gathering after work for drinks and a nice dinner. She especially missed massages and, oh yes, manicures. Her hands were a mess. At the moment, they were stained brown from a poor attempt at cleaning her tack.

She also knew there were certain things she couldn't do. She couldn't attach the bush hog to the tractor. A few months ago, she didn't even know what one was called. The other evening, Zane had patiently explained to her about diesel fuel and how to clean the filter screen to keep debris out of the tank. He had taught her how to make the necessary adjustments so the parts matched up and came together more easily. He even showed her how to balance the thing so that when she mowed, the cut would be even.

The next night, as soon as he arrived, he handed her a pair of gloves. "Use these. They will save your hands. And, may I ask a silly question? Why don't you hire someone to help you?" She didn't have a chance to answer before he had turned and walked away into the barn.

She liked the way he explained things. Nothing was demeaning in his tone when he talked to her. He said, "This has a protective sleeve on the pto, which is good, but you still have to be careful. I've seen too many bad accidents with people tangled up in them. Before you get off the tractor, disengage the pto so it's not turning."

He must have thought he read a questioning look. "You see how it spins? Without that protective cover, your sleeve or pant leg can get caught and that could rip off your arm or leg. If it didn't, you'd wish that it had. Understand? Oh, and another thing, watch out for trees. You get dragged off this seat and you could be chopped up by this damn thing."

She knew he was right. She needed to pay attention. The first time she mowed, she chose one of the fields with no trees. When she was finished, she backed the tractor and bush hog into the shed and headed up to the house. She had no sooner opened the back door than she heard the phone ringing. She made a mad dash for the kitchen, scattering the dogs. She was shocked when she realized who was on the line.

"Hey, cuz, how ya doin?" It was Waylon. She hadn't spoken to him in years. Waylon Kendale was three years older than her, but being family, they had been close as children.

"Hey, you. I'm okay. How did you get my number?"

"I called your mother. It's not like I don't know where she lives."

"So what's up?" She knew he wouldn't have called if there wasn't something to call about.

"We finally got fed up and moved to Alabama. We're in the midst of building a house. We're on Helene's family's land. Hey, listen, I need you to do something for me. My dad is sick. Can you go check on him?"

Catherine's thoughts were racing. It was just like him to pop back into her life and expect her to jump. She wasn't leaving the farm. Not now. Not for him. She wasn't going to do it.

"What's wrong with your brother?"

"We're wanting to be sure of what's going on. Justin's fine. It's just, well, you know."

The two boys had never gotten along. They just didn't, and somehow, she was always in the middle. Not this time. Not after all these years. They weren't kids anymore and things were too different.

"What would I do that he can't? Besides, how far can it be? Doesn't he live in Palm City?"

"You're smarter than both of us put together about that medical stuff. We need you for Dad."

He knew how to reel her in and how to manipulate her. But she was standing her ground this time.

"I can't go. I have a farm, animals. You can't ask me to go. I'm all alone. I have no one to take over for me."

"Your mother told me about your husband. I'm really sorry, Catherine."

She couldn't say a word as her eyes welled up with tears and she held her breath.

"Catherine, I'm scared. I've never heard Dad sound like this. He barely talks to me when I call him."

"I can't. I don't see how I can pull it off. I can't."

"Think about it. Take my new number. Just think about it. He needs you."

Catherine reluctantly wrote Waylon's phone number on the pad by the phone; then they said their goodbyes. She had a crushing feeling in her chest. She hadn't seen Uncle Walton in years.

~~~

It amazed her how the sound of Waylon's voice had made her feel so small. In an instant, she had reverted right back to her childhood, and then she had gone on the defensive. When they were little, she had followed her
~~~

cousin everywhere—he was her hero—but by the time she was twelve, they were fussing at each other.

Once Waylon had taken them into the woods, all four of them, frog hunting. Her little sister, Kiki, and his younger brother, Justin, were tagalongs. Waylon had a brand new bow, quiver, and arrows. The colors of the pretty feathers fascinated her. He used his pocketknife and cut her a spear from a palm frond. When they came out of the path at the pond's edge and onto the white sand, a small gray egret became startled, lifted quickly, and flew away.

"Stay right here," he had instructed them as he crept through the tall slender grass along the pond's edge. They watched as he placed an arrow on the string, pulled back, and released. Her heart was pounding. What she didn't expect, didn't know, was that the frog would scream. She covered her ears.

"Make it stop! Make it stop!" she shouted.

Waylon turned abruptly, glaring at her, then waded in after his arrow. "You wanted to come," he said over his shoulder. "What's the matter with you? You knew we were going frog hunting. What did you expect?" His face looked stern as he held up the arrow with the frog dangling by its leg. The shaft had gone through at the hip. The poor thing was still hollering, and it sounded to Catherine like it was saying, "Help, help, help!"

She kept her hands over her ears and tried not to look at its eyes. "Let it go. Let it go."

"It won't live with only one leg. Something will eat it anyway." His voice had softened a little. He took out his knife, pushed the frog onto the sand, and pierced it through the middle. She turned away just before he stuck it.

"Why did you have to shoot it? Why?"

"You asked if you could come along; now you ask me why I shot it? What did you think we were going to do?" He sounded disgusted.

"I didn't think you would really do it," she lied. "I thought we would just pretend." But she had known he would do it. She hadn't thought about it dying.

He pulled it off the arrow and threw the frog right into the middle of the pond. Kirsplash! The water rippled away from where it landed; she stood watching with her mouth hanging open.

"Now why did you do that?"

"We can't eat one frog, but some bass will. Food chain." He turned and started back down the path in the direction they'd come.

"Where are we going now?"

"Home. I'm done hunting with you."

Kiki and Justin had stood silently witnessing the whole thing. They fell in line behind her and Waylon. No one said a word as they trudged through the hot sugar sand. As soon as they came in through the back door of Uncle Walton's house, her mother had said, "Well, well, just in time girls. We need to go home."

Catherine remembered every detail just like it had happened yesterday. It triggered a whole lot of emotions and memories.

~~~

Her cousin's family lived in a perfectly square house. The two exterior doors faced east. One opened into the living room, the other into the kitchen. All of the windows and doors were jalousied—four inch wide individual panes of glass. A small bathroom was between the kitchen and boys' bedroom, making those two rooms
~~~

on that side of the house a little smaller. The entire house was made of Florida pine, harvested from out on the Martin Grade. Even the ceilings were pine. Catherine always loved the wood with all of the knots and indentions. She used to run her fingers over it when she went down the hall to the bathroom. She would lie on the couch and stare up at the ceiling, studying all the shades. She often heard her uncle tell people that he had "built it on a single sawhorse with my own two hands." The little house was exactly eight hundred square feet.

Her family lived with them in that house briefly the year her parents moved from Pennsylvania. Her mother and father told her it would be a great adventure. She had wanted things to remain the way they were. She was a happy five-year-old. She liked that she was in school on Buttonwood Street only one block from her house. She liked walking back and forth to school with her mother and feeling big. She liked coming home to her grandmother's cooking, and she liked living upstairs. It was the way a real family should be.

Then the adults began talking a lot. The next memory was vivid—the day they packed the car, put her and Kiki in it, and told them they were leaving. She had stretched up as far as she could to peek out the back window. Her grandparents were standing on the top step outside their house. Her grandmother raised her hand as if to wave, clutching a white hankie to her heart with her other hand. She didn't wave. She turned instead and ran back inside the house. Catherine wanted to scream, "Nanny, Nanny, Nanny," but she couldn't spoil it, not for her little sister or for her parents. So she sat down in the seat and made herself small, fighting back the tears until her face felt really hot. Inside her head, she did scream. She fought and fought the tears by clutching tightly the little white bear with the red ribbon collar her grandmother stuck into her hands just as they started out of the house.

Her child's mind couldn't comprehend that they were moving, or that they would never go back and live with her grandparents again.

"I love you, Nanny," she whispered silently as a big tear slid down her face. She didn't wipe it away. She didn't want her little sister to see she was crying.

~~~

Catherine was standing in the kitchen, lost in her memories. Champ pushed against her leg, let out a long low whine, and stretched. He knew when she needed him. Catherine's insides felt raw, like they were wrapped in a tight knot, a large pit sitting in her stomach. Scenes rolled around in her head; none of them helped her take a single direction. Every time she thought she could move forward, her mind took her back in the same circle. She didn't want to admit the phone call had caused so much chaos. She knew perfectly well how to distance herself from that side of the family. Hadn't she done it quite well for all these years? Except, of course, last Christmas when one afternoon she had sat down and written a letter to her uncle and sent him a few pictures. Her mother had told her that Aunt Josie had died some time before, and she had felt bad about not knowing. Finally, she decided to give this one chance and only one chance. She slowly dialed the phone.

"Buck, this is Catherine. I have a question." He was surprised when she asked him whether he knew someone dependable who could farm sit for a few days.

Buck immediately responded with, "What's wrong
~~~

with asking Zane?"

"I thought he was leaving as soon as his truck is repaired."

"He's got no place to be and I've been working on him to stick around anyway. You might as well put him to work."

She didn't know how she would ask him, but she wanted to finalize a decision soon.

"Do you know when he's coming out here?"

"No, but he's standing right here. Why don't you just ask him right now?"

Catherine stopped breathing. *"Please say, 'No'; please say, 'No.'"* He was instantly on the phone.

"Could you farm sit for me for a couple of days? I have to go to South Florida."

Without hesitation, he said, "Sure." What she didn't know was that Buck handed him a hastily scrawled note that said, "You have to do this!"

"Are you sure? I mean I have the dogs and all."

"It will be fine. They already know me. I'm sure we'll all be fine. I'll be over later. When do you want to leave?"

"In the morning, I guess. I'll leave in the morning." She was trying to convince herself.

"Write me a schedule. Tell me what you do when. I'll see you in a bit."

She had no idea what the hell she was thinking. She must be out of her mind. How could she invite him to stay in her house especially when she wouldn't even be there? She barely even knew him. All she knew was that ever since her cousin had called, she couldn't think of anything else. She had to see her uncle. Zane was right. She'd feel better if he had a schedule of her normal routine. It would be best for everyone, but especially the dogs. It would make leaving a little easier.

~~~

Buck couldn't have been happier with the sudden turn of events. Part of the reason he wanted Zane to stick around was to get him involved with the questions surrounding the death of Catherine's husband, James. If he could somehow figure out what had really happened, it would certainly put him in a different light in her eyes. At least that's what he was thinking. She was obviously quite distraught about her loss, and if he could relieve some of that pain, well, he'd do his damnedest. Meanwhile, he needed Zane because he'd have complete access to her house. Bill Brannan would love it! They couldn't have planned it any better, although she had set him back for a second when she called and said she had a question. It spooked him, but he knew at this point she was clueless. How lucky could you get? Still, he'd have to be careful what he told Zane.

~~~

Jotting everything down on a yellow pad, Catherine tried to think of every aspect of her day for the schedule. Zane was attentive as they did a walk through. It comforted her that the animals were always glad to see him. He had a certain demeanor about him. She decided that she would leave after the morning chores. That way it would be similar to the days when she went to town to do errands, but the dogs knew something was up. Champ stuck to her like glue, and every time she turned around, little Friskie was either under her feet or standing up on his hind legs spinning around in a circle. In spite of staying up half the night and checking and rechecking everything, she was scared.

Most men, it's true, do not carry the intuitive gene.

And, they don't have the nurturing gene either—the one that's required for taking care of children and pets. Still, he had two things going for him. First, he had an amazing relationship with his horse. She expected him to ride like a cowboy with his arms flopping up and down, doing the chicken, feet braced and forward. Instead, what she saw was a horse and a man become one. She found herself humming inside her head as if they needed music to accompany their dance. And, the second and most important thing—her dogs adored him. Still, she was glad she was only going to be gone a few days.

<center>~~~</center>

Right after her morning chores were done, Catherine was startled when she went out the back door for the last time and found Zane leaning against Buck's truck in her driveway. He tipped his hat and said, "Morning. I forgot to ask you about a key. Didn't want to call and wake you, but I didn't want to miss you either."

"Oh, yes, you're right." She had her key in her hand and just gave it to him. She'd figure something out later. "You can lock the door after I leave. When you leave, I mean."

"And, I wanted to know about the little dog. How often do you let him out?"

With the last question answered, there was nothing keeping her from getting on the road. She just didn't want to go. He knew.

"It will be okay. I promise. I'm sure we can manage for a few days."

Catherine frowned, "It's that I didn't expect to be doing this. Not now."

He'd seen that scared rabbit look before. Her eyes

98

said, "I know what's going to happen and I don't want to go there!" He'd seen the same look on his mother's face.

"Catherine, they'll be fine. You can call me every day, you know."

He gave her name such energy. "Cath-urr-inn." So much better than "Ma'am." She smiled.

"Thank you so much, Zane. It's hard for me. I'll call the minute I arrive."

She forced herself into the car; as she drove down the drive, she watched him in her rearview mirror. He was standing with his arms folded across his chest, her house framed behind him. She took in a deep breath and turned right toward the interstate.

~~~

Before she left her farm, Catherine told Zane all the dogs were locked in the house. "No sense having one of them follow me," she said, but he knew it was more than that. He had seen how deeply attached she was to each of them, especially Champ. Her body language and the expression on her face showed how difficult it was for her to leave.

Standing in the driveway, watching her drive away, Zane felt a little sad. The last several days had been nice. Dinner with her was easy and comfortable. He had talked more than he had planned. Now, he was alone at her house entrusted with everything. He was actually looking forward to a few days of solitude. Over the years, he had forgotten how much he enjoyed those boyhood days of going off by himself. He would head back to Buck's right now to pick up his gear. If he timed it right, Buck could drop him back off at Catherine's when he closed the store for lunch. It would also give him time to stop at the repair
~~~

shop and check on his truck.

~~~

The news was better than Zane had expected. The computer component would arrive on Monday. The mechanic would start right away, and without a hitch, Zane should have his wheels on Tuesday. Catherine would surely be back by then, and he would be free to hit the road again.
~~~

CHAPTER 11

Catherine was thankful for her cell phone. It eliminated the need to tell Zane where she was going, and it didn't give him a chance to find out inadvertently she would be at her uncle's house. She preferred to let him think she was away on business.

The drive would last four or five hours. She was glad she had left early on a Thursday morning. Even so, she encountered more traffic than expected. She set the cruise control, adjusted her seat, and pulled down the armrest. It couldn't be more boring, but she was determined to enjoy the scenery and keep her mind in neutral. The radio spilled out its cacophony as the miles ticked off.

North of Orlando, she pulled into Heron Creek Plaza. She took her time, got a drink and snack, and walked around watching people. She was about to push open the door out into the parking lot when a woman and a little girl rushed up. Catherine swung open the door and held it for them. The little girl glanced up at her and said, "Thank you." As they quickly passed, the woman also said, "Thank you," and continued inside. Catherine stood planted for a few seconds holding the door. She couldn't help but notice that the child looked remarkably like she had at that age. The woman was about the same height and body structure as her. As she followed them with her eyes, the little girl turned and continued to look at her until they vanished around the corner and into the ladies restroom.

"That could have been me with my daughter," she mused. It was the first time since James had died she had thought anything like that. She tried not to think about family, children, the kids that would never be. They made their decisions together one by one. Most of the time she had been too busy to have regrets, but now that he was gone....the thoughts tried to creep in. She didn't mean to, want to, but sometimes she would imagine what their children might have looked like. This woman, that child—it was like seeing herself in a mirror. They say everyone has an exact duplicate of him or herself somewhere else in the world. What if she had seen hers?

Soon enough she would be in the familiar house with her uncle. She had been about the same size and age as that little girl when they had moved to Florida. She would have looked like that the first time she could remember anything about her Uncle Walton. Soon enough the little house would surround her once again. She only hoped she would be able to face the secrets it held.

~~~

Catherine caught herself holding her breath, fighting back the tears. Nothing looked like she had remembered it. As soon as she exited the turnpike, shopping centers and developments replaced once wide-open spaces. Now there were sidewalks, four lane highways, and even concrete walls. It made her sick to her stomach. This land used to be cattle pastures and a dairy. Much of it had been pristine wetlands. It was so beautiful, a tropical paradise. Now, it was manicured. That was the only word she could come up with. There were tidy little
~~~

houses with tidy little yards and there were also gargantuan houses with their tidy little yards.

If it hadn't been for the road signs, Catherine wouldn't have found her way. It looked like anywhere U.S.A. It wasn't until she took the cut-off road, crossed the railroad tracks, and headed up the little hill at Mrs. Quinn's old house that things looked familiar. She slowed past the old trailer park, the laundromat now vacant, and the small restaurant that was still "Open for Business." She crossed the creek where her mother's friend, Sarah, crashed her car off the bridge. It had been the next morning before someone found her unconscious on the bank.

Catherine sighed as she rounded the last curve and turned right onto Elizabeth Avenue. She stopped. At the end of the street was her uncle's house. She had no idea what was about to happen. Catherine pulled into his yard, closed the car door as quietly as she could, walked empty-handed to the kitchen door, and knocked.

"Damn it, don't knock. Just come in." His voice was gruff.

She slowly opened the door and stepped in. He was seated right there at the end of the kitchen table with his back to the door. He didn't even turn to see who it was. "The damn cat tears me up when you knock. Don't knock. Just come in. The door is always open." He turned to look at her.

"Hi, Uncle Walton. It's me, Catherine."

"I'll be damned," he said, half-turning around. "I never would have recognized you. I'll be damned."

Catherine leaned down and wrapped her arms around his neck as he pulled her close and held her.

"I'm so glad you've come back to me. My God, Catherine, you've finally come back."

She couldn't say a word. The tears streamed down her face as they released their hold on each other.

"You sure are a sight for this old man's poor eyes. What the hell are you doing here?"

Oh boy! She knew she couldn't tell him that Waylon had sent for her, so she lied. "I have some business down here. Nothing major. I was wondering whether I could stay with you for a day or two."

"Why are you even asking? Now dry those tears. I can't believe it. I can't believe it." He handed her a tissue from a box on the table and took hold of her hand and gave it a squeeze.

Catherine dabbed at her eyes, but the steady stream of tears just wouldn't stop. Everything in the house was the same. The kitchen table looked the same as it had when she was little. Everything was in the same place. The only thing that was different was him. He looked very tired and his hair was almost all gray—not the raven black she remembered.

"I'll get a few things from the car and be right back." He let her hand slide out of his. She needed a minute to catch her breath. The neighborhood was basically the same. He hadn't even planted grass. The yard was still patches of white sand with Florida weeds. She loved it.

~~~

Catherine put her things in the boys' old room and walked out into the kitchen. When her uncle stood, Catherine was shocked. His bare feet were extremely swollen so that he could barely walk. He steadied himself, holding onto the table, made his way to the hall, and by using both hands on the walls, traveled down to the bathroom.
~~~

"It's good this is so narrow. It's hell getting old," he hollered.

He had looked so good sitting at the table that it was hard for her to grasp how difficult it was for him to get around. "How long have you been like this?" she hollered back, although she needn't shout in the small house.

"Not long, honey. Not long at all."

He shuffled back down the short hall, held onto the arm of the couch to move around the corner, and collapsed into the cushions. He scooted himself across, reaching for the remote, and turned on the blaring television. Catherine watched as he prepared to give himself a breathing treatment.

"I have to do this twice a day when I'm like this. I'm not sure it does a thing."

She was stunned at the number of bottles and cups on the table in the corner next to the couch.

"Do you take all those?" she shouted, pointing at the table. He had the tube in his mouth, but nodded with his eyebrows up and his eyes wide open.

She shook her head. "While you do this, I'm going to take a walk down to the river." She hated yelling. He nodded again as she headed toward the kitchen door. Stepping out into his backyard pulled her back into another time. The clothesline was in the exact same place. There were more mango trees, but otherwise, the yard looked the same. She took a deep breath.

So many times they had piled out of the car here in the yard and seen snakes hanging on that clothesline. Her uncle worked for the power company as a lineman, so he often crossed paths with large rattlesnakes out in the woods or on the roads. He would kill them and bring them home to skin. He was also an amateur taxidermist so there were always creatures in transition. She loved the tales he told about the captures and the killings. "The snakes wiggle until the sun goes down," he told her. They were never at his house at sundown, so she never knew whether what he said was true. He would bury them somewhere in the yard.

Catherine walked past the old rose apple tree in the middle of the front yard. Its branches provided a welcome relief from many harsh summer afternoons of so long ago. The narrow road had been paved and so was the path leading down to the river. Everything once was sand and native vegetation. Now the path squeezed between two precisely manicured yards, each sporting expensive large estates.

"Why didn't they leave it alone?" she thought. It was so unnatural now. She was relieved to see that the dock was nearly the same. Many hours had been spent right there, fishing and talking about everything and nothing at all. Her mother even fished back then. It wasn't important that you caught anything. It was the peacefulness of having tried, plus having nothing better to do. There wasn't anything much to think about then, and there was even less happening. She spent lots of time peering into the bottomless river, wondering what mysteries might become attached to her hook. She never knew what lurked beneath, and sometimes if she let it, the thought would scare her.

Someone had built a bench, so she sat there today, just staring at the sun playing on the water. She thought about how wonderful it was to pretend—pretend that you were little again and that nothing had happened. You could pretend that life was still full of wonderment and put no expectations in its way.

The tears rushed out as her emotions overtook her

and she couldn't hold them back. This was the worst possible time to come here. She was already raw and vulnerable from losing James, and she truly felt like she was being torn apart. The farm had kept her so busy that it enabled her to avoid the pain and all the nagging questions.

She felt like jumping into the river and swimming toward the sea. She knew she wouldn't make it. She would swim right out into the middle and then head toward the inlet until exhaustion came. Then she would begin to sink ever so slowly. It would take days to find her body in the brown murky water.

She was startled when she thought she heard someone call her name. Catherine quickly wiped her face on her sleeve and turned to look up the hill toward the house. A man was standing in the street. He motioned for her to come up. He was bare-chested and tan. If she didn't know better, she would have thought it was her father. She wiped her eyes with her shirttail and blinked hard looking back up the hill. The man was gone.

"Oh, God," she said out loud. "I knew I shouldn't have come here. Oh, God!"

CHAPTER 12

Celia Fenmore was eager to get off the interstate. She and Olivia loved it at Disney World, but they were both ready to get back home. Olivia's head was spinning with all the things she'd seen.

"Mom, those flamingos' legs are long and as thin as pencils." It struck Celia as funny that her daughter loved those birds the most.

"Oh, and I meant to ask you, do you think it would be okay to paint my room that color?"

"Flamingo pink? Now you know that's going to be pretty bright. Do you think it will keep you awake at night?" She was grinning. It wasn't a color Celia would choose, but then she wasn't five going on fifty! Besides, why stand in the way of a creative child. "I think we should paint it for your birthday. It will be a perfect way to celebrate your turning six."

"Can we go to the dollar store soon? I want to buy that pink flamingo we saw."

Olivia's artistic abilities were only surpassed by her "born to shop" skills. Her mother and grandmother had taught her well. She knew how to find a bargain. She also understood that Daddy worked very hard for their money and it was their job to mind the budget. Olivia got it. Whenever she wanted to buy something, she would get her piggy bank and sit at the kitchen table making little stacks of coins. Olivia had contributed eleven dollars to this mother/daughter trip. Celia would carefully sneak the money back into the bank the first chance she got. So far Olivia hadn't caught on. Once she said, "Mom, it seems like my money keeps growing." Celia had to turn away to hide her smile.

"Mom, did you see that lady?"

"What lady?"

"When we went to the bathroom. The lady at the door."

"Yes, but only for a minute. Why?"

"I don't know. I think she looked at me funny."

"Maybe she was in a hurry and we were in her way."

"No, she looked at me and then her mouth came open."

"I don't know what to tell you."

"She kept looking at me all the time until you pulled me away."

Celia didn't realize she had been pulling Olivia. "I'm sorry if you feel like I was pulling you, Olivia. Sometimes, I forget how little you are."

"It's okay. She was really pretty."

"I guess she was, but I only saw her for a minute."

"She had hair just like mine."

"Yes, I think she did."

"It was exactly the same color."

"Yes, I guess it was."

"Do you think I'll be that pretty when I grow up?"

"Oh honey, you already are that pretty. There's no question about it, but remember you have to stay pretty on the inside too. Now get me my purse because we're almost to the toll booth."

Celia hadn't paid that much attention to the woman, but Olivia obviously had. She was a striking woman, tall, pretty. They had made eye contact, but Olivia was feeling something more. That child amazed her. She connected with people and animals in a much different way than most people. It was a gift that came from Celia's grandmother. Mimi understood things at another level. Olivia was certainly a special child, and Celia felt blessed to be her mother. It would be good to be home.

"Daddy is going to be so glad to see us, and I bet he will be all ears tonight while you tell him your stories."

~~~

Celia loved having Cary Fenmore for a husband. His job allowed her to be at home with Olivia. The house was a gift from her grandmother. Mimi paid the down payment and the first year's taxes. It gave them a jumpstart so they could enjoy being newlyweds without the pressure. Cary had started as assistant manager of the furniture store, but it wasn't long before Ralph, the owner, announced he was retiring. He had pounded Cary on the back and winked, "Tag. You're it! I was like you thirty years ago when I took over this store. People will always need furniture and shoes." As manager, Cary had a sense of security and pride, and he knew he could provide for his family.

Celia's grandmother, Mimi, was exactly the grandmother every little girl deserved. Her arms were always wide open, and she had a huge, generous heart. It was difficult not to overindulge Olivia, but she managed.

Mimi told Celia, "I never imagined I'd be a great-grandmother. At first, the thought seemed to make the lines in my face look even deeper, but those are a small price to pay for this precious child." Celia's grandmother made sure every gray hair was in place, her makeup
~~~

impeccable, and her clothes crisply stylish with perfectly matching shoes. She was a stunning woman and the perfect person to help Celia raise her daughter.

~~~

Celia and Cary were extremely excited when she became pregnant. Celia had staged the surprise announcement on her grandmother's birthday. She purposely chose Mannico's because guests were seated in little rooms separate from the other diners. She was practically jumping out of her skin in anticipation. She made sure the waiter knew to time dessert after she handed Mimi the package. It was wrapped in plain pink paper with a big pink bow. Celia watched her grandmother's face as she opened it. Inside were a tiny pink dress and a pair of pink booties. Mimi's mouth hung open and her eyes began to tear.

"No! No! You don't mean it," she screamed as she jumped up and hugged her granddaughter. "A baby, a baby. Oh my God, a girl; it's a girl!"

Celia was shaking. "Open the card," she whispered.

There was a stork holding a little pink blanket with a baby, of course. The front said, "Happy Birthday, Nanny." She opened it. "Just wanted to say I'm on the way. I can't wait to be in your arms. Love, Olivia."

Mimi sobbed as she hugged the tiny pink dress and the card. "Where in the world did you find this card, and how long have you known?"

"Cary and I wanted to be sure everything was okay. We had some tests run. We're excited now that we know she's a little girl and she'll be perfect. Don't you love the card? I had my friend Danielle create it."

Just then, Cary appeared. "Congratulations, Great-
~~~

Grandma," he said as he hugged Mimi.

"So how did you get here right on cue, you stinker?"

"My wife is in cahoots with the waiter," he chuckled. And right on time, the waiter appeared with a flaming baked Alaska. They began singing "Happy Birthday," but she shushed them and made them quit. It had been the most perfect and exciting birthday Mimi could ever remember.

CHAPTER 13

Zane was awake before first light and watched the early rays of dawn spread across the pasture. He snuck out the front door with only Champ as a witness. He slid silently through the small gate and headed up across the field to the woods. He preferred the semi-darkness; he had used it many times to maneuver his way out of a bad situation. As a boy, his friends had teased him about being part cat. He had won every game of hide-and-seek at the ranch in the dark. The other kids never knew how many times he moved to a new hiding place.

The cool morning air made the dew almost freeze so it sparkled like a million tiny prisms. He was grateful for the time alone to regroup before moving on again. This woman probably had no idea what a pristine piece of land she owned. He stood quietly under the trees, looking back toward the house. A small gray fox leaped after a field mouse and never knew he was there. He was upwind from it, and it neither caught his scent nor sighted him and went about its business. He looped back around to the house and let the dogs out. It wouldn't take him long to knock out the barn chores and start working on the fence.

It was half past noon when he realized he hadn't eaten any breakfast, and worse yet, he hadn't fed the dogs. Even worse than that, he'd forgotten all about the little dog. He found the poor thing covered with hay and sticks and sitting on the back doorstep. His tongue was wagging probably from confusion and fear. Zane scooped him up, feeling bad.

"Sorry, little buddy. I can see why she keeps you in the house. We won't let this happen again." Maybe he could use the vacuum to clean off the little fuzzball. "Better late than never!" he said, looking into six hungry faces.

He found a brush with the dog supplies in the mudroom. "Women sure love being organized," he told Little Friskie, who sat perfectly still while Zane used his horse grooming skills.

He washed up and peered into the refrigerator. One thing was clear—this woman knew how to eat. She had left a plate with a note stuck on a toothpick in a sandwich, "Thank you." He would thoroughly enjoy the stacked roast beef with all the fixings she had left for him, even if it were a day old.

The machine was blinking with only one message. It was from her from the night before. "I have arrived. Hope all is okay. Call me if you need me." Her cell phone number was on a post-it stuck on the wall. The phone rang just as he started to walk away. He didn't intend to answer it, but he heard Buck say, "Hey, Zane. If you are in there, pick up the phone."

"What?" Zane asked gruffly.

"Hey, it's Buck."

"I know it's you, you darn fool."

"Is she gone?"

"Yes, she's gone; otherwise, do you think I'd have spent the night?" Zane was messing with him.

"Sounds like you're in a little better mood. Listen, we've got something we gotta do right away."

"If you need me to make a delivery, either load up the truck and come get me, or come get me and I'll help you load up, but remember I have to get back here."

"No, no. It's not about the store. It's about her. Bill called and we gotta get this done now."

Zane wanted to get mixed up in this about as much as a rabbit wants to see the shadow of a hawk.

"Zane, listen. Bill Brannan is really pushing this, and since we've got access, he says it will be easy."

Zane was getting pissed. When was Buck going to listen? "I'm done, Buck. I told you to tell him you haven't seen me. I'm helping this lady and then I'm out of here."

"I'm telling you, it's easy. I'll be over after I close the store."

"No. I'm not doing it. No." Zane slammed down the phone. He had been so close to speeding past that damn exit ramp when he made the wrong choice again. There was no way he was giving in on this. Not this time. If Buck wanted to get involved, he would be running solo.

The dogs were ready to burst out the back door. He grabbed the leash and hooked it on Friskie's collar. He wasn't about to make that mistake twice. He had never imagined he would be walking a dog, but he knew if anything happened to this little mutt, she would be even more heartbroken.

<div align="center">~~~</div>

Buck showed up like he said he would. "There's a whole lot more to this story than she knows. I need to tell you what's going on."

Zane kept walking toward the barn to do the evening chores. His jaw tightened and he closed his eyes. Nothing was ever simple with Buck. This was exactly why he'd tried to fight stopping here in the first place.

He spun around into Buck's face. "No. Don't tell me

another thing. I'm not interested, and I'm not listening to any story."

"She has no idea. Don't you understand? She has no clue about her husband's murder. She could be in danger."

"Buck. I have done everything I ever intend to do for those people. I'm dead serious. I'm done."

"Look. We don't know if she has a secure line or not. I can't talk about this on the phone. That's why I came over. Please, let me tell you what they want us to do; then make your decision. It's not that complicated."

"Damn it. No. Now get the hell out of here. I've got chores to do."

Buck had never seen Zane like this. Under any other circumstances, he would have kept at him, but Bill also told Buck he was glad they had quit when they did. He told him, "Zane's medical report was a little shaky." When Buck questioned him, Bill said, "You'll have to ask him. That's all I can tell you, but it was a good time for him to retire."

"Sleep on it," Buck told Zane. "Just think about it. I'll come by and talk to you tomorrow."

~~~

The damn dreams were relentless. Zane woke up as some strange man was yelling so loud it felt like his head was about to split. Lately, the characters in his dream didn't have identifiable faces.

The clock on the dresser showed two o'clock exactly. He folded his arms over his chest and stared at the nearly black ceiling. There had been so many close calls, too many dead bodies, and all the ugly distorted faces constantly jumbled up in the restless nights. Even
~~~

the places were now mixed up in his mind. He wasn't sure if he tried, whether he'd be able to recall the actual events accurately, and now the dreams jumbled everything even more.

It had been exciting, an adventure, challenging, when they were young. They were commissioned to create a new training facility and program. They had carte blanche to develop the site and choose the people. The damn place near Williamsburg now sported a plaque at the entrance that declared them "American heroes." They had purposely placed it near the CIA's covert facility. Yes, he was proud, but he was also silently ashamed. He kept it bottled up inside. The life he had chosen was far removed from the peace and harmony of a Montana ranch. When he allowed it, many questions haunted him. What if he'd stayed on the ranch? How different would his life have been? Would his mother have had grandbabies? Who would he have married? He rubbed his hands over his face. Zane had worked hard at not lingering on those thoughts for very long, but now they kept cropping up.

Their work took all their time and energy. It wasn't very different from the television shows he watched where the cowboys were fighting the Indians. He convinced himself it was on a higher, different level. But in the last few years, it had become so technical that Zane and Buck had begun to hate it. It became extremely difficult to identify the enemies. He knew he had left at exactly the right time.

When there had been down times, they recharged. Buck arranged unforgettable hunting trips. And, yes, there had been plenty of women over the years. They blew into this town or that and spent a couple of days cavorting, and then they were gone. That was it. No emotion. It had allowed the physical satisfaction of rolling in the sack with some woman's legs wrapped around you without any of the complications.

Zane threw off the covers and got out of bed. The bathroom was straight across the hall. As soon as his truck was ready on Tuesday, he would head north again. Whenever he sat still for too long, he started to think too much.

He stared into the dimly lit mirror and ran his hands through his salt and pepper hair.

Zane walked down the hall and stopped at her bedroom door. Suddenly, something moved. "Hey," he hollered as he felt on the wall for a light switch. Then he heard the dog thumping his tail. The light revealed Champ in the middle of her bed and Friskie on her pillow.

"I don't think you two are supposed to be in here," he said as he fumbled to flip off the light. He intended to push the dogs off the bed, but Champ lay as flat as he could with his ears swiveled back. Friskie didn't move, not even a whisker.

"She's not even gone that long, you two." He could smell her in the room. A slit of moonlight filtered through the sheers. Zane lie down and put his arm over the big dog. "She'd kill us if she knew we were in here." It wasn't long before the three of them drifted back to sleep.

~~~

Buck didn't show up again the next day, but the following day, right after he closed the store, he was in the driveway at Catherine's. Zane knew he'd be relentless because he had a double agenda. First, Buck was out to get the girl, and second, that man still wanted to stay close to the Association.

"Goddammit it, Buck, I told you I'm not doing it."
~~~

"Listen to me. Then decide. Okay?"

"No, it's not okay, but how do I stop you? Tell me that?"

"You don't. Here's the deal. They said her husband was a computer genius, but no one knew it at the drug company where he worked. They put him in there for a reason, and I'm skimming the surface for you here. He did his job and stumbled into a huge problem, so they got rid of him. They used some high powered taser right on his chest to stop his heart. They killed him and used the SUV rollover gimmick, bad tires, blah blah blah. Then they torched his vehicle, hurled it off the ridge, and presto, he was toast."

"Okay, convince me why I need to be involved?" Zane was irritated. "And, exactly where does she come into the picture?"

"They think there's some info still in his personal computer. No one knows where his laptop landed, but they suspect that she's got it. If she does, she could have everything they need to nail those sons of bitches and also jump one step ahead of the bastards."

"So, say the laptop is here. What do you do with it? You can't steal it."

"No, they just want us to copy and erase some files. She'll be none the wiser."

"So we clean the clock and then that's it? This sounds like we're back in kindergarten. And, then, what about the murder?" he asked emphatically. "Do we just tell her, oh, by the way, James was murdered? Ooops, we goofed. Someone should have told you. So sorry! Come on, Buck; don't you think this sounds pretty damn lame. Tell me the God damn truth, Buck. What's really going on?"

"I'm telling you the fucking truth. It's that simple. They don't really care what she knows about his death. I think she should know. Someone should have told her, and they should have protected him. They didn't have to let them take him out."

"I don't give a flying fig about any of it. We need to leave it alone and me out of it."

"And what if something happens to her, Zane? Can you live with that? I can't."

Zane honestly didn't know what he could live with anymore. A few days ago, Catherine hadn't even existed in his world. Now, well, here he was, stuck. "Okay, so say you go in there, locate the laptop, download the shit, erase it off the hard drive, and they just miraculously know to get off of her tail?"

"They'll set them up. They'll make a deal with the assholes; give them a laptop with some bullshit-encoded crap on it, and she won't be involved anymore. They have people at the pharmaceutical joint where he worked already in place. Something was in the works even before they killed him."

"Why the hell don't they give them any laptop then?"

"Because the one she has, if she has it, contains some pretty intense stuff. That's all they told me. And, the sooner you let me into the house, the better."

"If this is so damn critical, where the hell were you yesterday? I'm not getting this."

"I was busy with the store. My store." The truth was Buck had visitors yesterday who had given him a crash course in what they wanted him to do. He didn't want to have to do this without Zane's okay.

Zane finally had enough. He gave in. "I'm going to stay in the barn with the dogs. If anyone ever asks me, I'll swear I said goodbye to you and I thought you left. Got it?"

"I'll go get the job done and then I'm out of here."

A minute later, Buck slid into the back door and let out a long low whistle. He sure liked this lady's house. It was damn cozy. He had no idea where to look. Zane disappointed him. This was fucking bullshit. It could have been so easy, and they could have had this done in no time. Now he had to fart around searching for the damn thing. His biggest fear was that she had it with her. They warned them if she accidentally opened one of the files, well, shit, things would be fucked up.

And then, there it was, a laptop sitting on a green chair in what looked like her office. Okay, so maybe this was his lucky day. They told him to expect the battery to be dead. He pulled an electric cord out of his jacket pocket and plugged it in. Without a hitch, the laptop came alive.

"Almighty God, thank you," Buck shouted.

It took him over an hour, but he got the job done. He was sweating bullets by the time he finished. He placed the computer back on the chair and let himself out. Zane was nowhere to be seen. Buck had no idea why he'd been so adamant about not getting involved. He figured it had to have something to do with Zane's condition, because he was pretty damn edgy.

As soon as Buck had the data off her laptop, he mailed the flash drive to his contact, who conveniently dropped it into a mailbox in Las Vegas. As far as Buck knew, the case was closed. It was the easiest job he'd ever done. Bill called and said that everything was taken care of. There should be no further problems. Buck still thought he and Zane should talk to Catherine; tell her something. At the very least, knowing might protect her, but he would leave Zane alone, like he asked, for a while.

CHAPTER 14

When the phone rang, Zane was glad to hear her voice on the machine, not Buck's. "Hi, Zane; it's me, Catherine."

He picked up the phone. "Hey, Catherine, I'm here."

"Oh, I'm glad I caught you. I know I said I'd only be gone a couple of days, but is it possible for me to stay a little longer?"

He drew in a breath. It was cold and windy outside. The reports across the country were bad. Old man winter was furious. They said it was going to be an early winter. It certainly wouldn't hurt him or Trouble, for that matter, to stick tight for right now.

"It's not what I was expecting. My truck will be ready on Tuesday, but the weather has turned bad. I'll make it work. Is everything okay?"

She reversed it. "I was about to ask you the same question."

He bent over and picked up Friskie, who was dancing by his leg. He told her, "Say something," as he held the phone to the dog's ear.

"It's your mommy, Frisk. Tell Mommy everything's okay."

He surprised her. She didn't think he'd be that kind of man, putting a dog on the phone.

She said, "Hey, baby," into Zane's ear.

He lied. "He's wiggling all over. He misses you. I

caught him and Champ up in your bed."

"I suppose that will be okay for a day or two, if they aren't too dirty. I'll call you as soon as I know when I'll be leaving." She still hadn't mentioned to him that she was at her uncle's house. She didn't even say goodbye. She couldn't say another word, not with the rather large lump in her throat. Tears rolled silently down her cheeks. She wanted to go home.

~~~

Catherine was relieved to have the option of staying a few more days, because her uncle had a doctor's appointment that would enable her to get the information she needed for her cousins. If all went well, she could go home and Zane would be free to leave pretty much on schedule after all.

She helped her uncle out of the car and held his hands as she walked backwards, inching the short distance to the office door. By the time they were settled in the waiting room, he was gasping for each breath.

After the exam, the doctor told Walton he would be back in a few minutes. He motioned with his eyes toward the door so Catherine would follow him. As soon as the doctor was out the door, she said, "Oh, Uncle Walton, I left the car unlocked. I'll be right back." He barely grunted.

Outside in the hallway, the doctor pointed her toward a small office. He said, "I'm glad to meet you. He tells me so little, never about family. It's good you are here now. I guess you know the prognosis is grave."

Her heart was beating so hard and fast that she could hear it in her ears. The doctor continued in a voice that now sounded muffled, "The main thing is keeping him comfortable. Doing the chemotherapy is his choice."
~~~

She tried to say it, "Chemo. Chemotherapy?" The words wouldn't come out. She stood there as her body began to shake and she leaned back against the wall.

The doctor continued, "I can't predict how this will go. That's why I'm not pushing him. It may be too little too late."

She was stunned. She thought it would be something as simple as taking a water pill. The swelling would go down in his legs and feet and he would be able to walk again. This was complicated.

They drove home in silence.

Her uncle wanted to think about it. She was terrified. Chemo meant cancer with a capital "C." It meant being aggressive. She had seen too many people slip away. They faded with each treatment. Most had been very, very sick from the fight to stay alive.

When they were settled in his house, she tried to talk to him. "Uncle Walton, it will make you really, really sick. You are already very weak. Why not just let the cancer take its course. The prognosis isn't so good. Why should you suffer? You might have more time without the treatment. Your mind will be clearer so you can make decisions."

He was quiet for a while, and then said, "I don't need any time, honey. I miss Josie. I've already taken care of everything. The house is in the boys' names. So is the car. Look around. I gave away anything that mattered. The rest of the stuff isn't worth anything. I'm done."

Catherine wasn't surprised at what he said. He and Josie had lived simply. He was right. The house was almost bare except for the essentials. He sounded like a man who was accepting his death. He had always been that way—straight up—matter of fact—true to the core.

"After I'm gone, Matthew will live here." She'd

forgotten all about him. Matthew was his grandson, Justin's boy. She saw him once when he was a baby.

"Matthew? How old is he now?" Her voice cracked a little.

"He's eighteen. He's a good boy."

Catherine was glad the house would stay in the family, although she wondered how in the world the boys had agreed on that. She didn't dare ask him.

"It will work out just right, honey. You'll see."

~~~

She felt exhausted until she crawled into the small bed in the tiny bedroom. She stared at the painting hanging on the wall. She'd forgotten all about it. It was an African jungle scene her father had painted when they first got settled in their own house. He had dabbled in oils and spent many silent hours bent over a canvas. It was one of the good things she remembered about him. After staring at the ceiling and the walls for about an hour, she fumbled around in her bag and pulled out her journal.

She wrote: *I need to go home, but how can I leave him like this? Waylon told me he would come later, but not now. So far, Justin hasn't returned my call. How can they just expect me to leave my farm, my animals? And, worst of all, why would I leave everything with a complete stranger? Why I haven't even discussed any kind of fee with him. It makes me feel sick to my stomach. I don't know how I am going to do this. I don't know what I'm doing.*

It took her a long time to drift off to sleep.

~~~

Catherine was surprised her uncle's cats were hiding. For several days, she only caught a glimpse of them. Finally, Sissy came out. Eventually, Blackie, her big brother, showed himself too. He was gorgeous, solid black with sleek fur like an ermine. Her uncle's secret was fresh venison. He fed it to them every day.

"When Waylon comes, he fills my freezer. There are a lot of deer in Alabama," he said.

She needed to call Zane again. Ask him whether she could stay longer. If he said no, she'd have no choice but to leave her uncle and hire someone to care for him. His doctor's office had provided phone numbers for resources to her. At the top of the list was hospice.

CHAPTER 15

When Zane finally walked into her house, it was nearly dark. All that was left to do was feed her dogs and figure out something to eat; then he could settle in for the night. He fixed himself a plate, and as he placed it on the table, he noticed a manila envelope with his name penciled on the front. Buck couldn't leave him alone. He slid the envelope across the table, slammed down his plate, and sat down. Whatever it was, he didn't need to know about it.

It was late in the night when he gave in and removed the pages from the envelope. The chair in the living room was comfortable on his tired back as he began to read. The first report said that James' murder was staged. They had ambushed him in a sparsely populated area of Pennsylvania. They were fairly certain that a taser-type device hyped up with enough voltage to stop his heart had been used. The SUV was then torched and pushed over the ridge. The massive contusions to his chest cavity from the steering column and the taser had barely mattered because of the fire. They were smart and they got lucky. Everything went off without a hitch. Even the autopsy report was solid and left no doubt. They made sure there were no loopholes. Zane gained nothing from reading the material. He had already heard parts from Buck. The very last piece of paper was smaller, and on it, he recognized his best friend's handwriting.

"Hey Buster—(Zane hated the stupid nickname Buck had given him years ago)—*Listen, I know you're hot to get on with your new life, but I have a proposition for you. Why not stay on with me here in Highberry? We can buy some cows. I'll get a dog or two. Hell, you can take in a few horses—either train them for other people or buy, train, and resell them. What? What did you say? Oh, about the lady. Well, let the best man win. Once she's back, we'll be on the same turf. We can play our cards and see who wins the game. You've played and lost before, man. Where the hell do you think you're gonna go this time of year anyway? You and that horse can spend the days alone on my farm while I'm at the store or you can help me. I'm offering you whatever you want, but it would mean a lot to me if you could stay, even for a while. What's it gonna be? I love you man. I said it. Tuff.*

Zane shook his head. The idiot wrote like a girl. Was he begging? Tuff? Like hell!

~~~

During those first few days, Zane created his own rhythm on the farm. The chores flowed easily, and the animals were content with his consistency. As promised, he kept Friskie on a leash, giving him no chance of being forgotten or lost. Under any other circumstances, Zane would have bowed out and gotten the hell out of Dodge, but the timing had worked out, so he was glad to do it for her. He didn't really mind her dogs.

When he was a boy, he had begged his father for a long time to let him have a puppy, but the answer was always the same. "Got no use for a dog. Sides, you got no time for one." Then one November, out of the blue, his father had come home with a dog. It was a mixed breed,
~~~

mostly Border Collie and Australian Shepherd. Zane was excited until his father pointed his finger at him and said, "This here is my mutt, and I don't want you messing with her. Understood?" His mother shot Zane a look that meant, "Don't say a word" as she walked away. Right then, right there, at the age of eleven, Zane knew he had to get out of this place. He had to get away from this miserable man. Creating a plan made the worst nights bearable. Still, the thought of leaving his mother tore at his heart. Now, he could only hope one day, when he got the courage to go home, she would forgive him.

He felt better in this moment than he could remember. He'd set Buck straight yesterday telling him, "Look, Buck, you got what you wanted from me. Now, back off. The best thing you can do for me now is to leave me alone."

~~~

The part Buck kept to himself was exactly how much information the CIA had actually gathered on the case. James had warned several of the agencies about a particular drug combination. In an adapted form, it made a person's medical state mimic the dramatic effects of a stroke. In the beginning, no one took James seriously. By the time they had, it was too late. One world leader was already fighting for his life due to the devastating brain damage. There was no way to determine whether his stroke had really been drug induced or the poor bastard's rotten luck. The officials were assuming the worst, but keeping it under wraps. That's what the so-called counterterrorism assassination program wanted. They wanted to keep people guessing, keep them right on the edge. What they didn't want was the drug information to
~~~

get into anyone else's hands. The media had no clue, thank God. Either way, that particular country was now in the throws of a changing of the guard. It made Buck wonder whether this was only the tip of a giant iceberg. Were the other dominos about to fall? Frankly, there had better be an adequate amount of special agents investing time and energy in what the hell was going on; otherwise, there was a lot at stake for everyone.

Sometimes he really missed the excitement of his job, but mostly Buck was glad they had retired when they did. He would, however, always be ready to serve from this new found distance. He was slowly understanding that Zane felt vastly different. He knew now the less stress he caused Zane, the better. In the meantime, the pretty little lady was safe and they could both sleep at night. Still, Buck worried if he left Zane alone too much, he would make the wrong decision. Running was for wild horses, not men. It didn't solve anything. He was concerned about Zane's mental state. He knew Zane still blamed himself for their close call. "It weren't nothing but a thing," Buck had told him. "It was inevitable. It could have happened any time, anywhere. We were lucky. We're both still here." No matter how many times Buck said it, Zane didn't hear him.

~~~

When the phone rang, Zane was sitting in her kitchen, relaxing over a cup of coffee.

"Hello, Zane. It's Catherine. How's everything?"

"Everybody's fine."

"Good. Good. That's really good. I have something I need to ask you."

"Okay."
~~~

"I don't quite know how to ask, because this is hard for me."

"All right."

"All right then. So here's my dilemma. I came here because of my uncle. My cousin said he was sick, but it turns out he's..." she lost her voice. Zane knew in the pit of his stomach what she would say. She cleared her throat. "He has cancer and it's really bad." He could tell she was holding her breath now, trying not to cry. His mind was racing.

She continued, "I understand if you can't stay, but...."

He interrupted her. "Catherine, it's okay. I'll stay. I'll stay as long as you need."

There was a long silence. He waited. Then she said in a weak voice, "Zane, thank you. You have no idea. Thank you," and she was gone.

~~~~

Later, in the evening, when her uncle was asleep, she gathered up her strength and called him again. She explained about the chemotherapy, her cousin Waylon building a house in Alabama, her other cousin, Justin. She sounded stronger, more in control. She was glad to talk to him again because he gave her the confidence in him she needed.

"I have some questions for you, now that I'll be staying on for a while. It would help to know if I have the dogs' names right and your gray mare is a bit off."

"Off?" she asked.

"Yes, she's lame on her right front."

"Oh, you mean she limps. Yes, she does that sometimes."
~~~~

"I found some Bute; started her on that. I've been hosing the leg, using liniment, wrapping it. She's better."

"Whatever you think needs to be done, please just do it. I'll trust your judgment."

"Oh, and do you want me to work any of them?"

She hadn't given a thought to the horses being ridden, but she knew how he handled his own horse.

"I've only ridden the gelding. Would you mind?"

"No, not at all. Have they all been started?"

"Started?"

"Started training, under saddle? Do you know how much training they have had?"

"Yes, I think they have. The one mare, the bay, they showed her until she was three. Oh, and I haven't discussed paying you. We need to talk about that."

He didn't need a thing. He felt like he should be paying her. "Catherine, I really don't need anything. The roof over my head and a place for my horse is enough."

"No, really. Don't be silly. I insist. It's a lot of work."

"What else would I be doing?"

"We'll discuss this when I get back."

He didn't want to argue with her.

"Oh, I hear him getting up. I better go."

"What's his name?" he asked. She was surprised he wanted to know.

"Walton. My Uncle Walton. He's my father's brother." And with that, she hung up the phone.

~~~

Zane didn't understand her choice of horses. He didn't understand much about women, mostly because he had never needed to. The best horse of the four was her gelding. There was no way he was pure Arabian with his
~~~

thick neck and full heart girth. Zane was betting he was part quarter horse. The lame mare was put together pretty nice, but he didn't care for gray horses—high maintenance. The other two mares weren't anything special, but at least they had some color. The sorrel mare sported a strip and hind stockings. He wasn't crazy about white feet either—too soft. Now, the little bay mare, well, she was all right. She had a small star a little offset to the left. Her enormous eyes kept track of him and he liked that awareness.

Zane spent some time in the little bay's stall letting her get used to him. He ran his hands all over her, found a few spots she responded to, and watched her switch eyes when he passed behind her. He slipped a halter on her, then cross-tied her in the aisle and started grooming. The barn was set up fine for a small operation. She had it well stocked with grooming supplies. Her tack room sported a cabinet chuck-full of everything you could think of. He was sure his good ole buddy had a hand in that. Buck would have seen this as an opportunity to make some money and also rack up some points with her.

Her saddles and bridles weren't anything he'd be using. It looked like someone saw her coming. She had a fairly standard looking jumping saddle, one he thought must be dressage, and a fairly generic western saddle. Her bits didn't make much sense to him. He preferred a loose ring or just a plain snaffle.

The bay mare seemed fairly secure in herself. He turned all four of her horses out together and it didn't take them long to establish a pecking order. The bay was at the bottom of the heap, but he figured it was because she found it easier to go with the flow.

He threw his western saddle on her back and gave it a good shake. She stood firm. He took her out into the bright sunlight and quickly slid up into the saddle. She moved off his leg and allowed him to push her over to the gate, side-stepped so he could open it, and turned as he closed it. She was easy. He rode right into the pasture with her other three stable mates. Once he got her stepping forward and warmed up, he spent a while moving her toward the other three so she would learn to be more aggressive. She caught on to his game quickly and soon was moving with little resistance. At last, he could apply the principles he'd had in his mind for all these years. He was proving, if only to himself, that you don't have to use the downright cruel tactics he'd watched his father orchestrate.

To say that Zane's father was a strict disciplinarian was an understatement. There was no question about the rules or the punishment if you broke them. You got your ass beat. Zane learned early not to push his father. Fortunately, his mother and Parker Iron Crow, the ranch foreman, looked out for him. Zane was given a lot of freedom to explore the ranch. He had spent many hours watching the herds of horses. He had learned a lot by observing their pecking orders, how the mares taught the foals, and how a free roaming herd operated. He had realized quickly all horses want is to survive. They eat, drink, and find ways not to get eaten or captured. Humans are the ones who create situations for horses where none of that is possible. Thinking about horses kept things balanced for him when it got tough. He had promised himself if he ever got the chance again, he would treat them differently.

He had acted impulsively when he bought Trouble. At first, he thought he made a bad choice when he decided to head to Florida. If he believed in all the crap about everything happening for a reason, then he might convince himself that being on the farm was no coincidence. He could call it fate or take it a step further and ponder his meeting Catherine to give it an even deeper meaning. Or, he could simply complete the task and execute his plan just to get the hell out of Dodge. For now, he was content with fooling around with the horses and catching his breath for a spell. Catherine's place was giving him an opportunity he had never expected.

CHAPTER 16

She found her uncle standing in the doorway of his bedroom. "My damn legs won't work. The doctors told me do what I can, but I can't do a damn thing." He shuffled across the hallway and into the bathroom. When he finally came out and made his way slowly to his chair in the kitchen, she was standing at the sink staring out the window.

"I have to sit down to take a piss. It's not good for my manhood."

"Nobody cares, Uncle Walton."

"I do. Your aunt is probably laughing at me—a grown man sitting down to piss."

She set two full plates on the table. They ate in silence.

~~~

Later that evening, she was sitting in the chair straight across from him in the living room. If she stuck her legs straight out, her feet landed square in the center of the room. It amazed her. The house had seemed so big when she was little. Hanging on the wall above her head was a plastic picture of a buck jumping over a log in the forest. It was her uncle's favorite and hers too. It had a light behind the plastic. She bent down, plugged it in, and flipped the little switch. It still worked.

He said, "That's nice, baby."
~~~

She moved onto the couch next to him. Sitting there looking at the picture made her feel like a little girl again. She felt small and vulnerable.

Her parents' arguments had escalated one night in December. There had been bitter accusations that her mother fervently denied. Her father cursed, threw things, and began acting strange. One night he threw a glass ashtray. Catherine tried to clean it up. The broken glass, the smell of stale cigarettes, and suddenly, both of her parents were screaming at her. She was almost eleven at the time, and it scared her. She stared at their distorted angry faces and then ran into her bedroom where her little sister, Kiki, was sleeping soundly. Catherine just pulled up the covers and silently cried herself to sleep.

As she hurriedly pushed them into the car, her mother told the girls they were going to see her cousins. It seemed strange going out after dark. It was two days after Christmas. She remembered it vividly. They had gone to her Uncle Al's house, next door to Uncle Walton's. The six kids were in the living room playing with the toys near the Christmas tree. All of a sudden, there was a commotion in the dining room. Catherine heard her father's voice and she stood up. Then she heard him shout, "God damn it; if I can't have them, no one else will." She saw the gun in his hand. Someone screamed. There was yelling and a struggle and she heard her Uncle Walton say, "Jesus Christ, John."

Her mother was yelling, "Neil, Neil, I told you not to take him anywhere. What the hell's the matter with you? Why did you bring him here? Get him out of here. Get him the hell out of here." Catherine remembered locking eyes with her mother for a second, and then she watched the three men grab her father by the arms and drag him out of the house.

Later, her mother told her that her father was sick. Catherine cried and begged her mother to let her go live with him.

"Mommy, please, let me go take care of him."

Her mom promised, "If you stay with me and Kiki, we will get help for him."

They lived in a little white cottage with dark blue trim off the highway in Stuart for a while. They'd driven by it hundreds of times and she had always thought it looked like a gingerbread house. She had never expected to live there. Sometimes, she would think about something, even imagine what it would be like to be inside a building, and then she would end up doing exactly what she had imagined. Like with the little cottage. They didn't go back to live at her house for a long time, and when they did, her father was gone.

Catherine picked up a pillow from the couch, hugged it tightly to her chest, pulling up her knees. This was exactly why she'd stayed away so long.

~~~

Three weeks of treatments had taken their toll on Uncle Walton. His once raven black hair was now dull gray and so thin you could see his scalp. He sat on the couch, head back, mouth wide open, and his eyes closed. His face was pale and drawn. She called to him, "Uncle Walton." She tried again, "Uncle Walton." He stirred very slowly and opened his eyes.

"Hey, handsome," she smiled at him.

"Handsome, my ass. How long was I out?"

"About an hour. Want anything?"

"Some cold water would be nice." She set the glass on the table in the corner.
~~~

"Sit with me for a while, will you?" He patted the couch softly. It seemed like all she'd been doing was sitting with him or taking him to appointments. The little house was starting to feel very small. She wouldn't have done this for anyone but him. She couldn't have. She needed to be there for him.

"Uncle Walton, things aren't going so good for us." She secretly wondered whether he hadn't chosen to do the chemo in hopes it would speed up the dying process for him. She couldn't bring herself to ask. None of it mattered now anyway. He was definitely losing ground.

"I know, honey, but it will be okay. You know how much I miss your aunt. I'm ready to go. I want to tell her I'm sorry."

"Sorry? What do you have to be sorry about?" she asked.

"When she was sick and lost her mind, I didn't take care of her like I should have. One day she was in our bedroom and she had her damn underwear on her head. Her arm was all caught up in them. I yelled at her. I had to cut her out of them and then I yelled at her. She didn't know what she was doing." Tears slid down his face and he was huffing, trying to breath.

"You were probably exhausted from taking care of her, don't you think? It happens, you know. You weren't mad at her so much as you were mad at the situation. Don't blame yourself. I should have been here for you then."

"I didn't need you then," he said gruffly. "I didn't need anyone to see her like that. I took care of her."

"I could have helped."

"No one could have helped."

They sat in silence for a while, and then he reached out and took her hand. "You're here now. Now is when I need you. You know how the boys will be. They'll need you when I'm gone."

~~~

The next morning she asked him, "What happened to the boys? What made Waylon and Justin dislike each other so much?"

He turned his head away from her, staring out the front window toward the river. He spoke without looking at her. "They were different. Justin was like his mother, not quite a momma's boy, but more like her family. You know, British. He needed a lot of attention as a baby, because he was sickly. Now Waylon, he's bullheaded. Strong willed. The two of them butted heads about everything. Waylon picked on his little brother and I thumped on Waylon the hardest because of it. I didn't know any better back then. It's all I knew to do. It set up a kind of rivalry between them."

"They turned out to be okay as adults."

"Yes, but they keep their distance from each other. They remind me of two tomcats."

"As things get worse for you, will they be able to forget about that and make decisions?"

He finally turned and looked at her, "I think they'll leave that up to you. As long as you are here, they'll be okay. They'll listen to you."

"I sure hope so, Uncle Walton. I love you so much." She moved over and put her arm around his neck and hugged him. She took a deep breath and said, "There's something else I've needed to talk to you about for a long time."

~~~

Catherine's life had allowed her to avoid the truth about what had happened before her mother had called it quits with her father. She remembered bits and pieces, the majority of which were vividly unpleasant. Part of her just wanted to deny her first twelve years and pretend her life had begun when her mother married Hamilton. He was the man who had cared for them for all these years. Her mother had been smart when she chose Hamilton for her and her girls.

Catherine's old memories had been carefully avoided all these years, but here she sat next to her biological uncle, her father's brother, about to ask some hard questions.

"I guess this is as good a time as we are going to get to discuss this, Uncle Walton. There's something I need to talk to you about. I remember that night, the night you took the gun away from him, my dad. I remember it like it happened yesterday. I can see the scuffle in the hallway at Uncle Al's house. I remember seeing your face and your hands up in the air struggling to take the gun away from him. I want you to know how much that meant to me. I mean, you put your own life on the line for my sister, me, and our mother. It could have ended differently. I have thought about it hundreds of times. What if the gun had gone off? What if he had shot you?"

He sat staring straight ahead, showing no sign of emotion. His weathered wrinkled face had grown so thin.

She went on, "I don't even want to think about what might have happened. I want you to know that I knew, and I've wanted to say thank you for a very long time." She moved over next to him and hugged him long and hard. She felt relieved to have finally said it out loud.

Catherine had one more thing she needed to know. "What happened to him?" she asked. "What happened to him to make him do that?"

She'd heard her father shout, "If I can't have them, no one else will."

Her uncle thought for what seemed like a long time, then said, "He wasn't like that before the war. You know we both enlisted during World War II. I became a medic and he repaired the planes. He even did some of the art work on the fighter planes. He came home from England a different person. We all did. He wasn't right, not after what he saw. It changed him. He never was the same person."

Catherine said, "Other people went to war and didn't come back like that. You didn't. I don't understand why he took it so hard."

Her uncle drew in a deep breath. "He was one of those sensitive souls. He couldn't get over the pictures in his head. It was seeing the kids that hurt him the most. It affected him."

"But didn't he see us, his own two kids? We were right in front of him and we needed him. Why didn't he see how he was affecting us?"

"I don't think it occurred to him like that. He couldn't think that way. Honey, he did the best he could. The alcohol took the rest of what was left of him. He sort of shriveled up inside. There wasn't anything anyone could do. Your mother tried. We all hoped. Let it go."

She sat silently next to Uncle Walton. It was true. She had been too young to make much of a difference to her father. It was after her mother had left him, after they moved back into their old house. She had been twelve when she confronted him about his drinking. He was totally wasted, standing swaying in the middle of the road. He'd sent some young man to take her and her sister home from his girlfriend's house. He hadn't even stayed with them during their visit. Instead, he'd gone off to some bar. He was shouting at her, and she yelled back at him and called him a drunk. She ran with her sister in tow into a stranger's house where she called her mother to come and get them. It was confusing. He hadn't even cared they were there and yet her mother had sent them to him.

On the way home in the car, her mother had said, "My land, little girl, you'll have everyone in this town minding our business." Catherine knew how to solve it. She refused to go see him again. She hardly knew who he'd become any more. She made up her mind not to miss him.

Her uncle reached over and nudged her, "Leave it alone. You've spent enough years trying to figure it out. Don't let it drag you back. You did everything you could do, honey. It was his choice. The V.A. would have paid for his treatment. He refused. He didn't want it. Sometimes, I think he drank himself to death because it was less painful than living."

"The first day I came here when I walked down to the river," Catherine confessed, "I was sitting on the dock and I heard someone call my name. When I turned and looked up the hill, I thought I saw him standing there waving for me to come to him."

"I don't think he's found his peace yet, honey. Maybe your coming here will help all of us find our way."

She sat motionless, staring at the floor. Catherine wanted to bury herself in her uncle's arms and cry, but she didn't do it. She couldn't hold back the tears, though.

He reached over and caught one with his finger. "No tears now. He did what he did. So did your Mother. You've got to get past it. He was always proud of you even if he never said it. We were all proud of you. I still am."

She took a deep breath. "Thank you for being who

you are, Uncle Walton."

Catherine got up and walked into the bathroom. She blew her nose, splashed water on her face, and stood looking into the mirror for a long time. She had finally done it. She had asked the questions and finally told him thank you. She had known for a long time that she needed to do this. She sometimes thought she felt her father's presence, but she never told anyone. That's why when Waylon had called and asked her to look in on Uncle Walton, she had known deep inside that she had to do it. She just didn't know how she was going to accomplish it, but it had all worked out with a complete stranger coming into her life at the right time. Often things would happen for her that way. Almost as if someone were in control of maneuvering her through things. Like after James' accident. That morning when she had arrived at Arianne's apartment, the door had quickly opened and there stood Arianne. Things often happened she couldn't quite wrap her mind around, but were too coincidental. Catherine wiped her face on the towel and neatly hung it on the rack. Her hair was a mess; her eyes looked sunken in. She barely recognized herself, but she had to do this for him and for her.

"How about I fix us some soup? There are some fresh veggies, stew meat."

"Whatever you like will be fine by me. I don't feel so sick today."

She stood at the sink peeling potatoes, looking out the window. "Did you ever make that rattlesnake skin jacket you wanted?"

She heard him chuckle. "You remember that? No, I never did."

~~~
~~~

Her father had drank himself to death. His wife of about five years had cancer, and at the funeral, she told Catherine and Kiki she'd be the next to go. She died a few months later. Looking back, the whole thing was surreal. Kiki had decided to attend their father's funeral at the last minute. Uncle Walton wasn't at his own brother's funeral, but Waylon and Justin were there. They had looked odd in their suits, and it had been strange to see them all grown up and together. They'd hugged her, but said nothing. After the funeral, she couldn't find them anywhere. They had quickly disappeared.

CHAPTER 17

Zane could say in earnest that he loved her farm and being alone. He enjoyed taking his time without an agenda. He knew he was fortunate to have this opportunity. The weeks flew by quickly. It was hard to believe he'd been there over a month. Sleep came easily now in the quiet of the nights, but the dreams came as well.

Catherine was riding the little bay mare cantering across the pasture toward him. As she came closer, he saw her smile and wave. He walked to the gate as she slowed to a trot and met him there. She got off the horse and led it through the gate. The mare whinnied to her stable mates as Zane closed the gate, reaching out quickly to turn Catherine around and kiss her. She stepped back as he said, "Good morning. You two are out early." Just then, the mare shoved her nose into her back, pushing her into his arms again.

They had been laughing when he woke up. The dreams were more and more frequently about her, but sometimes about his escapades with Buck. Often they were distorted and confusing, and he awoke disoriented and uneasy.

One night the dream was about a horse that was cast in the stall, stuck up against the wall. He rushed to get a rope, wrapped it around the front leg to flip the horse over. He woke up in the hallway about to fall down the stairs. Another time he was standing along the bank of a stream and she pushed him off some rocks into the cold water.

Zane grabbed the extra pillow, placed it on his chest and folded his arms around it. This was the first dream where he'd actually kissed her. He swore he could smell her, taste her, and feel her soft lips. He let out a long sigh. This was not good. The sooner she got back and he could get out of there the better.

~~~

It was suddenly December. He called his mother every Christmas. He imagined her with a roaring fire in the hearth, and the long table set for the feast she prepared. She was wearing her traditional Christmas apron. He always told her he was fine. This time, it was true.

"Actually, Mom, I'm staying on someone's farm. Her uncle is gravely ill and this just sort of happened."

"I guess you retired at the right time. How long have you been there?"

"A month—just about a month. They've called in hospice. It probably won't be long."

"It's always hard, but especially so around the holidays. It's nice of you to do that for her. Have you known her long?" she asked.

"No, not at all. She's a customer of Buck's. Have I told you he bought a feed store, a farm?"

"Oh, so that's why you're there. For Buck?"

He knew she blamed Buck for his leaving. He knew she probably thought he wouldn't have gone if he hadn't had his buddy to go with him. They never discussed any of it. She never asked and he barely told her anything.
~~~

"Yes. I came to tell him goodbye before I head west." He knew hearing that would please her. He knew she'd wanted this for a long time, had been waiting for him a lifetime to do what he was afraid to do – go home. He continued, "It will be a while. I'll be leaving as soon as the weather allows. I figure Trouble and I will end up that away about the end of spring, beginning of summer." He avoided saying the word—home.

He heard her take a deep breath. He was sure she was thrilled her son was finally coming home after all these years. She simply said, "Trouble? Did you mention Trouble?"

"He's my horse, Mom. I picked up this little horse. I want to take my time bringing him out and look around a bit on the way."

"Zane, you know I can't wait. I'm so proud of what you did with your life. And, it's so nice what you're doing for the lady. I'm so excited for you, for us. I know you will get here at just the right time."

"Catherine will come back here right after she loses her uncle. I'll see how she does and then I'll head out."

"Don't make it too long, Zane. I love you. You just gave me the best Christmas present ever."

"I love you too, Mom." He hadn't said it often enough and he knew it.

"Oh, here they all come. The guys are all coming in. I wish you were here. The snow has drifted almost to the roof and they were out throwing hay to the cows."

"Enjoy your day, Mom. Tell old Iron Crow I said hello."

Maggie winked at Parker Iron Crow and mouthed, "It's Zane." He came over and slid his cold arms around her warm body.

She said, "I will, Zane. He's right here. Merry

Christmas. I love you."

"Bye, Mom. Merry Christmas."

~~~

That night, the moonlight was crisp and bright as he finished his chores and scooted the dogs through the back door. He started a fire and sat quietly in her living room. Heading home had been a long time coming. After his father had died, there had been no reason why he needed to stay away. He could have made arrangements, taken a vacation, a leave of absence. It didn't seem so important until now. Meeting Catherine and living in her house, for some reason, brought thoughts of his mother flooding in.

The phone conversations with Catherine over the weeks turned from informative to something deeper. Recently, he had told her the bookcases had arrived and asked her where she wanted them. He received her okay to put them together; then he had asked about the books. She was reluctant at first. She had a funny feeling about him looking at her things.

"No, no. Leave them. I'll do it when I get back."

Zane convinced her. "Just give me an idea of how you'd like them organized. I'm not illiterate. I can do it. You can always rearrange them later. At least they will be out of the boxes." He enjoyed it. She had a strange assortment, most he'd never read.

It was the last box that surprised him. It was full of her scrapbooks, some photo albums, and journals. He was respectful and didn't read her private stuff, but he did look at some of the pictures. He discovered a lot about her in the scrapbooks. There were photos of her with banners saying "The Missing Link Foundation," group pictures that
~~~

were taken at fundraisers, and photos of her life in New York.

When the phone rang, he snapped the photo album shut. It was Catherine. "Listen, there's this one box of personal stuff—my scrapbooks." He stopped her.

"Been there, done that!"

"You did not?" She sounded scared.

"No. I didn't. Your secrets are safe." It was a half-lie meant for her peace of mind.

She sighed with relief. "Did some storage boxes arrive yet?"

"Those pretty flowered things?" he teased.

"Yes. Could you just put those personal things inside those boxes?"

Sure he could. He had nothing but time. In some of those photographs, she was smiling, and she looked absolutely beautiful. He wanted to see Catherine smile like that and hear her laugh. It made him think a lot about the fact that he'd never seen his mother smile like that, not once, not ever. He couldn't remember ever hearing his mother laugh. It made him realize even more that it was time to go home and do something about it.

CHAPTER 18

Catherine sat on her uncle's screened porch. An old boat tilted idly on a rusted trailer in the yard. It began to rain and the wind was a bit chilly. The weatherman said the seas outside the reef were four to six feet. The river sported whitecaps from the brisk 30 mph winds. Even in the light rain, the blues of the plumbago, orange of the royal Poinciana, and the lush tropical greens painted a delicious view. She could hear the hum of a few silly boaters who launched without any concern for the risk. Off in the distance, a rather large foreboding thunderhead burst brightly with a bolt of lightning and the roar of thunder. The wind shifted, spraying her with mists of rain. She gave it up and went back into the house.

"I didn't know you were up, Uncle Walton. The lady from hospice should be here soon to help with your bath and shave you." He didn't respond. She had no idea how he had made it to the couch. It became increasingly difficult for him to breath. He saved his energy for important things—things he wanted to tell her. No sense wasting it on words that didn't matter. She fixed him a cup of coffee. He called it his luxury item. It was the one thing that still tasted good to him.

It didn't seem so long ago that they had been able to carry on long conversations. Catherine felt comforted filling in the blanks of both of their lives. It hurt her the day he told her, "I would have never recognized you. I could have walked right by and never known you." It was hard, but true. So many years separated them. So many things had happened to change her—not just aging. She felt what he said deep inside her core. She had been robbed of the one thing that sustained most people—her family—the feeling of connection. It was like finishing the connect-the-dots, but the picture was not whole. She had never felt it. Her heart felt fragmented, out of beat. She couldn't quite get the puzzle together. There was always something missing.

She poured hot water into a cup and added a lemon tea bag. That was her luxury item, a cup of comfort on an increasingly sorrowful path. She went to sit with him and wait for the hospice lady.

Blackie was curled next to him on the couch, both front paws on his leg with his head resting on them. Uncle Walton's hand was resting on his back. He was becoming weaker every day.

There was a light tap on the back door and then it opened. Roberta, the hospice nurse, came straight through the kitchen into the living room. The nurses were good now about not startling the cats once they understood how spooky they were and how they tore away pieces of her uncle as they bolted away. Roberta said, "Good morning," to both of them and set about her business, taking Uncle Walton's vital signs and assessing his decline. She chattered away at him, patting his arm every so often and reaching up and touching his face. They eventually made it into the bathroom. Roberta set the walker out in the hallway. The bathroom was so tiny two people could barely fit in there.

Catherine knew it would only get worse. She'd keep him home as long as she could. The tears welled up in her eyes and her chest felt like it was being crushed. If she had ever had even an ounce of courage, she was going to have to find it again soon.

Roberta settled him back on the couch. Blackie returned immediately to his side. Sissy appeared from under the corner table and settled above his head. He reached up to pet her. Roberta pulled Catherine by her arm through the kitchen and out onto the porch. "He's deteriorating. Take today, tomorrow, and say everything you've been holding back. The cats are very aware of what's going on. I know he said he's okay with his son taking them. They know. We will keep him here at the house as long as we can. I think it's important to him." Catherine couldn't say a thing except to utter a weak, "Thank you." Roberta squeezed her arm and was gone.

~~~

As Catherine stood in front of him, he patted the couch for her to sit. He gulped hard and said, "I'm done." She sat down and took his hand gently in hers. He said, "We need to talk now." He pulled his hand from hers and pointed at her. "You and me—we're different." He stopped and took in a few breaths. "My mother, your grandmother, was half Blackfeet." Catherine was trying to process what he had just said. She barely believed what she was hearing. "You are Native American." He fought to keep going breath by breath.

Catherine replied, "My sister always said there was something different about us. We were dark, so brown; we tanned easily. We thought we'd been adopted—were Puerto Rican. For the longest time, we thought our mother would tell us." She began to laugh. "We felt silly about it. Now it makes sense. Why didn't anyone tell us?"

"Don't know," he said. "Maybe she was ashamed?"
~~~

"Ashamed. We should be ashamed. I always admired them, the Indians. They went to hell and back. They still do. I wonder why our mother didn't tell us?"

"You knew." He took her hand and squeezed it. "It didn't matter. You knew, and I knew you knew." He sat looking straight into her eyes with his black piercing eyes. "Nobody had to tell you." She hugged him. Everything was suddenly making a lot more sense.

~~~

Catherine spent all her time with him that day and the next, the last day he would live in his little house "built with his own two hands with one sawhorse." He had recently shown her the photos of the construction.

She'd gone out a few days before to pick up groceries. Roberta was there and told her she'd stay until she got back.

"I'm off the clock. Don't worry about it. Take your time."

It was a relief to get away for even a little while. When she got back, Roberta's car was gone and a strange car was parked in the yard. She hurried to the back door. When she opened it, a man was standing in the kitchen. The minute she saw his eyes, she recognized him. It was Justin.

"Hey, gril!" he said. She laughed because when they were younger he had a speech problem and had always called her "gril," instead of girl. She was surprised by how tall he was, and how he'd filled out into such a large man. He bear hugged her. There was little either of them could say under the circumstances. He didn't stay. He said goodbye to his father, hugged them both, and went home.

~~~

"Shall I call the boys?" Catherine asked. "They need to know you're leaving in the morning."

"They won't come," Uncle Walton said, matter-of-factly.

He was right. When she talked to him on the phone, Waylon said he'd be arriving from Alabama sometime the next day. Justin said he'd see his Dad at the hospital. They more than likely didn't want to see him in his house like this for the last time. It was hard enough for her.

The next day in the middle of the morning, the ambulance arrived to transport Uncle Walton to the hospital. He had time earlier to hold Blackie and Sissy and kiss them goodbye. She watched him with them until she couldn't hold back the tears and stumbled out onto the porch where she sobbed as quietly as she could. There was barely enough room for the men and the stretcher in the house. He took one long last look around his house, caught her eye, and winked. He lay back peacefully on the stretcher. She knew he saw her tears.

"It's okay, honey. It will be okay."

"I'll meet you at the hospital shortly."

They shut the backdoor of the ambulance. As soon as she'd watched the ambulance pull away, she staggered into the house and down the hallway, throwing herself onto one of the beds in the boys' room. She cried herself to sleep. She hadn't planned on sleeping like that, but it was the first time she'd slept that deeply since she had arrived. She awoke startled. She had a jagged crease across her cheek, and her eyes were swollen and bloodshot. She couldn't have looked worse.

~~~

The pink lady at the front desk directed her to the
~~~

elevator. The nurse's station was directly in front of her when she stepped out; Uncle Walton's room was just a little to the right.

"He's in the hospice room. It's very nice," the nurse told her.

It was a private room with a bathroom. He looked pale and small in the oversized hospital bed. She sat in a comfortable chair at the side of his bed for a while before he stirred and opened his eyes.

"Hi, Uncle Walton."

He said, "Hi, honey." He sounded just a little bit stronger.

A nurse came in, took his vital signs, fluffed his pillow, and gave him a sip of water. She took a damp cloth and wiped off his face and adjusted the oxygen mask.

"Are you his niece?" she asked.

Catherine nodded.

"Roberta was here when he arrived. She wants to get together with you and his sons tomorrow." She reached in her pocket and handed Catherine a card with Roberta's phone number.

"Call her and set it up. I'm Diane. Let me know if you need anything. Just come to the nurse's station."

~~~

Catherine left him after dark. The cats needed to be fed, and she was exhausted. No one else had shown up at the hospital all day. Because she had forgotten to turn on any lights when she left, the house was totally dark. She hadn't even thought about locking the door. It was going to be very strange in the house without him, without anyone. In fact, she had never been in this house by herself before. No matter how hard she wished, life would
~~~

never be the same for any of them.

In the predawn hours, Sissy came into the room and jumped on the bed. Catherine drifted back to sleep on her stomach. A little while after that, she stirred when she felt something walking on her back. By the weight and feel, it had to be Blackie. She tried to roll over, but Sissy was curled up between her legs right in her crotch. She giggled. In less than a day, they had a new plan. She carefully pulled her right leg up and over to get both legs on one side of the cat. She slid sideways, slowly spilling Blackie off her back. She sat up and lifted them both off the bed and onto the floor. They had actually let her sleep until six-thirty, unlike the three o'clock ritual they had with her uncle. She paddled to the bathroom, and then crawled back under the covers.

"Just five more minutes, guys, okay?"

When she finally crawled out of bed, for the first time in a long time, she fussed with her hair, put on makeup, and dressed in her best shirt and jeans. She drove slowly to the hospital for the meeting with her cousins and the hospice staff. A nurse came out of his room, just as she got to his door.

"He's comfortable at the moment."

Within a few minutes, Justin arrived. He hugged her, glanced at his father, and said, "I came from work. Lannie should be here soon."

Lannie was Justin's wife; Catherine had not seen her in years.

A few minutes later, Waylon pushed open the door. She rushed out into the hallway before he could come in, grabbing her cousin to hug him. He lost his balance, stepped back, and caught them both by crashing into the wall. "I missed you too," he said with that crooked grin of his. His wife Helene stood a little behind him. Catherine briefly spoke the usual greetings. Once they'd gone into the room, Waylon took one look at his dad and stepped right back out into the hallway. She gave him a minute and then joined him.

"He's ready to go," Catherine said.

Waylon didn't say a word. She took his hand; Lannie arrived just as they were going back into the room. Catherine felt like she barely knew any of them. They decided Catherine should sit in the middle chair between the boys, while Lannie and Helene would stand.

There they sat, the three of them at the foot of his bed, silently waiting. Catherine said, "I always thought we were Cherokee. No one ever talked about it."

Waylon said, "Cherokee? Where did you get that idea? We're Blackfeet."

"I know," she smiled. "He just told me the other day. Why didn't anyone ever talk about it?"

"I guess it didn't matter. We all knew. No one really cared."

A few minutes later, a woman burst into the room and introduced herself as Jeanne. Roberta was with her. The room was suddenly crowded.

When Jeanne called his name, Walton opened his eyes.

She said, "Walton, your family is here." He slowly looked at each of them. She continued, "Roberta and I will be coordinating Walton's care. We are here to help all of you through this stage of Walton's life." She asked each person's name; when she got to Catherine, she said, "Oh, is this your daughter?"

Her uncle spoke right up, "No, she's too pretty to be mine." Everyone laughed.

"No, I'm afraid I'm his eldest niece," Catherine said.

Jeanne explained about the hospital's care and

services, its responsibilities and those of hospice, and how the staff would help to make him more comfortable. They each received a packet that provided information on what they could expect. Jeanne spoke directly to Walton before she left, "I'll be here every day to monitor your care, Walton."

Once Jeanne was gone, Waylon pulled Catherine out into the hall. "I won't be much good to you. You know I can't." He hugged her and quickly walked away. He could have let his guard down with her. He didn't need to be her fearless leader anymore. She didn't care. All she wanted was to be there for them, but she secretly wished she had someone to be there for her. She watched Waylon get on the elevator.

When Catherine turned back toward his room, she nearly ran into Helene. "I know how hard this is for you. Before we moved to Alabama, I spent a lot of time with him. We sat and talked. He loved you. If you need anything, let me know. We'll be at our house here." She squeezed Catherine's arm and headed toward the elevator. Justin had to get back to work so he and Lannie left next. Catherine couldn't help but notice Waylon and Justin hadn't said a word to each other.

Catherine stayed with Uncle Walton as long as she could. Her back was hurting and her legs were tired by the time she headed back to his little house.

~~~

The next few days and nights became a blur with promises of moving him to the hospice house and nothing being done. The promises always fell apart. Jeanne stopped coming, but Roberta was there as much as she possibly could be.
~~~

Late one night, when Catherine came back to sit with her uncle for awhile, the nurse called her out into the hallway. "It's not right what they are doing to him. You know they can't do this. They have to take him regardless of his financial status. They have him in their hospice room here, but utilizing our staff. They simply can't do this. They need to honor his wishes and transfer him. Call them in the morning and demand that they move him. He's only hanging on for that. You know how much he wants to get to the hospice house."

"I know. I expected them to come through for him. It's breaking my heart."

They heard someone coming up in the elevator so the nurse darted back to the nurse's station and Catherine headed back into his room. Later that night, a respiratory therapist came into the room. He didn't even do the treatment. Instead, he got out some oil and rubbed it on her uncle's back and arms. He said, "The treatment makes no sense at this stage of his illness." Catherine had watched it make him cough miserably for the past several nights. The man was just about to leave when he said, "They're not doing right by him. Everyone is talking about it. They've had a bed available. It's all about the money. Like he doesn't deserve to go over there? It's just not right."

The next morning, she called hospice. The receptionist informed her that all the staff members were in a meeting. When Catherine identified herself to the woman, she was shocked by what she said. "Oh, you're Mr. Kendale's niece. He's very poor, isn't he? It's such a shame when someone doesn't have anything when they die."

Catherine felt her blood boiling and rushing to her face as she became infuriated. She managed to swallow her rage, and said sternly, "Poor? This man, my uncle, was never poor. He chose to live simply, but with purpose. We could all take lessons from him on how to live with grace and dignity." She wanted to climb through the phone and slap the stupid woman. For now, it would have to wait.

~~~

Uncle Walton was restless. His eyes were searching her face. She went to the nurse's station hoping to find the nurse who had told her about hospice. She was greatly relieved when she saw Diane coming down the hall.

"He's been on a lot of morphine," Diane explained.

Catherine said, "Morphine? Why? He doesn't seem to be in that much pain."

"No. It's because of his son, Waylon. Yesterday when he came in, his father shouted at him. He was yelling, 'Shoot me. Get the damn shotgun and shoot me!' Waylon was quite upset and he asked the doctor to order morphine to keep him knocked out. It's more for your cousin's pain than your uncle's. There is a lot going on between your uncle and his two sons."

~~~

Uncle Walton had been telling Catherine things all week, things he wanted her to tell his sons. Catherine felt somehow cheated by her family and now cheated by the morphine. During the day, he was mostly passed out. At night, when the drugs wore off, he would try to tell her things. On the last night, Diane asked him in front of her, "Do you need a shot?" He almost shouted at her, "No more. No more."

Diane told Catherine, "Ask him questions. He'll be

able to respond that way. You'll know what to ask."

Sitting by his bedside, Catherine attempted to read a magazine, but she watched as his labored chest rose and fell. Listening to his breathing, she forbade herself to wish that it would stop. She knew he would be at peace then, but she wouldn't let herself think a thing that sounded like she was saying goodbye. He had been waiting for her to come back to him. She knew it, plain and simple.

Uncle Walton had stood for everything good, honest, and real. He was the one everyone could count on. Now, he was leaving. He was getting the morphine, but she was the one in pain. If they kept giving it to him, there wouldn't be anything left of him to cling to. After the injection, he would sleep, less restless, more at ease. In those quiet moments, the memories would come and play in her mind. In those memories, she would hang on to every part of him even harder. When he would come out from the drugs, he would be able to speak for a little while, communicate with a few words and motions. The nurses interrupted occasionally, but as the end grew near, the interruptions were less frequent. Catherine tried to be brave, to keep it together, but she was silently screaming inside.

~~~

It took the hospital four more days before Uncle Walton was transferred, but by that day, no one on the staff was going to forget Catherine anytime soon. They made absolutely certain, after she was done with them, that he was transferred into the exact same room where her Aunt Josie died. Catherine had finally reached her breaking point and had let them have it with both guns.
~~~

The last night in the hospital, Uncle Walton was extremely restless. Diane said, "Just keep asking. He's trying to tell you something." She checked his vital signs and said, "I think you need to call the boys."

Catherine felt like she was about to pass out. Diane saw her turn pale and pulled her into the hall. "Take a breath. You can call them when you're ready. It's getting very close. That's all." Catherine couldn't breathe. Her chest hurt. He wanted to die at hospice, not here. *"Please God, please, give him the strength to hang on just a little longer."* Still, she didn't know. They promised they would move him in the morning. He wanted to die in the same place where he had said goodbye to his wife.

She dialed Waylon's number first. It was a little after midnight. Helene answered sleepily. She woke Waylon and asked him.

"He's not coming. He said he'll see his father at hospice tomorrow. I'm sorry. Take care."

The phone rang three times before Justin's wife, Lannie, answered. She sounded breathless, startled. Justin told her the same thing. He didn't want to come in the middle of the night. Catherine tried to tell them it could be too late. Tomorrow might be too late. Lannie softly said, "Call me if anything happens."

About an hour later, her uncle became even more restless. His eyes searched her face. "What is it, Uncle Walton? What do you need? I love you so much. I wish I knew what you wanted. Do you want Waylon? Helene? Justin? Lannie?" Then it finally dawned on her. Why hadn't she thought of it? "Do you want Blackie?" How could she have been so stupid? There was no doubt in her mind. Finally, she knew what he wanted, needed.

She found Diane. "He wants his cat. Oh, God, he wants his cat. What are we going to do?"

Diane said, "It's okay. You can bring the cat here. It's really okay. Can someone bring it?"

Catherine hurried to the phone. She had no idea what Blackie would do. She didn't want anything to happen to him, but her Uncle needed him.

Lannie picked up the phone. "Lannie, can you go and get Blackie and bring him here. Diane said to come through the ER. She says it's okay. Walk on through. No one will bother you."

Catherine heard the elevator about forty minutes later. She met Lannie in the hall. There was no crate. There was no cat. Catherine was furious, confused, extremely angry.

She nearly shouted at Lannie, "How could you? He's waiting for his cat!"

Lannie's face was unemotional as she answered flatly, "We thought you were losing it. You've said so many things that he's told you. We don't see it. When we're here, he's out."

Diane came up behind Catherine and placed her hands on her shoulders and softly took control. "It's the morphine. During the day, he's on the morphine. At night, he's able to communicate. He needs his cat. Can someone bring it?"

Lannie was fishing around in her purse for her cell phone. Diane said, "Use the family phone in the hall." Lannie dialed her son, Matthew, and then she and Catherine waited silently in his room.

It seemed like only minutes when a tall boy with long black hair appeared at the door with a crate. Catherine was struck by how handsome he was. Matthew set the crate on the bed and slowly opened the door. Without a moment's hesitation, Blackie stuck out his head, looked around, and stepped out onto the bed. He walked right up on Uncle Walton's chest, kissed him on the mouth, and softly curled up in his armpit.

Matthew set the crate on the floor and walked to the other side of the bed where he sat down in the chair. He scooted it closer and took his grandfather's hand. Walton's eyes opened as Matthew started to talk. As he realized that Blackie was there, Uncle Walton wrapped his other arm around his cat. It was suddenly about these two, grandfather and grandson, who had somehow been given a way to say goodbye. Catherine and Lannie looked at each other, both fighting back their tears.

Matthew said, "I've been fishing a lot. I missed coming to your house, the dock. I'm sorry I haven't been to see you. I'm a senior now, you know."

Catherine's throat filled with a huge strangling lump as she fought to contain herself. She and Lannie grabbed hands as they stood silently at the foot of the bed. They didn't feel like strangers to each other anymore.

Matthew stayed as long as he could and then he said, "I'll see you soon, okay?" He leaned down and kissed his grandfather on the forehead, reached over and patted Blackie. "I love you, Pop Pop." He looked at his mother, with his eyes full of tears. Lannie hugged her son.

"I'm so proud of you. You know that."

He turned to Catherine and had to bend down to hug her.

"I can't believe you're so grown up. You're quite a young man. I know how much he loves you." Her voice cracked. "It means so much that you brought Blackie." They both looked at the sleeping cat.

Lannie said, "Blackie can stay. I'll bring him home later. You have school. Go get some sleep." She hugged him. He looked at his grandfather and then quietly slipped out the door. The women couldn't speak. They just stood holding each other's hand.

Uncle Walton slept peacefully at last. Once in a while someone would peek in the door, look at the cat in his bed, and be gone. Diane came in. "Everyone is coming to see Blackie. I'm sorry."

Sometime in the early morning, Lannie convinced her it was okay to go home. "I think he's determined to hang on until he's at hospice. Go home."

Catherine half-smiled. "Home. I don't really know where that is right now. What about Blackie?"

"I'll stay here for a while. I might as well take Blackie to our house. I'll swing by and pick up Sissy, if it's okay. That way they'll be together. We've had them at our house before when he's been in the hospital. They adjust. They'll be fine."

Catherine couldn't do anything but shake her head up and down. She took a long last look at her uncle. He looked sweet in the bed with his beloved cat. She bent down and kissed her uncle's cheek. His eyes opened. "I'm going to your house for a little while. Lannie's here. I'll see you at hospice."

Catherine hesitated at the door. "Thank you, Lannie. I know you didn't have to come. I'm glad you did. I'm glad everything turned out the way it did."

She found Diane. "I'm going home. I won't see you after he's moved."

"I'll make sure they move him as early as possible. He's very lucky to have you for a niece. It's obvious how much he loves you. You did good." Diane hugged her.

Catherine stumbled toward the elevator, then out into the night. In the morning, she didn't even remember how she had gotten back to her uncle's house.

CHAPTER 19

Zane was worried. Catherine hadn't called him in a couple of days. His heart sank as he realized her uncle must have taken a turn for the worst. He knew it was coming, but still—she hadn't even had a chance to recover from the loss of her husband. It seemed unreasonable, unfair. He wondered how long she would stay. Not that he needed to go, yet.

Once a week, Zane headed to town to pick up supplies, which included stopping at Buck's feed store. He tried not to linger, even though they were okay with each other now.

Zane asked, "So how's that darling of yours, Deb? That's her name, isn't it?"

Buck had a toothpick stuck between his teeth, and he nervously flipped it up and down with his tongue. Zane knew that look.

"You didn't. Tell me that you didn't." Buck looked sheepish—embarrassed. Zane kept at him.

"I mean it. Tell me that you did not boink that redheaded mouth of the South."

Buck shook his head as he spit the toothpick into the wastebasket along with a soggy plug of tobacco.

"It was a weak moment," he said. "She just showed up at the house. In the dark, it's not like you can really tell the difference."

"Not if you're drunk. Tell me you were at least

drunk."

"Drunk enough." Buck felt the beads of perspiration starting on his forehead.

"You are going to regret this one. She's leechy."

Buck was frowning. "Leechy?"

"Yes, she'll attach herself to you like a leech, and you'll never be able to shake her off. You haven't ever lived this close to one before." Zane was trying not to smile.

"You're probably right, but ever since I laid my eyes on that pretty little piece of ass, I've just been horny. It's Catherine's fault."

"Catherine? You asshole. Stop it. Why the hell don't you grow up?"

"All I did was screw her for Christ's sake." Buck was arguing with himself, not Zane.

"Yeah? Well, ask Deb what she thinks you did. I'll guarantee she's telling a whole different story around this sweet little town of yours. She has no idea you put Catherine's face on her body."

Buck drew in a breath. "Oh, Christ!" He hadn't given an ounce of thought to his behavior.

"Well, that's a good start. Maybe Christ and his Almighty Father can get you out of this one, 'cause you're gonna need a whole lot of help. I gotta get out of here before Deb shows up and I have to explain to her what's wrong with you."

"Say, man, this shit never bothered you before. What the hell's up with you?"

Zane turned quickly back into Buck's face. "You never lived in the town where you shopped before. Think about it. These people know your business. If you're gonna mess around, take it out of town. Remember that little ditty. There's a reason for it."

Zane grabbed the bottle of liniment off the counter

and left Buck standing there with a puzzled look on his face. He couldn't help but chuckle at how naïve his buddy could be. What a tangled web....

~~~

"Surely Deb didn't think it was anything more than a nice romp in the sack." Buck thought.

The truth was Deb hadn't been so bad in the dark in his bed. In fact, they'd fallen asleep in each other's arms afterwards and he hadn't moved until morning. The even worse part was that she looked damn good in his blue shirt, standing in his kitchen in the morning. When he'd pulled her toward the bedroom again, she never said a word. She just followed along like a silly teenager, and what they had done that time seemed really naughty, but felt really good. When she said, "I better go home," he reluctantly watched her dress and quietly walked her to the door. They kissed silently and tenderly, and she held his face in her hands and just looked up at him. It was the first time in his life Buck actually saw the woman on the other side of his desire. It was also the first time he'd ever seen Deb Albom not talking.

~~~~

Deb turned, walked away, and got into her car without looking back. She knew if she looked back, he would see her crying. For the first time in her life, she felt filled up. That empty hole inside her didn't hurt. Yes, this cowboy had almost turned her inside out.

"Dear Lord," she whispered, "forgive me for what I just did, but could you please make it happen again, forever." She giggled. She had never felt like this before. This guy was something else. She wasn't about to tell a single solitary soul about it. There are a few things that happen in your life that are so precious that if you share them with anyone, you spoil the magic. No. This was way too precious and special to tell anyone. Not yet. Not now. Maybe never.

~~~

Deb wanted to hear Buck's voice worse than anything, but she was too scared to dial the phone. She shook from head to toe every time she thought about what she'd done. She had let down her guard, defied her own rules, and slept with him. She had been so caught up in the moment, lost in the—God forgive her—heat of it that she couldn't even remember whether he'd taken the time to use—. Oh, God! She felt really sick to her stomach. She'd not only done it; she'd probably really gone and done it. What the hell had she been thinking?

It was one thing to behave as if you were foolish, but it was quite another to actually be that foolish. Now, she had to face him and worse yet, herself. Okay, she would admit that she had waited a very long time for just this exact moment, but now, today, she felt like shit about it. Yes, she went to his house. Yes, she was hungry for sex. Okay. She said it. Sex. But, she hadn't really expected him to do it the first time she showed up at his door. In that moment, Deb Albom became the person she wanted everyone to believe she was. Now, she actually was that flippant redheaded slut, and it didn't feel very good. Never mind what she thought about herself; what had Buck been thinking?

She wanted to stop the internal dialogue, but the only way she could halt the chatter was when she slept. She had already slept away a day and a half. It was tough,
~~~

but she had made her bed, so to speak.

She picked up the phone and dialed. "Hi, Mom!"

~~~

Buck was glad it was Sunday. The store had been unusually busy all week and he was tired. Plus, he wanted to sort through the two boxes his mother had sent him from the ranch. He had no idea what they contained. He cut through the tape with his pocketknife and pushed back the flaps. On top was a white envelope.

"Congratulations on your First Home!"

It hadn't even occurred to him. His first home! Leave it to his mother. Inside the largest box were household items—dish towels with cowboys on bucking broncos, a shower curtain with running horses, forest green bath towels, a soap dish, and last a toilet brush. Buck smiled.

The second box had an old photo album of his, some mementos from his room and an afghan he was sure his mother had made. It was dark shades of brown. Chocolate—his favorite. He checked his watch. She'd be awake. Buck dialed the phone.

"Hello, Mom!"
~~~

CHAPTER 20

Catherine sat in the quiet of Uncle Walton's house at his little kitchen table, sipping a cup of tea. When they were little, Catherine, Kiki, and the two boys learned how to fish. They had begun with short cane poles, line, and a hook. Later, they had graduated to real fishing rods and reels. Her cousins learned how to shoot and went mostly duck and deer hunting with their father. Other than those times, the men had been fairly absent, mostly at work. Once in a while, a few of them would gather at the kitchen table, drinking coffee and smoking cigarettes. Sometimes, the kids had been allowed to sit on the linoleum floor and listen.

Back then, the kids were seen and mostly not heard. The boys usually retreated to their room. On rare occasions, they sat in the living room. Once the boys entered high school, their dad began to treat them differently, or maybe it was the other way around. Maybe they treated their dad differently. It was like watching three bulls trying to survive in a small pen.

Coming back to this area and spending time here made all the old memories Catherine had been avoiding crop up. It seemed like as soon as her mother left her father, things had never been the same between any of them. In fact, once Hamilton moved in, she only saw her cousins at school. She almost never saw her aunt and uncle after that. She had no idea what had caused so much friction. She and her sister, Kiki, tried hard to get used to their new lives, and their mother and new stepfather pretty much controlled their whereabouts.

It had shocked the girls when their mother sold their old house in just one day, and by the following weekend, she had moved them to Jupiter. The out of state buyer had no idea they were in the imminent path of a hurricane. They rode out a fairly powerful storm in that new house. It was only about thirty minutes south, but to them it could have been on the other side of the state. The move separated them completely from Uncle Walton and their family.

Catherine gasped. She hadn't even thought to call her mother or sister, although she doubted Kiki could handle seeing her uncle like this. Catherine didn't really feel strong enough to deal with them right now. It was just difficult. She had spent years trying to figure it out, had talked to several counselors and asked for advice. Her last counselor told her, "Call them when it is what you need. Do it with no expectations. Take whatever good comes out of it and leave the rest." He had been right.

~~~

When Catherine heard Lannie pull into the driveway, she glanced at the clock. It was nearly six in the morning. Catherine had slept fitfully, but at least she had slept. She hated giving up the cats so soon. The house would be too quiet without them.

Lannie set the crate inside the kitchen door. Blackie immediately began to shake the door. She said, "I was thinking maybe the cats could stay for a while."

Catherine was relieved and grateful. "Oh, Lannie, you read my mind. Thank you."
~~~

Lannie reached down and opened the door, releasing Blackie, who stepped out, stretched and walked to the food dish. Sissy came tearing around the corner, gave him a swat, and darted away.

"I guess she's glad he's back," Lannie said, laughing. "Walton sure loves them. Well, I have to go make sure Matthew gets up."

Lannie started to open the door when she stopped and said, "Thank you, Catherine, for insisting we bring Blackie. I think that moment needed to happen for Matthew. He was afraid to see his grandfather—worried he wouldn't know what to say. He wouldn't have come if it hadn't been for you."

"I'm glad it worked out for both of them."

"The nurses are certain he's just hanging on until he gets moved to the room at hospice. I'm sorry we didn't help you more with that. I'm sorry we didn't believe you." Lannie quickly opened the door and stepped out.

~~~

The hands on the clock were creeping ever so slowly. At exactly nine o'clock, Catherine called and made sure her uncle was scheduled to be moved. She had no sooner hung up than the phone rang, startling her.

"Catherine, this is Mrs. Benchmark at hospice. I had no idea about the difficulty with transferring your uncle. I assure you that the problem has been corrected and he will be moved soon. In fact, Ms. Atward is probably arriving at the hospital as we speak. I am so sorry."

Catherine wanted to tell her how she really felt, but held back. It would do no good today.

"Please notify me when he arrives there." The transfer should have happened last week, not today. She
~~~

had plenty she wanted to tell Mrs. Benchmark, but it would have to wait.

"Please have someone tell my uncle that I will be there this evening around six."

"I'll be sure he gets that message. And, again, I am so sorry about your uncle."

She wasn't sure whether the woman was apologizing for their inadequacies or for the fact that her uncle was leaving, but it didn't matter. She'd have plenty of time to deal with them after he was cared for properly. She didn't even tell the woman goodbye as she quietly pushed the button on the phone.

Catherine had decided during the night that it would probably be better if she gave her cousins and their wives time to be with Walton. She had watched him pass through so many of the stages, and she knew he was very close. She would have time to say goodbye tonight when everyone had gone home and they were alone. She knew it wouldn't be easy for any of them. It was going to be a very long day.

~~~

Catherine busied herself cleaning. Before her arrival, her uncle had hired a cleaning lady to come once a week. Mysteriously, the woman had failed to show up the week Catherine arrived. He had figured she'd finally left her abusive boyfriend and moved back up North with her mother. He had never heard a word from her.

She peered into the refrigerator. There wasn't a thing she could trust in there, so she cleaned it out and headed to the grocery store. She would only buy enough for a couple of days.

The shade under a palm tree made a perfect
~~~

parking place for her and caused her to chuckle. They trimmed all the coconuts and dead fronds off the trees these days. Not at all like when she was little and an unsuspecting tourist would find telltale dents on their cars. Once in a while, a coconut would actually shatter someone's windshield. Not anymore.

The store was busier than she had expected. There was an old man in a plaid shirt with striped baggy shorts trying to get two carts apart. She helped him, took the other cart, and headed in the opposite direction. She didn't even have an appetite, but she knew she had to eat. She'd probably fix something simple like a hamburger before she headed out to hospice. She was standing in the bread aisle, looking for onion rolls, when she heard a child's voice say, "Mommy, there's that lady."

Catherine was surprised to see the woman and little girl she had bumped into weeks before at the turnpike plaza rest area.

The woman said, "Shhhh, Olivia," as she took the little girl by the hand and pushed the cart down the aisle.

"I know it's her, Mommy."

Catherine watched as they turned the corner and went out of sight. Was it purely coincidental? People's paths often cross. It didn't necessarily mean anything. It just happened.

Catherine headed toward the produce department for onions, lettuce, and a nice tomato or two. She didn't want to stare, but it was uncanny how much that little girl really did remind her of herself when she was that age. She was a very pretty little girl. Catherine placed a few more items in the cart. She could always take the stuff back to the ranch with her.

<p style="text-align: center;">~~~</p>

The phone was ringing as she opened the back door and shoved the bags on the counter.

Lannie said, "We were there when he arrived, all four of us. He smiled when they put him in that beautiful big bed in the hospice room. They propped him up so nice with a lot of soft pillows around him. He looked all around the room, folded his arms on his chest, and smiled. We thought maybe you would be there."

"No, I wanted you to have today with him. I thought the boys and you needed time alone with him without me."

"The guys are actually okay. They're talking."

"I'm just glad that Uncle Walton is happy. I'm glad they came through for him at last."

Lannie said, "Justin said not to tell you, but Walton got furious at us."

"About what?"

"I hate to admit it, but we were all talking about you, Catherine. He got very upset."

"They've always talked about me in a bad way. They kept me in the middle. I just hate that he was upset."

Lannie asked, "Is that your teddy bear? They brought it with him from the hospital."

"Yes, I gave it to him."

"I put it in his arm. I thought maybe he'd think it was Blackie. They told him you were coming later. He was calmed down when we left."

"I just picked up a few groceries. I want to eat and then go over to sit with him this evening."

"Call me if you want some company. You know I love him."

"We all do. Thank you, Lannie."

Later when Catherine began to drive toward the hospice house, her hands began to shake and sweat. She was clutching the steering wheel so hard that her palms hurt. She told herself, *"Calm down. He's all right. Take your time."* She became impatient with the traffic, the time the lights took to change; suddenly, all she wanted was to get to Uncle Walton. She felt panicked. She didn't like it when she got these feelings.

~~~

The gardens along the main courtyard were beautiful. Signs guided her to the entrance. She began to shake even more as soon as she parked the car. Catherine took a deep breath and opened the door. Three heads popped up at the front desk at the same time. The look on their faces frightened her. For a second, she wanted to back out the door and run. A blonde gentleman quickly walked toward her.

"Are you Catherine? Justin Kendale said you would be here. I'm so sorry to tell you that your uncle just passed."

She felt her knees begin to buckle. The man grabbed her elbow and steadied her. He said, "Justin is on his way. Do you want to wait for him here?"

"No. No." She could barely speak audibly. "It's okay. I want to see him alone first."

The man directed her, still steadying her by her elbow. He opened the door and guided her in. The dim lights made her uncle appear to be sleeping. The man said, "He passed just like that. He took in one breath and was gone. It was very peaceful. I'll be sitting right outside the door if you need me." He quietly let himself out of the room.

She stood by the side of the bed, looking at her uncle. The teddy bear was nestled in his arm. She sat down on the chair and buried her head in the soft
~~~

comforter. She had to get this done before Justin showed up. Her uncle wouldn't want her to cry for him. She took a tissue from the box on the nightstand. He had earned a room like this; they both did. Not just for dying. They should have had it for every day because they both deserved it.

Catherine knew he had planned it this way. He'd slip away right before she arrived. He'd still be warm. Still have a little color in his face. He always made her feel safe; he protected her even in the last moments of his life. He could do this for her, keep her from watching him die. She sucked in a deep breath just as the door opened.

Justin was escorted in. He hugged her and said, "I was trying to get here before you did. They called me and I tried to beat you here. I didn't want you to be here alone."

They were staring into each other's tearful eyes. She was moved that he cared enough that he was trying to take care of her.

Justin said, "I wasn't going to tell you. I mean we decided not to tell you, but I just have to say this. We were all here today, and we were talking about you. I was saying how I thought you had always been a little crazy, but now I knew it because of some of the things you were telling us Dad said. He got very upset. I didn't think he could hear us. He started beating on the bed with his fists and shaking his head. He was very angry. He straightened us all out, just like always. He set us straight about you. He wasn't just going to lie there and let us get away with it. I need to tell you I'm sorry I didn't believe you. Waylon said to tell you too. We are all so sorry. We knew you had something special with Dad. Maybe now we are old enough to accept it without being jealous."

She took it all in as she shook with waves of emotion. Everyone had received what they needed from her uncle. He had finally received what he needed in order to go on.

Justin said, "I don't want to leave you here alone. I'll stay with you or I'll sit outside and wait until you're ready to go." He could barely look at his dad.

"I already said most of my goodbyes to him. I think I'm okay. We can go." They stopped arm in arm at the door, looking at him lying so peacefully in the beautiful bedroom.

At the last second, Catherine said, "There is one thing. Is it okay if I take the teddy bear?" Justin walked over and gently lifted it from his father's arm, touched his father's cheek, and walked back, handing it to her. They turned and silently walked out.

"My nanny gave me this bear the day we left Pennsylvania for your house so many years ago. I always take it with me everywhere I go. It has seen me through a lot."

Justin walked her toward her car. "It's good you came to be with him. Everything went just the way I had hoped. You made it special for him, and you helped us get through it. We couldn't have done it without you, Catherine."

"I loved him a lot you know." She fought the tears. "I just wish I could have been here before for him."

"You were here when he needed you the most. You were here when we needed you the most. That's all that matters."

Justin closed her car door once she was inside and said through the open window, "Make sure that when you leave, you take that painting from our bedroom. The one your father painted of the jungle. That's yours. He wanted you to have it."

She reached out the window and patted his arm.

There was nothing else she could say tonight. She slowly backed up the car and drove out of the parking lot. Justin watched her go.

Uncle Walton was gone.

CHAPTER 21

Zane hadn't heard from Catherine in days, maybe more than a week. He felt sad for her; he knew she must be so involved with her uncle. She had been trusting, leaving him to care for her house and her animals. It felt good having someone trust him like that, someone besides Buck. He and Buck had been good at their jobs, holding each other accountable to the agency, but this was different. Catherine had just driven away, leaving him completely in charge. He finished shaving and ran his fingers through his hair. Maybe the graying would slow down now that he wasn't under so much stress. But the simplest thing would sometimes set him off.

The meeting had been setup because someone was going to squeal. As soon as Buck and Zane had stepped away from their car, all hell broke loose. They dove for cover in separate directions. When the gunfire ceased and Zane found Buck, he wasn't responding. Zane groped around in the darkness of the doorway, found the warm oozing blood, and applied pressure with his bare hands.

"God damn it, Buck. Don't do this to me now. Hang on, damn it!"

He removed one hand long enough to shout into his cell phone. He could hear a siren off in the distance and prayed for them to hurry.

Zane shook his head, trying to bring himself back to the present, but no matter where he went or what he did, he couldn't escape it. None of it had ever made any sense. Some said they had just been in the wrong place at the wrong time. It was a miracle that Buck had survived. The bullet shattered the top of his pelvis. The surgery took hours, with Zane waiting in agony. One of the nurses eventually saw Zane sitting there, covered with blood. She brought him a lab coat, helped him take off his blood-soaked shirt, and showed him where he could wash up.

Zane had been surprised when he looked in the mirror. His face was splattered with blood; his hands were caked with it. It wasn't worth it anymore.

When the doctor slowly walked toward him, Zane's heart sank. "Tell me something good, doc," his eyes were pleading. The surgery was successful. The bone fragments were removed. Buck would have a lot of pain for a while. If no infection set in, blah, blah....All Zane had needed to hear was that Buck was alive. The rest was a piece of cake. When Buck had come out of it, Zane told him they were done. They'd quit this fucking shit together. They would go out, just like they'd come in—side-by-side.

On cold damp days, Zane watched Buck limp, but Buck would laugh about it and say, "It sure beats being dead!" Buck never complained, not once, about the therapy, the pain. He just took it like the man that he was. Tough.

~~~

The phone call Zane needed finally came. Not wanting to seem anxious, he waited. On the third ring, he grabbed the phone.

"Hello."

"Zane. Hi. It's Catherine. I'm sorry it's been so long since I checked in." She hesitated.
~~~

"Everything is fine here."

"Oh, thank you. That's so good to hear. I know I've interrupted your life so much, but my uncle...." She lost her voice. Catherine cleared her throat as he silently waited to hear the inevitable words, "My uncle, he died, and I'm...."

"I'm so sorry, Catherine," Zane said.

"I know how anxious you are to leave, and I hate it, but...."

He spoke very quickly. "I can stay. It's really not a problem right now. Take as long as you need." His voice was calm and certain and comforting.

"I think I should have everything finalized by the end of the week."

"Just let me know. Truthfully, everyone is doing fine."

His words put her at ease.

"Catherine, I am really sorry you're going through all this."

She tried not to cry; she didn't want to sob, not on the phone with him.

"Stay. Stay as long as you need, honey, okay?" The word popped out. He'd never said it to anyone before.

She grabbed a tissue and dabbed at her eyes and nose. Then she nervously giggled.

"What's so funny?" It was good to hear her giggle.

"You. You called me 'honey.' My Uncle Walton called me that. He was the only one who ever called me that."

"I think I'm just a tad tired. Forgive me."

"Oh no! It's okay. Really. I know the farm is a lot of work."

"I needed it, the work I mean. It's been good for me. Thanks."

"I'll be home as soon as I can."

They said goodbye and she hung up. Zane sighed. Her coming home meant it would be over. The transition from what he'd been to what he was becoming was quietly happening. The solitude gave him time to think and sort it all out. Being with the horses brought him full circle back to that young man, the one who had run as hard and as fast as he could the minute he had graduated from high school. When he was riding, he felt just like that kid again. His body didn't feel that much different, but his mind had a thousand questions. He wondered whether those questions would ever be answered. Would his mother forgive him? What had his father done, felt, if anything, when they had discovered he was gone? Had his mother paid for it?

~~~

That night, Zane crawled into bed, thinking Catherine sounded very fragile. Her voice was weak and tired. She'd been through a lot—the death of her husband, changing her life so drastically, and now the illness and loss of her uncle. It was a damn shame she wasn't there to enjoy the beautiful day he had enjoyed on her farm. Maybe the best part of her life would begin for her right here when she came home.

Champ pushed his head up under Zane's hand. The dog had taken to sleeping on the floor next to his bed, abandoning little Friskie, who still spent his nights curled on her pillow in her bedroom. He patted Champ.

"It's all about to change again, buddy, in a few more days."

~~~

He galloped straight to the creek, jumped off his horse, and started throwing rocks into the water. Suddenly, a black horse appeared in front of him and he hurled the rocks at it. The horse just stood staring down at him. The rocks were getting larger as he threw them harder and harder, each one tearing away at the horse's flesh. He clawed at a huge rock, trying to loosen it. He soon realized that even if it did come loose, he would never be able to pick it up and throw it. His fingers were bleeding, and his breathing was heavy and frantic. Suddenly, the water swirling around his feet turned a dark deep red from the blood running down the horse standing in the creek in front of him.

He started screaming. "If I had any guts at all, I would have knocked you on your ass the first time you hit my mother! I should have killed you! I should have killed you, you bastard!"

His breathing was so hard that he could hear his own heart beating in his ears. The sound grew louder and louder until Zane woke up drenched in sweat. That dream was always the same. He had never had the courage to stand up to his father. Not in a dream. Not in his life. He had never had the courage to say anything or to protect his mother. He had watched silently as she took his father's rage. Zane had decided two things when he was still quite small. He would never treat a woman like that, and as soon as he could, he was getting the hell out of there.

When he was older, he had tried to talk to his mother about it. She refused. He had told her, "I'll make it right. As soon as I'm big enough, he'll stop doing this." In the end, he couldn't protect her. It was difficult when he decided to run, but it was even more difficult over the years when he began to understand the depth of what he must have done to her by leaving. It had taken him all these years to find the courage to face it.

He'd only seen his father show kindness twice. The first time was when he came home with that puppy. The second was when he'd actually bought a ball and was out in the yard playing with the mutt. Zane tried to fight his feelings, telling himself he would rather ride his horse alone than play ball with his dad. Later that same night, when he curled his arms around his pillow, he discovered a brand new set of reins. He fell asleep thinking about how much his mother loved him. He knew too that Iron Crow was the one who made those mecate reins from horse hair. The best part for the three of them was that his father never even noticed his new reins.

As these old thoughts and memories kept piling in on him more frequently, they made him uneasy. For the first time, he allowed himself to sit in them. He knew it was about time he was headed home.

~~~

The next morning, it was barely daylight when Zane let the dogs out and snapped the leash on Friskie. He was looking forward to a nice walk after the night he'd experienced. Several of the dogs were barking at something in a woodpile. Peanut was lunging back and forth, and Gem was just standing barking. He figured it must be a field mouse.

"Okay, guys, come on. Give it up!" They were persistent. When he finally got them under control and knelt down, way back at the end of a log in the woodpile were two tiny eyes peering out at him. Its tiny face was surrounded with gray fur standing straight on end. At first he thought it was a baby possum, until it opened its little
~~~

mouth and let out a pitiful "Mew."

"Jesus," he said. "Where in the heck did you come from?" He wouldn't be able to rescue it until the dogs were put up. "You're gonna have to hang tight for a bit, little guy." He was half hoping that it would be gone by the time he got back. He called the dogs, hastily walked Friskie around the house, put him inside, and returned to the woodpile.

Zane lay on his stomach and stretched his arm into the hole. The kitten was just out of reach. He rolled over on his side and stretched out as far as he could and finally got his hand on a paw. The tiny thing never made a sound or resisted as he pulled it out of the darkness. He carefully cupped it in his hands up against his chest and hurried toward the barn. The cats they had on the ranch were strictly for rat control and hung out at the barn with the ranch hands.

He sat the gray fluff on a trunk in the tack room. The little kitten looked up at him and let out a long screeching "Meeeeowww!" He picked it up and held it in front of his face. "Your voice is bigger than you are." He put it down in the middle of the rug on the floor while he tried to figure out what to do with it. The little thing ran right up his boot, onto his pant leg and all the way up to his waist before he could grab it.

"You little son of a gun!"

In the end, he found a deep cardboard box on a shelf in her pole barn, put rags from the mudroom in one end and an aluminum cake pan filled with dirt and pine shavings in the other. He placed the box against the inside wall of the feed room in the warmest corner. It would have to do for now.

As soon as the morning chores were done, he heated some milk and took it down to the kitten. It didn't take long before the kitten stopped licking the milk from his fingers and lapped it out of the saucer. At least it was safe and had something in its tummy.

~~~

Zane hurried through the back door, dogs scrambling to get out of the way, as he rushed to the phone. The man's voice surprised him.

"Let me speak to Catherine," the man said abruptly.

Zane took a deep breath, paused for a moment, and asked, "May I say who is calling?"

"Just put her on the phone." The blood rushed hot up into Zane's cheeks. *Who the hell was this?*

"Sorry, buddy, she's not available at the moment."

"Where is she and who the hell are you?"

This was exactly the kind of man Zane loved to drag into a dark corner and pound into the pavement.

"At the moment, I'm her houseboy," Zane said, holding back the rage he was feeling at this jackass.

"What the hell? Stop jerking me around and get Catherine."

"I'm so sorry, sir; she's out and I'm unsure of the time of her return." Playing this yo-yo at least gave Zane a tiny bit of satisfaction.

"Then tell her Roger called and tell her to call me back as soon as possible. Take down my number."

Zane didn't bother writing a thing. "Got it." He placed the phone on the cradle without saying anything else. "Yeah, buddy. I'll tell her. My ass!"

~~~

It had been too long since Zane heard from her. He wasn't exactly worried; he was wondering how much time he'd be spending at this place of hers. He could barely remember a time when he felt so calm and healthy. His body was thriving on the fresh air, hard work, and good food. Yeah, as much as he wanted her home for her own sake, it would be hard to pack up and leave.

CHAPTER 22

When Catherine opened her eyes, it took her a minute to realize she was still at her uncle's house. For the first time in a long while, she had slept all night and deeply. To her surprise, the cats had let her sleep. Sissy was perched atop the microwave on the kitchen table, her eyes following the movement of the birds outside. Every day, her uncle had thrown seeds out the back door. There were blue jays, mourning doves, beautiful red cardinals, squirrels, and the controversial neighborhood peacocks. The peacocks had been around for as long as Catherine could remember. Her uncle had enjoyed them. Catherine opened the back door, causing a few of the beggars to take flight. She tossed a cup of cracked corn and mixed seeds onto the bare sand.

She really owed a huge debt to Zane. He had put everything in his life on hold for her. He had come into her life at the right moment; otherwise, she didn't know what would have happened these last few months. He had never complained, not once. The only comment he had made was when he had said, "You sure are organized." She'd taken it as a compliment.

Her uncle's life was that way too—orderly and organized. Everything had a purpose and a place. He hadn't cluttered up his life or caused any chaos. He had kept it plain and simple. She admired him for it. Once, she attended a seminar where a participant said he had "thing anxiety." The man said he was happiest when he was traveling in his motor home because he got to leave all his "things" at his home. Her uncle had been a perfect example of being happy while having only what you need. That woman at hospice had no idea of the man she had been talking about. He had been anything but poor.

Zane had been understanding and patient with her situation. She was extremely grateful and needed to tell him so as soon as she got home.

~~~

The house was so empty without Uncle Walton in it, like her apartment had felt without James. One afternoon, the television had been off and they had just settled down on the couch. Her uncle said with a twinkle in his eye, "Shhh! Do you hear it?"

Catherine had listened intently.

His face had crinkled up as he grinned.

"You can't hear it? Listen."

She had sat even more still and listened.

Then he said, "It's the silence of the house. I just love it. It's what I miss about not being able to go out in the woods. Sometimes you could just sit out there and not hear a single thing. It is incredible."

It was such a good little house. She hoped the boys would keep it. Blackie rubbed up against her leg.

"You are such a sweetheart," she said as she scooped him into her arms. Leaving was not going to be easy. "Thank you for bringing so much joy to Uncle Walton." Blackie was purring as he dug his nails into her leg.

Catherine felt raw and exhausted. Her insides were shaky. The entire time she had been with her uncle, she
~~~

had refused to allow her mind to think of James. Every time even a hint of him had crept in, she had pushed it far away. She knew she wasn't strong enough to carry it all.

In her head, she believed there was a reason for everything. At least that's what she told herself. But, there was also this empty painful ache that sent daggers of skepticism sneaking in. If God were so great, why were some people's lives so screwed up? Why did you go from one chaotic moment to the next? Was there really a yin and a yang? What happened to balance? Why did she feel like there weren't any answers?

The pain was so great when she did let down her guard that she knew if she let it, it would overtake her. Sometimes, if she allowed it, it sucked all of her energy, and she was left curled in a little ball somewhere deep inside herself. The world seemed very frightening and extremely dark. It was that same feeling she had felt when she was little and her family had fallen apart. Catherine had learned that lesson at a tender age. She pushed those feelings far, far away so they couldn't hurt her. But today, today her heart was aching, breaking. She knew that once she left this house this time, it would never be the same. The person who had always caught her was gone now too! She refused to let it happen. She wasn't going to give any part of herself to that feeling of total despair.

"Be strong. Be brave," she whispered.

~~~

She walked out onto the porch in the afternoon sunlight to catch her breath. One rare day, she had actually coaxed Uncle Walton out there. It had been after dinner, it had just rained, and the air was clean and cool. They were talking about how much they both loved all the
~~~

creatures and how lucky she felt to have lived in that area when everything was so full of life. She had told him this story:

"One day I'd gone down to the river near our house in Rio. I was alone in the woods looking for bugs and exploring. I sat down with my back up against a tree, enjoying the breeze and watching the sunlight play across the water. I heard a rustling noise to my left, and when I looked, I saw a mother armadillo and four babies.

"They came to me. I sat still as a stone, barely breathing. The mother came to my side and sniffed my arm, and then the four little ones crawled all over me. One even crawled up on my chest and smelled my mouth. I was scared and incredibly excited all at the same time. It took every ounce of determination in me not to move. I was only about ten at the time. The armadillo family continued on its way, rustling around in the leaves searching for grubs and bugs. I waited until they were completely out of sight, and then I ran home as fast as I could to tell my mother. Naturally, you know I got in trouble. She told me how they were wild and might have been dangerous. How they carried diseases. 'Don't ever do that again!' she said. I walked away, trying not to feel bad. I wanted her to be as excited as I was. I was disappointed I had never had anyone to share that with until now."

Her uncle had listened to her, watching her face get excited as she talked. Then he said, "They are drawn to you. They knew you would do them no harm. That's the way it is with us. They knew." That was all he had said. It was enough.

She wondered now why he hadn't told her then about her heritage. It would have been a perfect opportunity to explain to her why she felt so connected. He knew who she really was. Why didn't he tell her? She would never know the reason why he waited. Now she was left with more questions than answers about being Native American.

He had taught her a lot about life. He would ask her questions, give her tidbits, make her wonder. When she would come back to him later with ideas or more questions, he would lead her; tempt her. He had taught her a lot more than she had realized until now. Now she would have no one to check back with to see whether she was headed in the right direction. Why had she stayed away so long? Why hadn't she realized the mistake she was making, leaving him out of her life? Now she would have to rely on her own intuition and listen to the gifts he had given her. All she had left was that family blood running through her veins and a lot of questions.

In a whisper, she asked, *"Uncle Walton, why did you leave me now when I need you so much? I wish I had come home sooner. I need you. I have always needed you. You were the only one who knew how to love me. You were the only one who understood me. I don't know what I will do without you."*

She was talking to the air. She took in a deep breath and let it out. "I can't even cry," she said. "I have gone so deep inside that I can't even cry." She dressed and put on some makeup in an attempt to pretend to be alive.

~~~

She would call Zane later when she was more relaxed and he was finished with chores. Then she would ask him whether she could stay a little bit longer and they would figure out a plan. Meanwhile, she needed to pick up a few things and getting out of the house would be good for her.
~~~

She drove along the river, watching the sunlight sparkle across the water like a million diamonds. She passed her old elementary school. Her uncle had told her it was now an environmental center. She planned to visit before she went back to Highberry.

Turning left off Indian River Drive onto Jensen Beach Boulevard, she felt instantly transported back in time. At least this street still looked basically the same. As she crossed the railroad tracks and headed up the little hill, everything suddenly changed. It tore out her heart to see what the developers had done to the sand dunes, and farther west, the wetlands. She sighed. Here was where she had ridden the horses as a child in the savannahs.

Catherine thought she remembered seeing a bookstore so she drove north on US 1. Once she found the store and was inside, she went up to the counter where a woman directed her to the Native American section. She searched the shelves, not really knowing what she was looking for. Her eyes stopped on a pale purple box that said "Animal Wisdom Cards." She pulled the box from the shelf and read the back. She was intrigued. "These powerful cards provide insights into our purpose here on Mother Earth." She quickly paid the clerk and headed out.

Soon she sat at the car wash, watching the employees there work their dirt removing magic. She was glad to have today to herself, although she needed to touch base with the boys. Uncle Walton had made it clear to them all that he wanted to be cremated. He had told her, "I want no service. No one needs to cry over me. I've had a good life. Just throw my ashes along with your Aunt Josie in the ocean." At the time he had said it, Catherine had no idea he would be gone so soon.

She went through the KFC drive-thru and ordered crunchy chicken. Then she retraced her route to Uncle

Walton's house.

As soon as Catherine brought the fried chicken inside, Sissy and Blackie were all over her like fleas on a dog. She placed two small plates on the counter and pulled some skin and meat off the bones for the cats. Her rear had taken on an entirely new shape the last few months from sitting. She had been so absent from her own body and mind that she had been eating only out of necessity. Plus, she had fed her uncle whatever he wanted. What difference did it make? Today, the aroma and the flavor pulled her back from how far away she'd been. The chicken was delicious and the coleslaw was sweet and crunchy. She sighed and licked her fingers.

After carefully washing and drying the kitchen table, she sat in the chair where she could look out the window. She pulled out the Animal Wisdom Cards. There was a book that explained clearly and easily how to use the cards. She scanned the index searching for armadillo. She soon became lost in the reading and the travels of her own mind, hoping to discover the secrets of why she had the encounter so many years ago.

Reading that people actually considered the animals their brothers and sisters made her realize she had always been that connected to the creatures she had come in contact with. It said that the armadillo was passive in its defense. It spent nights digging for food and protected itself with its thick bony plates and horns that covered its back. The armadillo rolls into a tight ball when threatened. They keep to their own territory and often examine their boundaries using their natural defenses to protect themselves from potential threats. Solitary dwellers, they preferred not to have friends.

She sat quietly absorbing the words. Catherine certainly had enough hurt in her life. Had the armadillos tried to warn her long ago? Did they try to tell her then how strong she would need to be? If only she had known.

"Armadillo wears its armor on its back. Its boundaries of safety are a part of its total being. Armadillos can roll into a ball and never be penetrated by enemies."

There it was—wasn't that exactly what she did when she had too much? She took to her bed and curled into a tight little ball. That was the only way she ever survived everything that kept being hurled at her.

She got up and searched through her bag for a pad of paper and pencils. The exercise sounded interesting. While she was up, she grabbed a glass of ice and a coke, placing the glass on a flat stone her uncle kept on the table.

Catherine drew a circle on the piece of paper. In the body of the circle, she wrote all that she desired to have, to do, to experience. The instructions said to "include all things that give you joy."

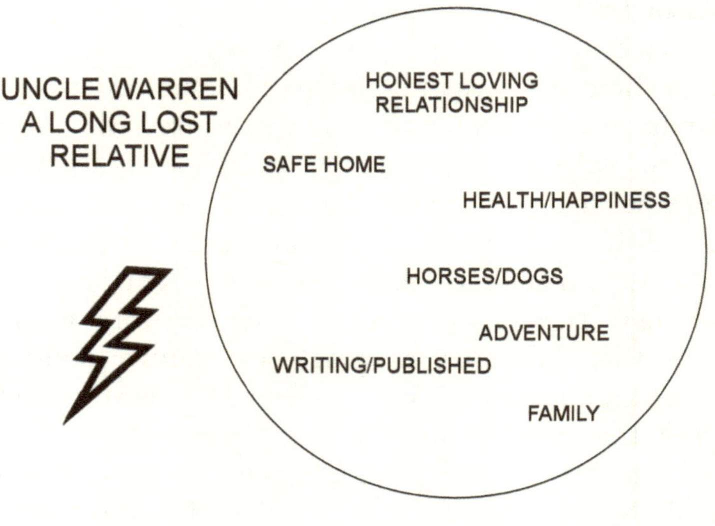

She continued reading. "Boundaries allow only our chosen experiences to be part of our life. These boundaries shield us from things that are undesirable. The circle represents a shield and reflects who you are and what you *wish* for others even on an unconscious level. The things outside the shield, represent what you are willing to invite in, for example, a long lost relative."

Catherine picked up the pencil and lovingly wrote outside the circle—Uncle Walton—a long lost relative. Now he was lost to her forever. Why hadn't she found these cards years ago? Why had she resisted coming here for so long? Even now, she was resisting by not calling her mother or her sister. They wouldn't have known how to help her, not with this. They just didn't understand.

Sometimes, she tried to convince herself it was a sign of maturity, keeping people out, but a friend had cautioned her, "Be careful. Sometimes people confuse setting boundaries with shutting down and building walls." Is that what she did with her family?

Everything had happened with her uncle so quickly. It was bitterly painful, and she didn't want to share that pain with anyone. She had been totally focused on his wishes and his needs. She had barely taken time for herself, let alone become involved with anyone else. This had been her chance to concentrate on the person who had been such a huge part in molding whom she became. His early lessons were the only pieces of her that connected her with that family and the roots that grounded her with the earth. She loved that secret part of her that she seldom allowed herself to explore. She knew now where it came from. She felt that somehow the farm would reconnect her with that part that had been pushed so far away. She had a few things to finish here, and then, well, who knew what might happen. She drew a lightning bolt beside the shield and looked out the window.

CHAPTER 23

Buck had no idea who was banging on his door. "I'm coming. I'm coming." He was not prepared for Deb Albom to be standing there. Without a word, she pushed past him into his house.

"There's something I need to talk to you about," she said in a soft voice as she passed him. He motioned toward the kitchen table, but she walked directly into his living room and sat down on his couch. He hurriedly followed her, turning on the overhead ceiling light.

"Is it possible not to have it so bright in here?" she asked quite softly.

Buck fumbled with the lamp on the end table. She was sitting on the edge of her seat and looking at the floor. This wasn't the loud flamboyant person he was used to dealing with.

"Is something wrong with you?" he asked.

"You might want to sit down."

"I'm okay standing." He wasn't at all sure of what to say to her. "What is it?" He sounded impatient.

"It's about us, Buck. We have a little problem."

"Us?"

"I don't know how to say it. I didn't mean for it to happen."

She didn't have to say any more. Buck knew. He let her sit there and wait while he just stood there for what seemed to both of them to be a very long time. Then he walked over and sat down next to her on the couch. He took her by her shoulders and gently turned her toward him. He was still holding on to her arms when he said, "What do you want to do?"

He waited for her to react. He hadn't given another thought to that little romp and certainly not about anything like this happening.

"I got myself in this mess and now I don't know what to do."

~~~

Deb Albom's life had a whole other story that no one in this town knew—most certainly not Buck. When she had suspected she was pregnant, she called her mother. She expected her mother to go nuts, crazy, like the night the cops had gone to her house and told her parents to go to the emergency room at the hospital. The lady doctor had pulled them aside and told them their daughter had been brutally raped. Deb hadn't expected them to blame her.

Deb never got over her father blaming her for the rape. He had been irrational, violently tearing the house apart. For the first time in her life, she had been afraid of him. He had said a lot of terrible things—about the way she looked, how she dressed, and the people she hung around. None of it was true. It didn't matter. The people she expected to protect her hadn't believed her. Not even her mother. And so she had done the only thing she could. She became the girl her father had said she was.

Thank God, this time, her mother asked the question very matter-of-factly. "What do you want to do?" Maybe it was because they were both older now. Maybe it was because her mother had a lot of time to think about
~~~

how they'd treated her. Maybe... In Deb's imaginary life, she was a real estate agent and Buck owned the feed store and they had met just the way she'd planned. He was crazy about her from the get go and they had fallen in love, married, and lived happily ever after. They would have two, maybe three children, and they....

Buck squeezed her arms gently and repeated the question. "What do you want to do, Deb?"

She was shaking. "I know it's not anything you want to be involved in, but I thought you should know before I do anything. My mother wants me to come home."

She still hadn't said the words, "I'm pregnant." He gently let go of her arms. They sat in silence for a while.

The thought of being a father, having a baby, had never really entered his mind. Not, at least, in a way that made him want to settle down, marry someone. He'd sometimes wondered what his kid would look like, but he had never pictured himself with one. It was too easy to think of women in terms of what they could do for him. He had never let himself get past that. Women were just something more or less to play with. You didn't want to own one. He'd always used them, but hadn't abused them. It made what he did with them okay in his mind.

Buck hadn't expected it himself, but now he simply got the urge and turned her gently toward him, leaned in, and kissed her. He quietly and tenderly kissed her. When he stopped kissing her, they sat just looking into each other's eyes.

"I didn't mean for this to happen. Not like this anyway. I'm not really the person you've known, not who you think I am," she barely whispered.

He knew the Deb sitting on his couch did not act like the person he'd been dealing with recently. This Deb was calm, behaving rationally. Buck knew he needed time to think.

CHAPTER 24

Celia sat across the table from her daughter, drumming her fingers. Olivia was right. That was the same woman. There was something strangely familiar about her. First, they had seen her at the turnpike plaza and now at the local grocery store. What were the chances of that?

She carried the pile of laundry into the bedroom, accidentally knocking a frame off the dresser. It was a photo of her mother. "I do really miss you, Mom," she whispered. She placed it farther back against the mirror. Her mother had managed to stay alive long enough for her daughter to marry, but she had never known about her granddaughter. Her mother would require an entire book to explain. It was only because of her grandmother, Mimi, that Celia grew into the person she'd become.

Olivia called from the kitchen, "Mom, can you please open this jar."

~~~

When Celia was born, her mother was seventeen, almost eighteen. The young mother and new baby came home from the hospital to Mimi's guesthouse. All of Celia's early memories were of her grandmother. Her mother, Nyla, had refused to tell anyone the name of the father, but from the beginning, Celia was told he was a handsome and wealthy businessman. Nyla included all the details
~~~

about how they had met and fallen in love. She told Celia he had wanted to be in their lives, but....this was where the story changed, depending upon how much alcohol Nyla had consumed, whether she'd been out the night before, or the phase of the moon. By the time Celia was a teenager, she knew a lot more was going on with her mother than Mimi wanted people around town to know. Mimi covered Nyla's lack of parental skills, but it was impossible to protect her daughter's reputation because of the way she behaved.

One day when Celia was about fourteen, her mother was going on and on about what a wonderful man her father was and how much he loved them. Celia had heard it one too many times. She stomped her foot and started screaming at her mother.

"If he was so great, where the hell has he been for the past fourteen years, Mother? For God's sake, he hasn't done the first thing for either one of us, ever."

"Celia, baby, now stop it."

"No, Mother, you stop it. The truth is Mimi has taken care of us, not him. He's never done a thing for us. I don't even know who HE is!"

"I have told you a hundred times, baby, that I can't tell anyone. I promised."

"I don't think you even know who he is. I think you made the whole thing up. Look at the mess you've made of your life."

Celia's words bit deep into her mother. Nyla's face showed the pain. She never expected her daughter to be so angry or to question her. They stood staring at each other, and then Celia turned and ran. She ran right up to Mimi's house and into the arms of the person who made her feel safe. Mimi knew, without either of them saying anything, what had finally happened.

"I love her, Mimi. I really do, but she makes me sick when she tries to turn him into some kind of hero. You're the one who has taken care of us, not him. Why can't she admit it?"

"Oh, honey, it's complicated. Your mother is fragile."

"Fragile. She's strong enough to go traipsing all over town at all hours, but she's too fragile to get a job. It makes no sense. She could at least take care of herself."

"She sort of lost herself years ago when she was just a little bit older than you. Until then, she was a wonderful child. We were very proud of her."

"What happened to her?"

Mimi drew in a deep breath. She had dreaded the coming of this day for a long time.

"She was barely sixteen. Your grandfather and I bought her this pretty little car. She and some friends were supposed to go to the movies. Instead, they called some boys and told them they would meet them at the Royal Castle. There's this curve, you know, the one by Mr. Winn's vegetable stand. It had rained right before they left the house. I told her to be careful."

Celia waited. Her grandmother was staring at the floor.

"What happened, Mimi?"

"Your mother was inexperienced. The car hit a deep puddle and shot straight across to the other side of the road and into a tree. They said the steering wheel saved her. She imbedded her nails into her hands holding on to it. Her best friend, Nancy, was in the front seat. Two other girls were in the back. Nancy didn't make it. Your mother was devastated."

"But it wasn't really her fault. It was because of the water."

"That's exactly what the police report said. They did finally do something about that dip in the road because that wasn't the first time someone had lost control there. The whole town was talking about it."

"So my mother blamed herself for Nancy's death?"

"No one could convince her otherwise. We all expected her to withdraw, become depressed, but she was the opposite. She went crazy. It was as if I didn't even know my own daughter. Years later, we finally found out the truth."

"What was that, Mimi?"

"It happened when Dr. Pentock got a new younger doctor in his practice. He's the one who figured it all out. He was treating your mother for some medical problems and he saw the accident report in the file. He was surprised the hospital hadn't done a brain scan, but things were different then. They told me to watch her. Not to let her sleep for twelve hours."

"So what was it?"

"He suspected that your mother had an undiagnosed brain injury. She had signs—personality changes, moodiness, and even her posture and the way she walked changed. She gained weight. He thought too that it affected her ability to make the right choices even when it came to her sexuality. I was stunned and relieved all at the same time because it finally made sense."

"Why didn't you tell me this before?"

"You're fourteen now. How was I going to explain to you about your mother's behavior? You're older now and able to understand."

"It might have helped me to know that she was handicapped."

"She's not. She has a hard time thinking."

"Mimi, there are kids like that at school and they

call them mentally challenged.”

“She’s not. She’s not like that. She functions fine. She does the best she can.”

“No she doesn’t. You do. You cover for her.”

Mimi didn’t know what else to say. She had kept this secret deep inside. The day the car hit that stupid tree, her beautiful daughter disappeared and a stranger came to live with her and her husband.

~~~

The day they buried Nyla, Celia sat stone straight next to her grandmother. The worry and the wondering were finally over. Her mother’s life was finished. Celia barely heard a single word the minister said at the church. She stood solemnly on the hill at the cemetery, staring out at the river. Mimi was rigid, emotionless. They had been perfect parents full of dreams for their lovely little girl. Mimi never expected to bury her husband and then her only child. Everything changed the day her daughter had the car accident. Mimi knew it had taken a toll on her husband’s health. Then Nyla had come home from who knows where one night, fallen asleep in her bed, and died. They said it was her heart.

Celia drew in a long breath. She came to terms with her mother’s condition the day her grandmother told her the truth. Deep in thought, she jumped when Mimi touched her arm.

“Are you ready to go? Do you need more time here?”

“No, Mimi. I’m okay. Do you?”

“Yes, I’m ready to go.” People stopped them, hugged them, whispered words Celia could not hear as they moved toward their cars. There was nothing left for either of them to say. They were both feeling slightly guilty about
~~~

their sense of relief. There would be no more sleepless nights worrying about Nyla's whereabouts. Not anymore. Cary walked to the car with his two ladies on his arms. He had been their rock. He loved his mother-in-law in spite of her unusual life. He was very grateful that Nyla had decided to keep the baby who had become his wife.

~~~

Mimi sat silently in the garden, her hand wrapped around the pretty cup Olivia gave her for her birthday. Celia's father was no great mystery to most of the people in town. Nowadays, no one would have given it much thought, but back then, well, there was a stigma about unwed mothers and illegitimate babies.

Her daughter had been courageous in Mimi's eyes. Nyla was only seventeen, almost eighteen, when she gave birth to Celia. From the moment Mimi held that tiny baby, she and Celia shared a secret. They could communicate without words, even from great distances, as if their thoughts bounced happily across the airwaves. That silent language was even deeper, stronger between Mimi and Olivia.

Mimi had planned the rather large party for Celia's twenty-first birthday. That night, it was her dear friend, Julia, who brought along her nephew. He became the best birthday present ever! Celia couldn't take her eyes off him from the first moment they were introduced. When they began dating, Nyla fought it tooth and nail, pitching fit after fit and saying all sorts of unimaginable things. In the end, Cary was wise and won her over. He had told Celia, "I don't mind courting your mother a little bit if it means I get to keep you." And that's exactly what he did. He brought Nyla flowers, invited her out on their dates, sat for
~~~

hours watching television with her and helped her fix things around their little house. Mimi and Celia believed it was God alone who sent Cary to them. It had been painful for all of them that Nyla had died before her granddaughter was born.

Olivia was beautiful from the moment of conception. She began tiny flutterings early in the pregnancy, adding to Cary and Celia's excitement. When Olivia arrived, there was no doubt the planet would never be the same. She was already a mover and a shaker. When she started school, her teacher had sent a note home to Celia, "Check out the crystal or indigo children on the Internet. Your daughter was sent here to teach us." Mimi was well aware of that.

~~~

The image of the attractive dark-haired woman crept into Celia's mind as she worked the dirt in the herb garden outside her kitchen door. The air was cool and crisp. Droplets of dew hung tear-shaped from the leaves. It wouldn't hurt to speak to her, that is, if she ever saw her again. It was odd that Olivia felt somehow drawn to her. She wiped her hands on her jeans, sat in the little chair in the garden, and pulled the phone from her back pocket. Her grandmother was probably out in her garden this morning too.

"Hi, Mimi. Just checking in. Isn't this morning gorgeous?" The morning chats were a ritual that kept them connected.

"Mimi, do you ever cross paths with someone and have it bug you?"

"You mean when you can't place how you know them?"
~~~

"Sort of. More like you don't know them, yet they seem familiar somehow."

"Yes, I've done that. You see someone, and you wonder whether maybe you saw him at his job before, like when I first saw your grandfather, so you want to know more about him. Like that?"

"Yes. That weekend Olivia and I were in Orlando, I told you we saw that woman at the rest stop. Olivia somehow felt drawn to her. Then we recently saw her at the grocery store. Olivia spotted her and even said, "Mommy, there's that lady!"

"People just move around a lot more nowadays than they used to."

"There's something about her that feels familiar."

"Maybe you knew her in another life," Mimi chuckled.

"You're so funny. It doesn't feel like that. It feels closer, more recent. It feels like I should know her. If I ever see her again, I'll say something to her."

"What? 'Excuse me, but do I know you? Do you know me?' You have to be careful. This town isn't like it used to be. People are weird these days. Be careful."

"Oh no, she doesn't look like that, like someone I need to be afraid of. She was well dressed, really nice. Carried herself well. Anyway, maybe I'll never see her again. Who knows?"

"Well, so how's Olivia?"

"She's great. As a matter of fact, she's telling her story at school today about her trip to Orlando. She's growing like a weed."

Even though Mimi was Celia's grandmother, she felt more like her mother and her closest friend. Heaven only knew what would have happened if Mimi hadn't been there to oversee her own daughter's parenting. Mimi had made certain that Celia had everything she needed and nothing more. It was even easier for Mimi to spoil Olivia.

213

CHAPTER 25

Catherine couldn't figure it out. She was staring at the ceiling in her cousin's bedroom in a twin bed by herself. James had been a great husband. He was romantic, responsible, intelligent, and funny. He was a great provider. His company loved him. They held him in high esteem, called him a workaholic, a brilliant salesman. That's what she thought had killed him. He had invested too many long hours. He had told her he was "onto something. It will be a big deal. You'll see." That night, she had this nagging feeling. She had called him to tell him to be extra careful. When she finally reached him, he had sounded tired. She never imagined it would be their last phone call or that she would never hear his voice again. Even if she had been certain of why she felt so uneasy, she wouldn't have been able to change what had happened.

"Stop it! Stop it!" she shouted at herself out loud. "You've done this a million times and it always ends the same. James is gone."

She crossed her left ankle over her right, then crisscrossed her hands, grasping them together and folding them up onto her chest. She held her hands tight to her heart. *"Center, center, center. Breathe. You don't have to think these thoughts. You don't have to think these thoughts."* She stayed like that until the ceiling turned into a swirl of brown, and then she unfolded herself and crawled out of bed.

~~~

The glass shattered, sending sharp pieces all over the kitchen. It slipped right out of Catherine's hand as the phone rang. She bent to pick up the larger pieces, tossing them into the wastebasket as she said, "Hello." Helene's voice sounded tired.

"Oh, Helene, I'm so glad you called. I was going to call you to find out what the boys decided."

"There's no service at all, you know. They cremated him already."

For a second, Catherine couldn't say a word. It was done. She hadn't given much thought to it, except for the day that she was dusting above the television when he told her, "The smaller vase is your Aunt Josie. Mine is the larger one, you know." He had said it rather matter-of-factly. She knew it was what he had wanted. No fuss. He didn't want anyone crying over him and he'd told her that several times.

Helene said it for her. "He thought it would be so easy for us, but it's not. I've been crying ever since he left us. Waylon can't stand it. I have to hide or do it when he's not around. He's gone hunting this morning, and here I am drowning in my tears."

"I know. I know." It was all Catherine could say without losing her voice.

"I hoped for a memorial service, something. He lived here over fifty years. People wanted a service, but he and the boys decided. Waylon thinks funerals are barbaric. Plus, he keeps reliving that day that Walton asked him to shoot him." Her voice stumbled over the words. "It's tearing him apart."
~~~

"It's how we grew up. If something was suffering, they took out the rifle and put it out of its misery. A single bullet and it was over." She heard Helene sobbing softly. She could almost feel her shuddering through the phone.

Helene cleared her throat. "Listen, Catherine; there's something I want to tell you about his last day, the day we moved him to hospice. Waylon and Justin, in an attempt to avoid what was really happening, I think, started talking badly about you. Even Lannie got pulled into it because she was defending you while they were debating your sanity."

Catherine interrupted. "Justin told me about it that night in the parking lot. He apologized."

"He needed to because their behavior was ridiculous. All of a sudden, Walton's bed started shaking because he was so angry. He was trying to get their attention. When they looked at him, he slammed down both his fists. He had such a stern look on his face and he stared them both into silence. He made it perfectly clear to all of us that he was very present and wasn't putting up with their nonsense. I was relieved that he did it because it was really upsetting me too, the way they were carrying on. I can't imagine that Walton had that much strength then."

"It meant so much to me to have Justin tell me he was sorry," Catherine replied. "I had their dad's interest at heart always."

"We know that," said Helene. "Waylon is so shut down. He can't reveal his emotions for even a second, but he did tell me that he regretted treating you like that. He said the way he treated you was always wrong. I think he was jealous all these years because you could be so close to his father and you weren't even here. It was silly, really."

"It's hard to explain—explain our family that is. Waylon and I were the closest, but Justin and I talked the most. Waylon always picked on me, but I knew he loved me. I love them both in different ways."

Helene's voice was shaky again. "I loved Walton. I didn't always approve of the way he treated your aunt. After her stroke, sometimes he was mean. But after she died, I would go over occasionally in the evening to keep him company and we would talk. He told me how bad he felt about the way he had treated her. I think that's why he was eager to die and get to her, so he could tell her. It made me so sad."

"Helene, he loved you a lot. I know he did. He loved us all. Life had us so scattered. Everything changes. It was so simple when we were children. That little house he built, the life we lived, it was just a whole lot easier."

"I love that little house. I hope they keep it for awhile. I have no idea what Waylon is thinking. He doesn't tell me."

"I can't stay much longer. I have the farm, my animals. There's this man I hired who's living in my house. I want to clean this place up a little and then I have to go. I'm just so worried about Blackie and Sissy. I hope they'll be okay."

"Oh, they've been with Justin and Lannie before. They'll be okay. I better get off of here before Waylon gets back."

"Thanks, Helene. The only good part about this has been getting closer to you and Lannie. Tell Waylon I love him."

Catherine set the phone back on the receiver and retrieved the vacuum from the hall closet to clean up the shattered glass. Life was just like that lately, shattered. You never knew when it would slip right through your fingers and end up in a million pieces.

~~~

Catherine felt disjointed. The days had grown confusing to the point where she didn't know the month or the year at times. It scared her. She had always been so organized and in control, until now. It was difficult to remember what she was about to do. It seemed like her mind was jumbled up, playing tricks on her. She wanted desperately to complete a few things at the little house and then get back to her farm and her real life. She didn't allow herself to think about the farm too much because then she would really miss the dogs. She missed the horses. She couldn't wait to breathe in the scent of the barn in the morning mist again. She wanted her new life back.

The shards of glass were scattered everywhere as she carefully vacuumed the linoleum floor. She put the vacuum cleaner back into her uncle's closet. Only three pairs of pants and two shirts hung there. She pulled one of the shirts to her face and breathed his scent far into her heart. She could barely remember seeing him in long pants. He owned two pairs of shorts. One pair he wore while the other was washed by hand and hung up under the window awning outside to dry. He had exactly seven pairs of socks even though most of the time he was barefooted around the house. And, he had seven pair of underwear. He had a pair of shoes for good and an old pair "to knock around in." He told her, "Men have it easy. Think about it. We don't need much." It was true.

Women? Well, women drag a lot of stuff around with them. "Ever seen a woman pack for a trip?" he asked. "Men throw a few things in a duffel bag and off they go."
~~~

He was right. They just glide through life, like Zane. Look at the way he had just slid into her life. He moved into her house, took over her chores, with ease. Could a woman ever be that comfortable? She longed for a simple life, an easy comfortable existence and no complications.

She could ask Zane to stay for a little while to help her with a few things, to get her a bit more organized. She wanted to ride her horses, too, and with him around, the fear factor would be less. Someone would be there in case of an emergency, in case something went wrong. In fact, he had told her he was already working the horses. Why not watch him? She could use him to formulate a real plan for the ranch. If he truly were a ranch hand, then he would have no problem helping her get the place in shape. She shrugged her shoulders and cringed. She didn't even want to think about what the place must look like with a man taking care of it.

First, she would need to get back in shape herself. She didn't want to get anywhere near a mirror. It would be nice to blame her age, anything to make an excuse for how she looked, but the truth was she'd let herself go while caring for Uncle Walton. There was no point stewing about it. It had been her choice. All of her time had been devoted completely to him, and she had no regrets whatsoever about that. Now she had to get busy and whip herself back into shape and get her strength back. It was the perfect time to take a walk down to the river.

The sunlight was bright, making her wish she'd remembered her sunglasses. Life had been so intense lately she'd barely noticed the old rose apple tree still there in the front yard. It had been their sanctuary from the summer heat. The fruit had become ammunition at times to bean her cousin, Waylon, on the back of his head when he needed it. It comforted her that the old tree still stood in the middle of the front yard.

She walked across the narrow road and headed down the slope to the dock, straight across the river from the hospital. It seemed like only a day ago that she had stood looking out the hospital window toward his house. Life changed too quickly. She felt her chest tighten and pain settle in around her heart.

Suddenly, there was a poof sound and a small brown head popped up out of the water straight in front of her. It peered right into her eyes, and then in a swirl and splash, dove underwater and disappeared beneath the dark brown whirl. In all of the hours spent as a child down there on that dock, she had never seen an otter. She was certain this one had come out of Frazier Creek into the river. The recent rains pushed out more fresh water than usual, and with it had apparently come this unusual critter. She wished she could hurry back up to the house to tell Uncle Walton.

After lunch, she settled down with the Animal Wisdom Cards and a glass of coke on the porch to investigate what the otter had come to tell her. Maybe it was a message from her uncle. She quietly opened the little book.

Otter are very territorial and tend to live alone. Their wisdom teaches independence and self-reliance. They represent female energy, applying to both men and women. Their relaxed and happy attitude reminds us to laugh and enjoy life to the fullest. Because of their curious nature, they touch, sniff, or explore everything they come in contact with. The special message they bring is always to look at all aspects of every situation, event, or the people we come in contact with. Be open to new challenges. Otter are agile fast swimmers and remind us to deal with the problems of life with ease. They are good parents and nurture their offspring. Otter wisdom also reminds us to rid ourselves of fret, worry and pain.

The passage also spoke of expressing joy for others and sharing the bounty of your life. Isn't that exactly what she'd always done? Her work through the Foundation had provided so much for so many and continued even now without her. It seemed, too, that this philosophy had spilled onto the ranch. Look at Zane. True, he was there covering for her, but wasn't it the perfect set up for him right now? It was uncanny how things had worked out so easily.

The last sentence said, "Simply allow your life to unfold." There it was right on the page, exactly what she was thinking. All her life, she had worked so hard at getting it right. What if it could just happen like that? As if it were supposed to? No, not that she was supposed to lose James, not like that, but that life just played itself out.

Otter wisdom teaches the importance of not hanging onto material things that would become a burden.

Wow! Her Uncle Walton was a perfect example of being unburdened. And, hadn't she practically purged her apartment? Well yes, sort of.

The passage said to become otter and move gently into the river of life, flowing like the waters of Mother Earth. This was feeling weird, but also magical, mystical even. Here she was right back at the river, the very place that had taught her so much about life. And, here were these words on the pages of this book.

She hoped she could honor what they were

teaching her. Right now she felt weak and vulnerable. She was almost frightened of what was coming next. She needed to gain some power and soon. It was no fun at all feeling isolated and alone. She put the cards and book back into the box, and headed into the house. All too soon she would have to say goodbye to the little house. It wasn't going to be easy, not very easy at all.

~~~

Catherine was relieved that she wouldn't have to share her emotions with anyone this time. What she was feeling was deeply personal. With James, it had been sudden. She was deep in shock. So many people wouldn't have believed he was dead if they hadn't been at his funeral. Some needed so-called "closure." As far as Catherine was concerned, there was no such thing, not if you really cared for someone. How could you feel that way? As long as people were remembered, they were still alive, at least in spirit. Closure meant they were gone. The aborigines believe the stars are their remembered ancestors. Catherine now had two of the brightest stars in her sky.

Helene called to tell her that Justin would pick up his father's cremains and bring them to the house. Once they were transferred into his urn, Justin would arrange to take them out in the ocean and fulfill his parents' wishes.

Helene took a deep breath before she said, "They want you to put his ashes in the urn."

Catherine didn't say anything. She couldn't. She knew she had to do it. She would stay long enough to take care of her uncle one last time, and then she would leave. The rest would be up to the boys.
~~~

Justin called her the next morning, asked what she had planned for the day, and told her exactly when he would be there. While she was out on an errand, he had slipped quickly into the house and sat the cardboard box on the kitchen table.

She was barely in the back door when the phone rang.

"I put him on the table. I guess I missed you." He said it loudly and quickly. He lied.

She knew he had planned it, but it didn't matter.

"Justin, I know how hard this is. I'll take care of him. I promise." She choked back the tears.

She knew he must feel raw too. He was the one who gave in to his emotions. His father had seen him as weak, but she saw him as someone who felt something, at least once in a while. He had tried so hard to please his father, but often it had been too hard. She saw him struggle with it. Sometimes he would just fire the rifle, attempt to kill the deer, because he didn't have a choice. She saw the conflict in his eyes. She heard the unsaid words in his heart.

"Put them both on the kitchen table when you are done. I'll take care of the rest after you leave." His voice trailed off as the words fell heavily from his lips.

His words tore at her. She didn't want to leave. She wanted to be little again and feel the safety of the little house. She wanted it to be the four of them, little children playing in the sand just like it used to be. She didn't want her life to turn out this way. It was just way too hard. In almost a whisper, she said, "I'll take care of them. I'll call you and let you know when I'm leaving. You can take the cats whenever you like, you know."

He took a deep breath. "It's okay. There's no hurry. It will take me a while before I'm ready to let them go. I'll take the cats after you leave, but I'm not ready to take a boat ride. Not yet."

She knew he was avoiding seeing her. She really wanted to see him, hug him, tell him goodbye. "I'll call you," she said and they both hung up at the same time.

Catherine picked up the small cardboard box. How was it possible for a human being to fit in it? Not her uncle. He was big and strong. He had been so virile. Now, he was in a box made of paper. Tears poured down her face as she clutched him to her heart.

"I've got to get you out of there," she said, as she carefully set the box back on the kitchen table. But, could she? Did she have the strength? Nothing was ever easy, not for her. She put her hands up to her face and screamed.

~~~

Early the next morning, Catherine sat on the couch in the small living room, barely breathing. She could do it. She had to for herself, for them and for him. Today, she couldn't even think his name. It would make it too real. The boys were in no hurry, but she was. She had already stayed much longer than she had expected. She needed to complete this on the strongest day she could muster, and it was now, today.

The first task meant successfully moving the two urns from their precarious perch on the shelf above the television. He said he had put Aunt Josie up there so he could see her. The urns looked heavy and Catherine was scared one or both of them would crash to the floor and her aunt's ashes would just go flying.

Her aunt had died three years ago on the exact date that her uncle's heart had started acting up and they had
~~~

admitted him to the hospital. Helene had asked Catherine whether she thought he had fretted himself into his heart problem. Catherine never responded to that question. She had wandered off in deep thought, wondering whether people really did die from a broken heart.

Catherine had avoided the urns, not even attempting to dust them. She took a deep breath, pushed herself up off the couch, and walked to the television. She stood staring at them for a long time, sighed, and headed to the kitchen to the phone. Helene answered on the third ring.

"Helene, I'm so glad you're home. It's Catherine. I need some help."

Helene agreed with what Catherine told her. "Yes, I think I'd take her urn down first. It's bound to be the heaviest."

"I'll call you back when it's done."

String was tied around both of the urns and stapled to the pine wall. She found scissors in the kitchen drawer and quickly cut them away, releasing the smallest container. The narrow shelf was leaning forward from the weight so she held the smaller urn in the crook of her left arm while bracing the larger urn. She could just reach the kitchen table around the short wall that divided the rooms. She took a deep breath and blew it out slowly. Beads of perspiration floated together and one dropped off the end of her nose.

Removing the larger urn was easy now that both hands were free. She quickly set it on the table too. The lid on his urn was covered with several layers of tape that required scissors and a paring knife to remove. She wondered whether it had been shipped like that or he had put something inside. She was relieved when she could finally peer in and see only the artist's paperwork.

Now came the hardest part. She moved the small cardboard box in front of her and just stood there for a long time. This would be the end. Like the last scene in so many of the movies they had watched when she was a child and then just days ago. It wasn't fair. It wasn't supposed to be like this. THE END. She felt sick to her stomach. She slowly opened the cardboard box. A purple ribbon with a silver round metal tag was wrapped around the mouth of a plastic bag containing his ashes. She picked up the bag and held it to her heart. This was all that was left of him. She couldn't even cry. She felt empty and lost and worst of all scared.

"It's not fair. You were supposed to be here for me forever."

She couldn't bring herself to pour him into the urn. She didn't want any of him to get lost, not even in the air. She quickly pushed the bag into the urn and shoved the lid on. She moved the urns together at the end of the table up against the wall. They were really lovely, made of ceramic clay. His was strong and masculine, colored with deep shades of blue in swirls like the ocean on a summer day. Hers was smaller, green, not blue. It was just like him to choose something like that, like the earth. She patted each one tenderly, and only then did a tear slide down her face, mixing with the sweat. She licked the salty drop from her lip.

She slowly dialed the phone. "It's done. I did it. Nothing happened. I put them on the kitchen table. Together." Neither of them said another word. They could hear each other breathing, but they couldn't speak. They just quietly hung up the phones.

~~~
~~~

The next time Catherine looked at the clock, two hours had gone by. She didn't even know what she'd been doing, but the time was gone. She found a rag, some furniture polish, and returned to the shelf above the television to dust. Sitting below where the urns had been on a little ledge was a brown envelope. She turned it over and gasped. The postmark was a few days before Christmas three years ago. She slid out the contents and began to shake all over. She had completely forgotten about sending it to him.

There were pictures of her amaryllis in bloom, one of her with James, and an insert she had placed in his Christmas card. It was printed on green paper and read:

Life's journey has been mystical and magical, yet with some moments of intense pain. People have circled in and out; some have not returned. Some have left a lasting impression and most certainly altered the course of events. And so, I suppose that this is a tribute to the lasting effect that a word, a gesture, or a simple happening can have on a person. The turns their life shall take may well be guided by the people they come in contact with. I can't help but think of a grain of sand silently clinging to a hand that is put into a pocket and the journey it might take, most likely unknown to the bearer. We could be that grain of sand simply allowing ourselves to float about without guidance or direction, going through the motions of life, but seldom really living. I am one of the fortunate ones whose destiny was determined long ago. See how my story unfolds.

Handwritten at the bottom, it said, "Uncle Walton, Thank you for being one of the people who altered the course of my life. Love, Catherine."

There was a smaller card with a handwritten note

saying, "You must think I'm the worst niece in the world because I promised to come see you two and I didn't." She began to cry. At the bottom, she had also written, "Thank you for taking the gun away from Daddy. I do remember that night." She couldn't stop crying. She rushed down the hallway and threw herself on his bed. All of it came pouring out at last as she buried her face into his pillow. When she awoke hours later, the house was dark and still.

<h1 style="text-align:center"><u>CHAPTER 26</u></h1>

Catherine heard footsteps and then the back door abruptly opened and a man filled the space between the kitchen table and the stove.

"You scared me."

"I forgot to knock. I'm used to just walking in."

She hugged Justin for a long time. They both sighed as they turned each other loose. She hadn't known he was coming, but honestly, she was glad he was there. She watched him look at the urns on the table.

He said, "It's okay. It's okay. Just leave them there. I'm not ready to do anything, not yet. The ocean's kinda rough right now anyway. We'll wait." His voice wavered like the waves.

She watched tears sit on his lower lids, hovering. They didn't spill over onto his cheeks like hers. It seemed like once she'd started crying, she couldn't stop.

"I think I've cried the St. Lucie over its bank."

"Yeah. The tides are running really high. White caps. I wondered why, but now I know. It's your fault!" The words took them away from the truth that sat right there on the kitchen table. Neither of them said the meaningless chatter—"How are you?" "I'm fine." No. They talked about other things. The river. The cats.

"I'm not taking them until you leave—the cats, I mean. It will be soon enough then."

"Just promise me you won't let them go outside

right away. I couldn't bear it if something...." Her voice trailed off.

"I won't. I won't. Sissy won't go out anyway. She never does. She barely leaves my room. They'll be fine. They've been at our house before. I promise I'll take good care of them."

She didn't think of him like that, tender, but here he was saying words she needed to hear that made her feel a little better.

"I can't bear to take them away right now anyway. I'm not strong enough to...." He was looking at the urns on the table.

"I know. You don't have to say it."

She knew when the time was right he would take his mother and father out into the ocean. But it wasn't time just yet. None of them were ready to let any of it go right now. Knowing he would take care of the cats made her heart ache a little less, at least for the moment.

He opened the kitchen door and brought a second crate in from the porch. She knew he must have intended to take them, but coming into the house had changed his mind.

"I'll leave this here. They can check it out. Where are they anyway?"

The cats knew. Catherine and Justin found Blackie curled up on Walton's pillow on his bed. The large black cat barely raised his head, peered at them through slits, not eyes. She heard Justin take a deep breath behind her; she turned in the tiny hallway and they grabbed each other.

"I know, I know," she said as they sobbed together; she patted his back. She finally said, "I need a tissue before your shoulder is a soggy mess." One step and she was in the bathroom. She heard Justin go into his old room.

"This house used to be so big."

"We used to be so small."

He sat down on the bed. "He did love us. I know this has been hard on you, but we wouldn't have made it without you. He loved you so much. You were here when we needed you the most. That's all that matters."

She reached out and took his hand and sat by his side on the bed.

"Don't forget to take your father's painting. You should have it. Take it when you go."

~~~

Catherine knew it was time, but it felt like something was crushing her chest when she thought about packing her few clothes and leaving the little house. It was the part of her life that had felt solid and, well, normal. Even if she had kept it distant, she knew it was always there. Now everything she loved was going away.

She sighed as she parked the car and headed into the grocery store. It would most likely be her last meal at the tiny kitchen table. She wanted to celebrate every bit of what the little house had brought into her life. She wanted her comfort food. She glanced at her list: roast, potatoes, peas, apple pie. Her uncle had loved apple pie. She picked a few Vidalia onions and a small clump of garlic. A nice bottle of wine would make her mellow, soothe her. She added a few items for the trip back home.

Home. That word sounded strange. Would she ever really feel like she belonged somewhere? Would it be her home? Every time she started to feel safe, secure, something happened.

She sighed. She wasn't going to let anything spoil
~~~

her dream this time. It was all up to her. She was in charge of her destiny, and nothing was going to get in her way.

Don't kid yourself, Catherine. You know full well life just isn't that simple. You can have the best intentions, but fate or whatever the universe delves out will come and smack you right onto your backside.

She plopped the bags on the backseat and drove along the river past her old elementary school. She glanced at her watch, turned the car around and pulled into the parking lot. The roast would be the perfect temperature to pop into the oven when she got back to the house if she just stopped in for a few minutes. She imagined she could smell the aroma of peanut butter cookies and hear the laughter of children as she walked up the three steps into the entrance.

Oh, if only you could go back to those sweet and innocent days.

The old school was painted the same pale crème color. Nothing was changed structurally. She got goose bumps. The information center was located in the old principal's office. It felt eerie as she quietly opened the door and walked in. The woman had her back to her, but when she turned around, Catherine held back a gasp. She was face to face with the same woman, the woman she had seen at the rest stop, the woman she had crossed paths with in the grocery store. She closed her mouth.

"Hello, and welcome to the Environmental Center. How may I help you today?" the woman said.

Catherine thought she saw the woman shiver and saw the goose bumps raise up on her arms. She was feeling exactly the same way. It felt almost like an electric shock, but cold.

Catherine gulped. "Oh, I just wanted to look

around. Is that okay?"

The woman asked, "Did you want a guided tour or do you want to view the exhibits alone?"

Catherine hadn't even thought about the exhibits at the Environmental Center. She just wanted to spend a few minutes reminiscing about the years she spent at the school. She had begun first grade the year they moved to Florida. She cleared the lump in her throat.

"I think I'd like the tour," she heard herself say in an indecisive voice.

"My name is Celia. I'll be happy to show you our current exhibits and tell you about the area."

"Actually, this was my elementary school when I was little."

"Then you will find they haven't changed the building structurally. I'm sure since you grew up here, you will enjoy the exhibits. Everything should be very familiar." The woman opened the door and motioned for Catherine to go out.

"Do you work here every day?"

"Oh, no, I volunteer one day a week for a few hours. It's my little way of giving back to the community and helping the environment."

The woman had a soft methodical voice and calm demeanor. She quickly put Catherine at ease. The courtyard was exactly as Catherine remembered. Celia guided her to the first room.

"Oh, my gosh. This was my sixth grade class and the worst year ever. I had a terrible teacher."

"Who was it?" Celia asked.

"Mr. Brown." You could hear the disdain in Catherine's voice.

"You're not the first person to tell me about him," Celia chuckled. "Apparently he was an awful teacher and a horrific principal. It's funny because according to his family he was a great father and grandfather."

"That's hard to believe."

"He died just a couple of years ago. He had a heart attack at his grandson's soccer game. It was sad. The family gave a donation to the center. I can show you the plaque."

Catherine didn't waste a moment, "No. No thank you. I think I'll pass on that one."

Celia smiled. "I guess I can't blame you for that."

Next was her fifth grade classroom. "I learned to play the piano thanks to Mrs. Samplee," Catherine said. "She was a great music teacher, but my voice sounded just horrible. She told me it was heavenly, but I knew better."

Catherine was quite familiar with the items in the exhibits. There was a paper nautilus shell, porcupine fish, triggerfish, basic corals, and a display of a Seminole Indian village. She and Celia worked their way around room by room and were about to enter Catherine's first grade classroom when Catherine gathered up her courage.

"Celia," she asked, "do you recall seeing me before?"

"Yes, as a matter of fact I do. My daughter and I saw you at a rest stop on the turnpike and then again at the grocery store."

It made Catherine feel a little better that at least she was as aware of her as she was of them.

"Do you think it's odd that we keep bumping into each other this way? I mean, do you think there's some, well, how do I say this, deeper reason why we keep connecting like this?"

Celia took a deep breath. "Actually, I talked to my grandmother about it. I told her if I ever saw you again I was going to say something. I don't think it's so 'odd,' as you put it. I think sometimes people are put into our path for a reason. What do you think about it?"

"I didn't want to let it just go by, especially now with seeing you again today. I'm leaving in the morning to go home, and my stopping here was purely spur of the moment. It seems like one of those strange times when you can't figure out what the puzzle is about."

They walked into the last room. It was the wildlife room and had an assortment of stuffed creatures. The taxidermists had prepared them in various natural positions.

"This is nice, if you call dead animals nice. My uncle did taxidermy."

"Really," Celia said. "Who is your uncle?"

"Walton. Walton Kendale," Catherine said. "He lived on Elizabeth Street, not too far from here. That's why I'm here. He became very ill and I came here to take care of him until...." Her voice drifted off as she held back the tears. She was fumbling around, petting a dead otter. She reached into her purse for a tissue. "I'm sorry," she said as she dabbed at her face.

Celia placed her hand on Catherine's arm. "I'm so sorry about your uncle. You must have been very close to him. Some of these were his you know—the otter, some of the ducks, the deer head. He brought them to us not so very long ago. He helped me with a couple of the displays. He didn't like them unless they were authentic."

Catherine was trying to process this. Here she was at her old elementary school in a room where her uncle had recently stood. She was looking at some of his taxidermy from her childhood. It felt surreal. Here she was with a woman whose life entwined with hers in a strange and mysterious way.

"Your uncle was a very interesting man."

"Thank you for saying that. He really meant a lot to me." Catherine's voice began to falter, and the tears started to stream down her face. Without a moment's hesitation, Celia put out her arms and Catherine fell into them sobbing. She felt like she was with a dear friend who just wanted to comfort her.

"I'm so sorry about your uncle," Celia said.

Catherine pulled herself away, straightened her blouse, fussed with her hair, and pulled a tissue from her pocket to blow her nose. "I'm so sorry. I'm falling apart at the moment. This place brought up a lot of old emotions."

"You don't owe me an apology. This must be very hard on you, being all alone and losing him."

"My cousins have done their best to console me, their wives, you know."

"I'm glad to be here for you in any way. Your uncle was a very nice man."

"Thank you. Thank you very much. I guess I better go. I have groceries in the car. I think this will be my last night in his little house. It's right up the road on Elizabeth."

Celia smiled. "My house is right around the corner. Small world isn't it?" They strolled slowly down the corridor and back to the office.

"Let me get you my card," Celia said. She was back in a moment and handed the card to Catherine. "I wrote my home number on the back, just in case, you know."

"That's nice of you. Oh, and by the way, your little girl is beautiful."

"I know. She's amazing. She is a special child. I'm extremely lucky."

They both moved toward each other at the same time and hugged. Celia spoke first, "Take good care of yourself."

"You do the same. Thank you again." Catherine walked slowly away and then turned back around. "I don't think I told you my name. It's Catherine. Catherine DeLong." She walked out through the archway, down the three steps, and to her car. She took a long deep breath, gazing out at the Indian River. She didn't quite know what to think about all of this.

~~~

Catherine barely had the groceries in the house when there was a soft knock at the door. Waylon slowly opened it and walked in. She watched his face as tears filled his eyes.

"I couldn't let my favorite cuz leave without saying goodbye."

Catherine staggered into his arms, then they fell apart. The floodgates they had carefully guarded opened wide. They stayed that way until Catherine reached behind him and grabbed a paper towel. "I thought you had gone back to Alabama. I didn't know you were still here. I didn't think you would come."

"I didn't think I could," he said. "It's your fault. I couldn't let you beat me, you know. You've been so strong." He was grinning the same silly grin he used when he teased her so many years ago. The years had taken their toll on his face. There were deep crevices and his skin was leathered now. "I had to come tell you I'm sorry. I've always been so hard on you. I wanted to tell you I'm sorry for doubting you. You knew him better than any of us. I don't know how you kept from being mad at us. We deserved it our entire lives."

"I was mad. I was mad at you the day you tied me up and made me eat sea grapes. You went off and left me
~~~

there." She blew her nose hard into the coarse paper towel.

"How were they? The sea grapes, I mean." He grinned back at her. They were fighting hard to stay in the moment in order to keep the pain away.

"They were full of sand and made me puke, and I vowed I'd get even."

"I'm glad you didn't try because I was always bigger than you until now."

"You!" She punched him. "That's dirty. You can't pick on my size." They tried to laugh, but the tears still hung there behind the surface.

"Did you come to take some of his things?"

"No. He already gave me the things that mattered. We didn't have much, you know. There's nothing else."

"Do you want the picture from your bedroom? The jungle scene?"

"Oh, no. That's yours. We all knew that would go to you. Your dad painted it. You should have it. Take whatever you want, except for Dad's dresser. Helene asked if she could have that."

"Of course. Yes, she should have that. Where is she?"

"Helene? She couldn't do it. She gets too upset. She said she wanted to remember him alive, sitting on the couch with Blackie."

"I understand. I wish I could do that too. This is really tough. Oh, are you going to take the pastel of your mother? I remember when the neighbor drew her. Aunt Josie sat for hours for her. I always thought it was odd, but I loved it."

"It is odd. I still don't know why my mother did it. Here she was born in England and the woman draws her as an Indian squaw. It's not right."

"I don't think I got it until now. You know, the part about us being Native American. I think she might have done it for your dad. It's odd, but also kind of neat that she did it. I don't know. Maybe there's no real meaning in it. Who knows?"

"Not me."

"I'm going to leave in the morning. I want to take some pictures, go down to the river. Stay put. I want to take a picture of you right here in this kitchen."

She hated that he didn't stay longer, even for dinner. He said he had to go, get back to Helene. Then he told her, "Stick the key up on the shutter by the front door. I'll find it."

They hugged for a long time. "I hate this," she said. "I feel like I'll never see you again."

"I only live in Alabama, not Alaska. Come and see us. We put our house here up for sale. We may already have a buyer. It's time."

"What will you do with this house?"

"Keep it for a while. See what happens. There's no hurry."

"Don't do anything without letting me know first, okay? Maybe I can help."

Waylon nodded.

"I mean it. Be sure and tell me before you sell it."

He hurried out the back door. Everything had changed in an instant.

<center>~~~</center>

Catherine's clothes were packed; she placed her camera on top and zipped the suitcase. She put the few items from the refrigerator in a small cooler she had bought a few days before and walked slowly around the house one last time before she carried the last few things to her car.

She hadn't lingered at the river long; she took a few pictures, then did the same from the top of the hill, looking toward her uncle's corner. Now Catherine stood in the little house, trying to soak up every bit of his energy she could. Its walls held her tenderly. She listened. Silence. Sissy sat on her favorite perch atop the microwave on the kitchen table, peering out at the birds. Blackie was curled on her uncle's pillow. She could smell him in his room. Tears slid down her face again. She stumbled out and sat down on the couch, sticking her feet straight out into the middle of the room one last time. She got up and unplugged the television. Catherine stood staring at the picture of the buck jumping over the logs. It was odd that neither of the boys had taken that picture. She shouldn't take it because it belonged to one of them, but she didn't want anything to happen to it. She could always pack it up and mail it to one of them. At least it would be safe with her.

"This is too damn hard!" she shouted. "This is too damn hard, do you hear me? Everyone who has ever mattered to me is gone! Gone!" Her father, her husband, and now her uncle were all just gone. She didn't even know how to feel anymore. Yes, she did. She felt absolutely miserable and alone.

She suddenly remembered that she had never even called her mother or her sister when Uncle Walton died. Her purse sat by the door on the kitchen table. She fumbled around and found her cell phone. Her hands were shaking as she dialed her mother's number. The familiar voice made Catherine's shoulders sag and her heart feel heavy.

"Mother, it's Catherine; Uncle Walton died." She

stiffened and waited.

"Oh my God. Now they're all gone; isn't that something?"

"I'm okay, Mom. I thought I should let you know."

"Are you going to the funeral?"

"No, Mom. There's no service. He's already been cremated."

"Oh, then I guess there's no reason to send flowers."

"No, Mom. There's no one to send flowers to."

"I'm sorry for you, but at least that's over. I wish you were near."

"Actually, Mother, I'm here, but I'm leaving in a few minutes. Will you tell Kiki?"

"Oh, you're here? Well, why didn't you tell me; we could have met for lunch?"

"It was a little hectic, Mom. I really was busy with him, and now I want to get home."

"I'm sorry, I'm so sorry, but I've got to get going too. Hamilton needs a prescription picked up, and I have to get back in time for his lunch."

"Yes, Mother. It's okay. I'll be fine. Love you too! Bye."

Catherine tried her sister's number. No answer. She left a message. "Kiki, I was in town briefly, but I'm leaving right now. Uncle Walton died. I'll call you when I get back to the farm. Love you. Miss you. Bye."

She'd forgotten to call Zane. He didn't even know she was coming home. She glanced at her watch. He was probably out at the barn. She had to struggle to remember her own number. She left a message: "Zane. Hi. It's Catherine. I know this is short notice, but I'm heading home. I'll see you in a few hours. Thanks."

It's okay, Catherine. It will be okay. Whatever it is,

you can fix it. Get yourself back home.

In those last moments, before she forced herself to leave, she fought hard not to cry, but she couldn't help it. She allowed herself one last hysterical moment, and then she announced out loud, "Enough! I have to go. You have to let me go. I can't stay here any longer. But I love you and I will never forget you. I love you little house; do you hear me?" She wanted to fill her eyes and her mind with every little detail. She stroked Blackie and told him, "Thank you for taking such good care of him. I know Justin will be good to you. Please stay safe." She walked out to the kitchen and Sissy slid from her perch and arched her back up under her hand. "You too. You stay safe too and take care of your brother."

Her throat was dry and her right ear was ringing. Too much crying, she supposed, as she popped a soda into the holder in her car, set the cooler where she could reach it, and returned to the house.

This was the hardest part. She patted the urns that held her aunt and uncle. "I hate this. I absolutely hate this, but I'm glad for you. I know you two needed to be together." Sissy was purring loudly. "You're right. I know you're right. They are where they need to be, and now I need to be on my farm." She picked Sissy up, cradling her in her arms. Her face once again became distorted as she fought against her pain. Catherine gently placed Sissy back on the microwave, took one last look at the empty couch, ran her hand down the kitchen counter, and stepped out the back door. She fumbled in her pocket for the key, locked the door, and placed the key up on the awning by the front door. It was over. Somehow she had to find the strength to drive herself back to Highberry and home.

CHAPTER 27

Zane popped into the house in between chores to check the time and prepare the chicken he planned to cook for dinner. He found a roasting pan, skinned some potatoes, sliced an onion, and placed everything together with a little water and dashes of salt and pepper. He shoved the entire pan back into the refrigerator. The blinking light on the answering machine made him nervous as he pushed the button. He sighed when he heard Catherine's voice. Everything was about to change abruptly.

"The jig is up," he thought. It had been a good deal while it had lasted. It didn't make any difference to him at all; at least, that's what he wanted to believe. He and Trouble would hit the highway tonight. He figured he'd be well away before Buck had wind of it. He headed out to the barn to organize his gear.

Two hours later, he watched as Catherine drove slowly down the long driveway. He was finishing the chores in the barn. Some of the dogs took off to see who was coming. He smiled as they realized it was a familiar car and began barking and bouncing. She crept steadily toward her house. He made a vain attempt to call them, but his voice fell on deaf ears. As she opened the door, all of them were attempting to get to her, and he could hear her giggling and saying, "Get off of me. Get off of me." She pushed them out of the way and got out of the car.

The moment of chaos seemed to delight her as she stood back watching them as the bigger dogs raced around barking at the smaller ones. The only one that was missing was Friskie. Zane grinned as he strolled across the grass toward her.

"There's really no place like home," she said, smiling back at him, then turned her attention on the dogs. "Settle down, guys; just settle down." They surrounded her.

"Welcome home!" Zane said.

Catherine had her hands on her hips and surveyed the barn, the pastures, her house. "The place looks great, Zane. The dogs look wonderful. You must be exhausted."

He grinned. "Not really, ma'am."

She raised one eyebrow. She really had to remind him about calling her that, but right now she was so tired she was feeling a little woozy.

"I want to see the horses, but first I have to make a pit stop."

"Go right ahead. I'll just finish up a thing or two."

~~~

When Catherine turned to go up to the house, all the dogs followed her, but Champ. He watched as Zane headed toward the barn. He looked back and forth for a second. Zane turned and looked at the dog, then Catherine. "Go to the house, Champ." The dog looked at him for a split second and then whirled and caught up with Catherine and the pack. He nearly knocked her down as he flew past her. She walked up the back porch steps and into her house for the first time in what seemed like forever. She really didn't quite know what to expect. She'd never gone off and left a stranger alone in her house.
~~~

Little Friskie was bouncing up and down, walking on his hind legs. He was so happy to see her. She picked him up and let him kiss her face. His little black eyes were looking at her as if to say, "Where have you been?" She kissed his little face and put him back on the floor.

The aroma of the cooking chicken filled her nose. Everything was right where she had left it. The place was spotless. The dogs followed her into the kitchen. She was amazed. Nothing was out of place. No dishes in the sink. She opened the refrigerator. Tidy as could be. "God," she said, "maybe I should pinch myself."

She made her way to the staircase and peered into the living room. Everything was exactly the same. Champ was at her heels as she started to go upstairs. "What is this about?" she asked as she patted his big retriever head. He whined. "No, no! You stay down here. I don't care how much you missed me. You stay downstairs." He sat at the bottom of the steps, watching her go with his big old tail thumping on the carpet. "Now I wonder just exactly who spoiled you!" Everything upstairs seemed to be right where she had left it. It was so good to be home.

She took a few minutes to freshen up, and as she headed down the stairs, all six faces were staring up at her. "You scoundrels." It was so good to have them all there. So good to bury her face in their fur and look into their eyes. She picked up Friskie and carried him into the kitchen. She steadied herself with her free hand as she bumped into the wall. She suddenly felt dizzy. She hadn't eaten anything all day except a small bag of salted peanuts. She sat Friskie down. Maybe all she needed was a soda to bring her sugar back up.

Catherine saw Zane coming from the barn toward the house. He had such a nice walk. She'd forgotten how handsome he was, sort of a softer version of Robert

Redford. He wasn't rough looking at all. He skipped up the steps and into the house quickly.

"I'll just be getting my things from upstairs, and then I'll load up my horse and be out of here," Zane said.

Catherine was so surprised that she blurted out, "What did you just say?" She quickly recovered. "I mean, I don't think I understood you. Could you repeat that?"

He was surprised by her. "I need to get my clothes and stuff from upstairs, and then Trouble and I will move on."

"I guess I didn't think you would leave the minute I got here. I mean, I do understand that you were delayed, but I was thinking that I have fences that need mending and some equipment I need an opinion about." She was grasping at anything, anything she could think of to keep him there for a little while longer.

"I pretty much repaired the fences, and I took the liberty of checking the equipment for you, because I used it." Then he completely surprised himself when he said, "But, I suppose I could do that, ma'am—stay, I mean—but only for a little while. I really do need to move on. I can sleep in my truck or the barn if you like."

She was startled. Sleep in his truck? The barn? Why she wouldn't think of it, not with this big house.

"Sleep in your truck? No, no. That won't be necessary at all. You can stay right where you are. That's why I have a guest room. You'll do no such thing. That's ridicul—" She almost got to the end of the word before the room began to spin and her legs buckled out from underneath her. She felt herself half-floating, half-falling all at the same time.

~~~
~~~

Zane heard her voice trail off in the middle of the word, saw her lips grow pale, her face go white, as he caught her right before she hit the floor. He laid her flat, wondering whether he should start CPR on her, but when he touched her face he felt how hot she was. She was burning up with fever. He managed to bring her around with a wet cold towel. She told him where to find the aspirin; he helped her up the stairs to her room, only to have her pass out again. He didn't know exactly what to do. He unbuttoned her blouse, got her out of it and her bra, wiggled her carefully out of her jeans, and left her draped across the bed in her panties while he looked in her dresser for a nightgown. He picked one that looked like something his mother would wear, lifted her head, and slipped it on her. Her arms were limp as noodles. He should call 911. Instead he phoned Buck. Buck could tell right away there was something wrong.

"Hey, Buck. It's Zane. Listen, Catherine just got home and she's burning up with fever, and she passed out. I've got her up here in her bed, but I wonder if I should call 911 or something?"

"If you think it's an emergency, yes, do that, but I can see if Dr. Grant can come by. She's right down the road from there. I'll call you right back." Buck hadn't even waited for Zane to respond.

He walked to her bathroom, found a washcloth, wet it with cold water, and put it across her forehead. The phone rang, and he grabbed it before it finished the first ring.

"Marcia is on her way. She'll be there in a couple of minutes. Call me back after she leaves."

Zane didn't want to leave Catherine alone, but he had the chicken in the oven. He dashed down the stairs, flipped on the kitchen light, turned off the stove, and slammed the roasting pan from the oven to the stovetop. He vaulted back up the stairs. Catherine hadn't moved. This seemed serious. He felt like maybe he should have just called 911.

He dashed back downstairs when the dogs barked. In a second, he had opened the back door for a petite blonde woman. He pointed up the stairs, then found himself standing silently at the bedroom door as she examined Catherine.

"Are you her husband?" Marcia asked.

"No. I've been here taking care of her place for a few months. She's just back home thirty minutes ago."

"Where was she? Was she overseas? Out of the country?"

"Oh no. She was south. Stuart, I think. She was taking care of her uncle. He was very ill. He died about a week ago."

"Was he hospitalized?" Marcia asked.

"Yes. Yes, toward the end. Yes, he was." Zane's palms were sweating.

"She's burning up with fever."

"She just took two aspirin before I got her up here. Will she be okay?"

"This happens. I've seen it before. They spend all that time in the hospital sitting by the bedside. They keep it all together for the other person, but they forget to take care of themselves. Once the person's gone, it all catches up with them. They pick up something from the hospital or somewhere else. Their entire immune system is shot."

She pulled a pad from her black leather bag and started writing. "I'm going to prescribe something to bring the fever down. I'm also going to give her a shot. Once the fever breaks, she should come around. You can go to the pharmacy in Alachua. It's the closest. Get some electrolytes; one of the sport drinks is fine. Push fluids. As soon as she's able, get these antibiotics in her. Don't feed her anything tonight. She'll probably like some broth or something tomorrow. Chicken broth is good. Keep it light. I'll stop over in the morning early before rounds. Is 6:30 okay?"

"I'll be right here waiting."

"Here's my phone number at the house. I live down the street. Don't worry; call me tonight if anything changes. Oh, and get yourself some Vitamin C. Wash your hands a lot. If we get lucky, you won't catch whatever this is, and I won't have to hospitalize her. It's the last thing she needs right now." She handed him a card.

He walked her out to the car. The dogs sensed that something was wrong, and they were quiet, lying in the kitchen and hallway.

"Keep an eye on her temperature. If it goes above 103, call me. I left a thermometer on the nightstand. She's most likely simply worn out."

"It wasn't just her uncle. She lost her husband not too long ago. It's a lot."

"I know. Buck said she'd been through some tough times."

"Thank you. I'll see you in the morning."

The aroma of chicken filled the house. The dogs were being exceptionally calm and quiet. He bounded up the stairs with a bowl of ice chips. She was sweating, but still in the same spot. He rinsed out the washcloth and placed it back on her forehead. It upset him. She finally makes it back to her house and then passes out. Catherine made a slight sound and opened her eyes; she asked weakly, "Where am I?"

"You're home, Catherine. You're in your own bed. You have a fever." He watched her eyes slowly close and her body relax. He took an ice chip and gently rubbed it over her pale lips. They looked dry and pastey. He had noticed how bad she looked as soon as she stepped out of the car. Her clothes were loose on her. Her face was drawn. She looked incredibly tired. Her beautiful hair was now dull, lifeless. He could see how hard the last couple of months had been for her. He was scared. He hadn't ever felt this scared. Not like this. He touched her hair. When he undressed her, he felt like he was violating her, but he could see how incredibly thin she was. He knew this was really bad. She was in no condition to fight whatever it was that had invaded her body, but worse, she was in no condition to fight what had invaded her spirit either.

He quietly went downstairs, fed the dogs, and then prepared himself a plate of sliced chicken, a few potatoes and onion, and set it on the table. He would eat while he talked to Buck and then go get her prescription.

"Buck, it's Zane. Hey, listen; Catherine is really sick. She's got a fever; she's completely out of it. The doc you sent said she probably picked something up at the hospital tending to her sick uncle."

"Now what? What are you going to do?"

"She was in the process of asking me to stay for a little while when she just keeled over in the kitchen. She got really pale and passed out. I caught her before she hit the floor. What am I going to do? What can I do? I have to stay here and take care of her. What else can I do?"

"Honestly, man, I don't know. It's not like she has any relatives around here. There are a few old ladies who sit with people, but...."

"No, no. I'm not having some old lady in here. I'll manage. I have to leave now to go get her prescription. She's so damn thin. I can't believe how thin she got. It's a damn shame."

"Where is she?" Buck asked.

"She's in her bed. I managed to get her up there before I called you. I got her into a nightgown before the doc came."

Buck chuckled.

"What are you, stupid?" Zane's voice was angry. "This is serious. Catherine is really sick. Quit fucking around."

"Hey, man, you're the one who's always been the 'slam bam, thank you, ma'am!' What am I supposed to think? That you didn't look?"

"Damn straight. This is different. You're an idiot. I've got to go."

Conversations with Buck were ridiculous lately. Did he need this? Did he need any of this? Zane knew he shouldn't have come here, but if he hadn't....

As he drove toward Alachua, his mind drifted over the last few months. He really liked her little farm. He would stay long enough to get her back on her feet, but then he knew what he and Trouble had to do.

~~~

Dr. Marcia Grant arrived exactly at 6:30 a.m. like she had promised. She examined Catherine and then turned to Zane, who was waiting in the hallway.

"She's a very sick lady, but I don't think it's life-threatening. Your job is to keep her hydrated and give her the antibiotics. I picked up some supplies last night. There's a plastic cover for the mattress and some pads to place under her. It will help with the sweats from the fever, and I'm not sure she'll make it to the bathroom every time. Part of the problem is her immune system has been compromised by the stress, but I suspect mentally
~~~

she had a collapse." She paused for a moment and looked back at Catherine.

Zane asked, "How long before she comes back around?"

"If we get the fever down, she should show improvement by tomorrow. It's usually twenty-four to forty-eight hours. I'll give her another shot before I leave."

Zane stepped out while Dr. Grant gave Catherine the injection.

"I'll call you later to see how things are going."

As they walked down the stairs and out of the house, Zane told Dr. Grant how grateful he was for her help.

"It may be a long hard haul. The mind is amazing, but also mysterious. Let's plan on her coming out of this once we get her fever down and her body starts to heal."

As soon as Dr. Grant's truck was safely down the driveway, Zane let the dogs out. "You mutts stay out of trouble."

It had been a long night. She had slept fitfully, sometimes saying phrases that made no sense. She talked to James, sometimes giggled, sometimes whimpered. He watched her eyes dart back and forth behind her eyelids during bouts of dreaming. She had periods of drenching sweats followed by teeth chattering chills. He changed her nightgown several times, switched pillows under her head, and either tried to cool her down or warm her up.

Now, as he approached her bed, her eyes opened. He felt relief as she said, "Hi" ever so softly. Her voice was scratchy.

"Hi, back at you."

"The dream. You went off a cliff." A tear rolled down her cheek and then she was back into that place where he didn't want her to go. His heart sank because he knew she had thought he was James.

Zane rushed down the stairs and out to the barn. He would do the chores as quickly as possible and get back to her.

~~~

He found her on the floor in the bathroom with a toothbrush in her hand. He couldn't imagine how she'd had the strength to get there. He pulled the toothbrush from her fingers, scooped her up, and carried her back to the bed.

During the night, he used tepid water to cool her down. He had to remove her nightgown to bathe her, drying her off with a big fluffy towel. Her hair was soaked again. He changed the pillowcase, changed her nightgown again and carefully positioned her back in her bed. This had to end soon. She had to come out of it.

He was almost frantic by the time she finally began to stir. Sometime in mid-morning, he managed to get her to swallow more antibiotic, then washed and dried her bed clothes and linens and was putting them away when he heard her stir.

"What are you doing?" she asked.

"Just putting away some stuff. Welcome back!"

She tried to push herself up with her elbow and fell back with a groan.

"The doctor was here last night and again this morning. She gave you some injections." He lifted her forward and pushed a pillow behind her back. "You're supposed to drink a lot of this," he said as he handed her a glass of water. Her hands were trembling as she cupped them around his and they brought the glass to her lips. Her face was white as a sheet, and she had a big crack down the middle of her bottom lip.
~~~

"I'm so weak. I can feel every bone in my body. What happened?" She reached up to feel the tangled mess her hair had become. "My hair even hurts."

Zane couldn't help but chuckle. "That's a new one on me."

Catherine attempted a smile, but her lips cracked with pain.

"You've had a fever. Dr. Grant said it wouldn't hurt if you took two Tylenol. Maybe that will keep your hair from hurting," he grinned.

She pointed toward the bathroom. "In the medicine cabinet, Tylenol, I think. Probably wouldn't hurt for me to go in there," she said, rather shyly.

He didn't say a word as he gently moved the covers off of her, scooped her up in his arms, and carried her. It wasn't at all what she'd expected. He steadied her as she stood in front of the commode. She was thankful to discover she was in one of her long flannels.

"What can I do for you? How can I help?" He actually felt very anxious about the situation and fearful that she would fall.

"I think I can manage now. Just stand outside the door."

He knew how weak she was. She was sweating profusely and wilting. She'd been in there about five minutes when he heard her weakly say, "Oh Lord!" and then a thump. He found her sitting in front of the toilet with her head against the wall.

"At least you didn't break anything," he said as he scooped her back up. It had happened so quickly when she had stood up to rearrange herself.

She felt limp and unresponsive. As he slid her back into her bed, he realized she was gone again. Gone to wherever the fever took her and worse, wherever that place was where she was able to visit James.

~~~

Zane had no idea what Catherine was really like, her true personality. All he had seen was a good-looking woman. He and Buck had their share of women over the years. Their lifestyle hadn't allowed for relationships, not that either of them had wanted one. They had their certain women in certain places who didn't mind their popping in for a day or two. It had been exciting when they were young. Nowadays, things were different. It was a hell of a way to live, too dangerous. He was relieved to have that phase of his life behind him, and he knew how lucky he'd been avoiding God knows what.

One evening he picked up one of her photo albums. The cover said, "Reach for the Stars." It was a compilation of photos, clippings, and awards. He learned a great deal about her that night. Her involvement with The Missing Link Foundation, her non-profit, was amazing. She had accomplished a lot as its executive director, and he knew that the album didn't tell the entire story.

The photos were revealing. She was on a tugboat with a child with the Statue of Liberty in the background. She was surrounded in another by a group of kids in wheelchairs in front of the Capitol Building in Washington, D.C. She was in Cinderella's carriage with three little girls in pink princess dresses. There was a picture of her dancing with a little tiny boy in a tuxedo as he smiled up at her.

She certainly didn't deserve whatever was going on in her body now. She had lost so much already, and he just didn't want her to lose herself. He didn't think she was the type just to give up. Still, he just didn't know.
~~~

CHAPTER 28

Celia dialed the phone and was about to hang up when Mimi answered and said, "Hello" loudly. Celia could hear she was out of breath.

"What's wrong? What happened?" Celia asked.

"Oh, nothing's wrong! I was working in the garden by the front door and I had to run around the back to get in, that's all."

Celia couldn't wait to tell her the good news. "Mimi, remember that woman I told you about, the one I keep bumping into?"

"Yes."

"I was at the Environmental Center yesterday and she just popped in."

"You're kidding. That had to be interesting."

"It was," Celia continued. "I found it very comfortable between us, but it was sad. Her uncle has just died and she's leaving today to go back to North Florida."

"That's too bad, I mean about her uncle. So you two hit it off?"

"Mimi, it seems like it went even deeper than that. I felt connected to her. Apparently, she felt the same way because she actually broke down and cried. She was very close to her uncle and you could tell she was devastated. She just fell into my arms in tears."

Mimi asked, "Who was her uncle?" She tried not to

gasp when she heard Celia say, "Walton Kendale." She gathered herself for a second and then she asked, "Did she tell you her name?"

"Yes, she did, as she was leaving. She said her name was Catherine DeLong."

Mimi's heart sank. She knew this day would come. Now she had to figure out how to handle it and when she should reveal the secrets to Celia. She was thinking, *"What were the chances of this happening?"* when Celia spoke.

"What were the chances of this happening?" Celia asked. "I mean our paths crossing twice and then the third time at the Environmental Center. Do you think it means anything?"

Mimi was lost for words.

~~~

Celia knew by her grandmother's voice that something wasn't right.

"Mimi, really, is something wrong?"

"No, dear; I'm a little winded from the dash from the garden," she lied. Her mind was going a hundred miles an hour. She had plenty of time to prepare for this, but she still couldn't predict how Celia would react to what she had to tell her.

"I have a luncheon, so I better get the mud off and figure out what to wear. You know, we ladies dress for each other."

"I'll call you later," said Celia, "when Olivia gets home from school." They said goodbye and Mimi went back outside. She sat on the glider in the garden.

"Oh dear," she said out loud.

~~~

Nyla had said she was madly in love with him and expected to marry him. The truth was he was some guy she met in a bar. She had been belligerent, coming home late, and then defensive whenever Mimi would ask her where she had been. They argued. One night, she didn't come home at all. Later, when she understood what a mess she'd gotten herself into, she confessed to her mother that she'd been extremely drunk and allowed the man at the bar to take her home. She awakened in his bed the next morning, quickly dressed, and snuck out, figuring she'd never see him again. Mimi quietly arranged for her to see a doctor. Nyla had brought it upon herself. It was her way of punishing herself for screwing up her life. She was the one responsible for the car accident. Nothing would bring back her friend, her friend who would never have a life. The doctor sent her for counseling, and with her mother's patience and understanding, she came to terms with her pregnancy. After Celia was born, Nyla made up the story about him being a prominent businessman who intended to do right by them.

Mimi and the counselor helped Nyla focus on preparing for the baby, but it was short-lived. She started spending more and more time sleeping, while the baby grew steadily inside of her. Miraculously, the day that Celia was born, Nyla seemed to turn a corner. She was attentive and beaming, and she truly loved being a mother. No one really saw the depth of the heartache she had suffered over the years. Somehow, the baby helped to diminish what she felt she had done to Nancy.

Shortly before Nyla quietly passed away in her sleep, she had consoled her mother. She told her, "Mom, I have regrets about some things I did, but the accident just happened. I couldn't stop it. I know I've been a burden to you at times. I felt so responsible for taking Nancy's life.

She shouldn't have died, and I felt even worse for her family. When I first got pregnant, I was ashamed, confused, and angry. Then when Celia started growing in me and I felt that first little flutter, I knew it was going to be okay. I had finally done something right. Someday, you will tell Celia the truth. I know you will find the perfect time. It will really be okay." A few days later, Nyla was gone.

~~~

Celia knew she had exactly one hour before Olivia got home from school as she pulled the car into her grandmother's driveway. Mimi was in the garden, pruning her roses, as Celia rounded the corner of the house.

"Some luncheon, huh? Did you forget to go?"

"Okay, so you caught me. What are you doing over here so late this afternoon?" Mimi asked.

"I wanted to see for myself whether you were okay. You sounded funny."

"I was rushing to get to the phone. I told you."

Celia wasn't convinced. Something else was going on.

"I'll get us something to drink if you have a minute?"

Mimi took off her gloves and placed them with her pruning shears on the patio table.

"I need to get something out of the freezer anyway. Let's just go on in."

Mimi's kitchen was a comfort to Celia. It was like an old familiar friend. It was where all their family gatherings took place. Mimi poured them each a glass of tea and took out a package of frozen meat. She placed it in a bowl on the drain board. They sat at the table where they could
~~~

look out into the garden from the bay window.

"Okay? So what exactly is going on?" Celia asked.

"It's nothing."

"I know it's something because you keep telling me it's nothing."

Mimi took a deep breath.

"It's about your mother, and it's about you too."

Celia listened intently as Mimi began as simply as she could with Nyla's unexpected pregnancy and Celia's birth. The gossip in this small town had been difficult. She talked about how Nyla had never quite forgiven herself for the accident, and how Celia had brought them so much joy, but especially to Nyla. Mimi grew very still with her hands in her lap, thinking.

"Celia, honey, there is no easy way to tell this. A few days before your mother died, she told me one day it would be important for you to know what I'm going to tell you. She said that I should tell you when it felt right. I don't think it will ever feel right, but you do deserve to know. What you do from here is your decision."

Celia didn't know what to expect. She sat up straighter in her chair, placing her feet square on the floor as if to brace for the worst.

"Your father wasn't some prominent businessman. He worked at a glass and home supply company. When his wife divorced him, he couldn't take being away from his two little girls. He started drinking even more heavily. About the same time, your mother was having her troubles. She had this boyfriend she found out was cheating on her, and she said she broke off the engagement. The truth was that they were never engaged. She went through a really deep depression. One night, she ended up at a bar and then she went off with this man. You were conceived from that encounter. What your mother wanted me to tell you is that your father was John, Walton's younger brother. That woman you have been crossing paths with, Walton Kendale's niece, well, she's really your half-sister. Catherine DeLong is your half-sister."

Celia felt a sudden flash of heat move completely through her body. Mimi was staring at her as if she were waiting for something to happen.

"Mimi. I don't understand why? Why didn't someone just tell me?"

"I don't know. People didn't talk about such things. I guess I felt like if I said it, the whole world would fall apart. Even now, even though it only took a few minutes, I feel sick to my stomach. I guess we were all afraid of the consequences."

Celia sat completely still, not saying a word. She didn't know exactly what to think at that moment.

"Why didn't you tell me this before? Why didn't my mother tell me? Why did she lie? Why was it such a secret?"

"I think your mother wanted you to believe that your father was someone important so you would become someone important. We tried to tell her that it didn't matter, but she wouldn't listen."

"What happened to him? My father?"

"Oh, after she divorced him, Catherine's mother, his ex-wife, remarried. He allowed the two girls to be adopted by their stepfather. They attended the best schools, lived a fairly charmed life."

"You didn't answer my question. What happened to him?"

"They said he drank himself to death. It was a long time ago, Celia."

"How do you know all this? Why didn't you just tell

me?"

"It wasn't my decision to tell you. She was your mother. It was all so hard. I kept track of them—Catherine and her sister Candace, I mean."

Celia wasn't quite sure what to think about all of it. She looked at her watch. "I have to go. Olivia will be coming home. I'll talk to you later."

She kissed Mimi on the cheek and dashed out the door. She was stunned. No wonder she had felt so connected to that woman. Something had been drawing Olivia to her, too. Celia pulled into her driveway. She needed time to let this all settle into her mind.

CHAPTER 29

Except for the periodic walk to the bathroom supported by Zane, Catherine barely moved. She spent every moment in her bed. He had prepared the chicken soup the day after she collapsed, and he had carefully spoon-fed her small amounts of the broth whenever she was alert enough to swallow. He'd kept the dogs downstairs, away, as much as possible.

Dr. Grant stopped in and told Zane, "Keep doing what you're doing. It may take a while before she actually starts to feel better. If you need more antibiotics, just have the pharmacy call my office."

Zane had to rely on Buck more than he wanted, but the circumstances of Catherine's illness overruled the feelings he had toward his friend right now. He tried to give their recent incident little credence, given the fact that Buck had most likely been shit-faced at the time. Buck had a bad habit of sticking his foot in his mouth when he'd consumed too much alcohol. This little lady was just too nice a person for Zane to allow Buck or anyone else to talk about her that way.

~~~

After he had closed the store, Buck came by with a load of feed and hay. They didn't say a word to each other. Buck drove through the gate at the barn and just started unloading and stacking the supplies. Zane joined him,
~~~

and as they threw up the last bale of hay, he turned to walk out the door. Buck reached out and grabbed him by the arm, spinning him back around.

"Zane, look man, we've been friends too long to do this. I'm really sorry. I mean it. I was screwed up the other night." He stuck his hand out for Zane.

Zane looked him straight in the eyes. "She's a nice woman. She's had a rough time. You got me into this with her, and then you start ragging on me about her. She hasn't even been here. You're acting stupid and it pisses me off." He turned and walked out through the barn doors, leaving Buck standing with his hand outstretched. Buck wiped it on his jeans, shrugged, and climbed into his truck.

Zane was at the gate, holding it open for him. Buck hung out the window of the truck. "Zane, why the hell is this getting to you so bad? Don't you think it got blown out of proportion? We've never been like this before. Come on, man."

"You hit a nerve. I've spent a lot of time here. I know some things about her that you don't. She goes through all this, and then she comes home sick. It made me really angry. She doesn't deserve it."

"Lighten up, man. This is me."

"Yeah, and this isn't some gal you picked up in some bar. This is a nice woman."

"I know that."

"I need to get out of here. I need to load up my horse and get out of here, but I can't leave her like this. No one has even called her. No one from her fucking family even called to check on her. It seems like no one even knows she exists. What do you think would have happened to her if I hadn't been here when she got home? Who would have known? It's nuts."

"Zane, I've said it before; you see things different than me. I skim the surface and you go deep. You end up in the worst situations, but you always come out the rose. You can handle this. What else can I say? You're the good guy, and I'm a little jealous. The booze gives me the lip service to act like a jerk. You should be used to it by now."

"You're right about the jerk part, but I don't want to be used to it. Plus, I'm a little edgy right now. Dr. Grant says it might be another week before she rallies. It's not just the fever. She may have had a mental collapse or something. I need to get back in there and check on her."

Buck stuck his hand out the truck window. Zane shook it. "Zane, don't run away from something that feels different. Promise me you won't leave unless it really feels like the thing to do. Promise me you'll talk to me before you go."

"I won't leave without saying goodbye to you, jack shit! You are such an idiot!" They both smiled.

Zane hadn't felt this intensity for a while now. He'd always known what to do and he did it. Something was boggling his brain this time. He hurried into the house as Buck drove away. He boiled some water for her tea and heated up a cup of soup. He was startled when he carried the tray into her room and didn't find her in the bed. When he heard water running, his heart started to pound.

"Catherine?"

"I'm in here. I'm fine. I'll be out in a second." He set the tray on her nightstand and stepped back out into the hallway. He heard her footsteps on the carpet.

"Zane, are you still up here? Come in, please."

She had on a pale pink robe; her hair was wet and hanging straight around her face.

"I'm alive!" she said. "That shower felt great." She sat down on the bed, fluffed up her pillows and positioned herself under the covers. "Wow, this really smells good. Thank you."

He was happy to hear the word "shower." He had pictured her underwater in the tub for a brief second. He picked up the tray and placed it over her legs and turned to leave.

"Don't go. This is the first time I've felt coherent so I want to talk to you. Please."

He sat in the chair next to her bed. He watched her hand shake as she sipped a few spoonfuls of soup and began, "Zane, thank you for everything. You have no idea. I'm so sorry about coming home sick yesterday and having to put you through this, but I think I was really tired. Thank you for taking care of me and for taking care of my farm for so long."

He was stunned. She had no clue that it wasn't yesterday and that almost two weeks had gone by. He sucked in a breath and said, "I need to tell you something before you go on. You didn't get back here yesterday. You have been sick for almost two weeks. Dr. Grant has been here three times."

Her face showed her confusion. "You mean I've been sick in this bed all that time? What happened to me?"

He watched her eyes darting around; he waited until she looked at him again.

"You got home on a Friday. You passed out in the kitchen moments after you arrived. Dr. Grant came that first night and then again the next morning. She was here again yesterday. This is Thursday. You'll be back here two weeks tomorrow."

"What's wrong with me?" She couldn't believe what she had just heard.

"Dr. Grant felt that you probably picked up some

bug at the hospital, plus you were suffering from exhaustion from all that you've been through. Your body shut down."

"What did you tell her?"

"She knew you had lost your husband. Then Buck and I told her you were down South taking care of your sick uncle and that he had just died."

Catherine rubbed her face with her hands. "I'm so out of it. Who took care of me, dressed me?"

"I did," he said quietly, looking at the floor.

When he looked up, she was staring at her bedspread, not making eye contact with him.

~~~

She was trying to digest it all. She couldn't. For two weeks, this stranger had been taking care of her, bathing her, changing her. She quickly glanced at Zane and then down at the tray. She didn't know what to say.

"How did you get the doctor to come to the house?" she asked.

"Oh, she lives right down the road. Buck called her the first night and she came right away."

"Honestly, Zane, I don't know who sent you, but I must have an angel looking over me." Her voice trailed off as she thought about her uncle and then James.

Her face revealed those heartsick places in her mind. Zane quickly said, "I never took care of anything but sick calves before this, ma'am." He was teasing her.

She smiled. "Well, I hope I was less trouble and more cooperative than a calf."

"At least you didn't moo. You were pretty quiet except for a few nights when you were saying sentences that didn't make much sense. I better get back to my
~~~

chores." He quickly stood and moved toward the hall.

She looked at him standing there in the doorway. He seemed so tall and handsome.

"Did my attorney send you checks? Did you get paid?"

"I really don't need the money, ma'am. I didn't cash the checks."

"That's ridiculous. You stayed here for months, and by the way, please call me 'Catherine.'"

"The way I look at it, I owe you. Do you know what it would have cost me to rent a place like this and then have my horse here on top of that?"

"Well, I'm not going to argue with you. You earned every bit of it." Her head had started to pound. "We can talk about it later."

The phone rang just as he was about to go out the back door. They picked it up at the same time and he heard her say, "Hello."

"Catherine, thank God. It's Roger. I'm just checking in. My God, I'm so glad to hear your voice." Zane quietly pushed the button to hang up the phone.

"Hi. I actually do need to talk to you, but not now. I've been really sick for a couple of weeks and Zane has been taking care of me."

"Jesus, Catherine, why didn't you call me? Who the hell is this Zane guy anyway?"

"You know, the man I hired to take care of the farm. You do remember, don't you? My uncle was very ill."

"Christ, Cath. I forgot about your uncle. Hell, how is he?"

Catherine felt the pain move in deep around her heart again. She put her hand up to her chest. "He died," she whispered.

"Oh, Jesus Christ, Catherine. I'm sorry. Oh shit, I'm

such a moron. No wonder you're so sick, sweetie. What do you need me to do?"

"Oh, no. It's all settled. He didn't have anything from a legal standpoint that needed to be done. The boys got everything. But Zane, he didn't cash the checks. That's what I needed to tell you. I want him to be paid." She rubbed her temple as the pain in her head increased.

"No problem, sweetie. I'll have my girl check on that for you. We'll figure something out. What else?"

There wasn't much she liked about Roger, especially the names he called her and the language he used.

"There's nothing you can do. I've discovered Zane's actually been taking care of me the past two weeks. I've been completely out of it."

"Who the hell is this guy? Do you know anything about him?"

"Yes, Buck, the guy from the feed store. He recommended him. They've been friends for years."

~~~

Roger didn't like what he was hearing one bit. He knew exactly who those two guys were and he knew Zane and Buck's connections. He had to figure out a way to get that son of a bitch out of her house.

"Shit, Catherine, I have to go. Something's come up. Babes, I'll call you later. Get better, okay?" He abruptly hung up.

Roger was pacing, slamming his fist into his palm. This was not good. Those sons of bitches were snooping around Catherine's house. The two bastards were right there in the same town as Catherine. How convenient? He had to get to the bottom of this.
~~~

~~~

Zane took off his wet parka in the mud room and slipped out of his boots. He raced upstairs. He was finished early with the chores because the horses had to stay in the barn out of the nasty weather. It was still pretty cold for the end of March. The water came down in sheets sideways, pushed by gale force winds. The rain soaked clear through to his skin. He needed to change and check on Catherine.

She was still weak and pale as a ghost, but managing to get herself back and forth to the bathroom. She was eating a little better and gaining strength.

He had missed the fact that Dr. Grant's truck was in the yard because of the rain, but overheard their conversation from the hallway.

Dr. Grant said, "I think you have finally turned the corner of your recovery. Start slowly, do a few stretches in the bed when you feel like it. It's going to take a while to come back."

"You have no idea how wonderful it was just to wash my hair."

"I know, but don't overdo it. I'll be happy when we don't see these dark circles under your eyes and you get some color back."

Dr. Grant excused herself and hurried down the stairs and out the front door.

~~~

Zane peeked into her room. She was curled around a pillow with her face away from the door. The dim morning light made it hard to see her. It had become so natural, this routine of his. He would really miss the house, the farm, the dogs, and yes, he would miss her.

He managed to squeeze in some productive phone calls preparing an agenda to head slowly west by staying at horse-friendly layovers.

He moved down the hall to his room, took a quick shower, and redressed in dry clothes. He would fix them both something nice because he was starving.

Her eyes opened as soon as she smelled the aroma of bacon; she smiled as he came in her door.

"Now, that's what I've been waiting for. A big smile on your face," he said.

"Trust me; this isn't hard to get used to, except for the part where I move like an old woman whenever I try to walk to the bathroom. My joints are stiff and sore from being in bed so long. My scalp is even sore."

"You look mighty fine this morning," he said. "Do you feel up to joining me downstairs?"

She raised her eyebrows. "I don't think...." He cut her off.

"I'll tote you down the stairs. I think I can handle it."

"Better yet, why don't you bring your breakfast upstairs and join me?" she asked.

"I was going to grab a quick bite. The horses are stuck in and I thought I would groom and clip them today. The weather has been just terrible."

"Oh," she said sounding rather disappointed. "Okay, then just leave me up here all alone again." She was pouting with her lower lip sticking out.

He gave in. "I'll be right back." He juggled a cutting board and her tray and headed back upstairs.

Once they were settled, she began to question him, "How long exactly have you known Buck? I hardly know anything about you two."

~~~

Carefully, choosing his words, Zane began their story. They had been friends since childhood, even before elementary school. Both of their families were ranchers, and they had attended the only school near their homes. The people in that area were close because they needed the support of each other, especially during the frequent hard winters. Sometimes, the kids couldn't make it to school because of the weather. There was little entertainment available, so they would have special parties and celebrations during the year to bring the kids and their families together. Of course, there were the rodeos. That's where the two of them had excelled. In the beginning, the boys had been started off on sheep, then steers, and finally, bucking broncos and bulls. It was friendly competition, and at the same time, expected of them. They were thrown up on a horse as soon as they were big enough to hang on.

Zane told her, "The first time I worked cows with my dad, I was only four years old. He snuck me out early one morning before my mother realized I was gone. She was furious at him for days. When we rode back in that evening, the ranch hands were chuckling. There I was asleep on my pony, but I was still hanging onto the saddle horn. My mother didn't speak to any of them for a week. I don't know what they did to get back in her good graces, but it took her a while before she would let me out of her sight." Zane liked the way she looked directly into his eyes when he talked and the way she listened to him. Loved the way he could read her expressions. He was glad she was feeling better.

"I'd best get these things out of your way and get back to my chores."
~~~

"Thank you, Zane. Thank you for all you've done for me. I don't know what would have happened to us if you hadn't been here. It's really amazing. I never would have met you if your truck hadn't broken down."

Zane slipped quietly out the door. Yeah, it had been a real twist of fate that had brought him to Florida in the first place.

CHAPTER 30

Roger Halvesord was frantic. Buck Matthews and Zane—what's his name—involved with Catherine—it was the worst possible scenario. Of all the places in the world she could have landed, she had to pick the same town as them. What the hell would she think if she found out the truth about James? She would be devastated, not to mention what she would think of him. He had to protect her, himself, keep her from finding out.

James had claimed he had stumbled onto the information by accident. His task had been to keep the company one step ahead of the competition. He was responsible to stay abreast of the competitor's research projects, their connections to the FDA, and keep his CEO's on top. As their number one man in that division, he had been well-respected and admired. He had a certain way about him that made people open up. Every company had its own people strategically placed, but James had an uncanny ability to uncover their new products and information without seeming underhanded or illegal. His latest tactics, however, had put a lot of key people in precarious situations. What James had known would have insured that some top executives ended up behind bars and then caused a huge domino effect across the country.

The authorities had suspected someone close to James had gained access to his computer and key files. Everything abruptly turned ugly. Some said James had been set up. Roger knew how James had been reeled in. They lured him with important information and then set up a meeting. That's where James had been headed when they made it look like an accident. Roger knew it was no "accident." The government quietly and methodically pursued its investigation. Roger cut a deal with them so Catherine would know nothing about it, including their final determination. He lied to Catherine when he gave her the settlement checks. One was from James' insurance and the other was from the U.S. Treasury. She had looked at the checks for a long time, astonished by the amounts, and then begun to question him. All Roger told her was not to ask and not to tell. The newspapers and television news bulletins stated simply that Robadeaux Pharmaceuticals was under investigation for illegal tactics involving top executives. They showed several men being led away in handcuffs trying to hide their faces. A separate story told about James' accident without connecting it in any way to that investigation.

The coroner's report showed severe burns over 90 percent of James' body, smoke asphyxiation, chest contusions, and a fractured skull. James' car had careened to the bottom of the ravine. His body was in very poor condition because the entire vehicle had been incinerated in the fire. They had said it launched off the road, and because of the impact, crushed his chest cavity and face. Roger appeared heroic in his push to determine the real cause of James' death, but the coroner told him it would be difficult and time-consuming to identify which trauma occurred first. In truth, the government didn't care.

Roger cleverly played the good guy. His only motive now was keeping Catherine from knowing the truth about him. With James out of the way, she was fair game. He told her he was pushing the investigation; that he would get to the bottom of what had really happened. He wanted her to think another car may have been involved, anything to steer her away from any suspicions about him.

Now these two sons of bitches were mixed up in her life. Was it some half-assed fluke that they were in the same town? He didn't think so, and he needed desperately to find out what the hell was going on. The last thing he wanted was for Catherine to find out he had been the one to lift the information from James' computer. They had lied to him. They had told him it was a simple task. No one would get hurt. Then they had told him what they were going to do to James. He had felt relieved, but at times, he felt like he should watch his own back. They told him nothing else was going to happen to anyone. But now, with Buck and Zane right there with her, he had to think something else was going on. It made him feel really uneasy.

He had been in Washington, D.C. when he read about them in the paper. There had been a retirement party. The photographs were carefully shot so they didn't reveal too much of their faces. *"Must be nice,"* he thought, *"going out in a blaze of glory after all the miserable things you've done."* They were called heroes. The paper said, "The incredible two worked undercover for years to bring down...." Blah, blah, blah. Now these ruthless bastards had somehow ended up with Catherine. What the hell? Roger pulled his suitcase off the shelf and began packing. He had to go see for himself. After all, hadn't he promised James that if anything happened to him, he would take care of her?

~~~
~~~

The only flight Roger could catch was from New York to Tampa. He called ahead and rented a car, heading immediately upon landing toward Gainesville. He would call Catherine when he got a little closer to give her a heads up. He would lie, tell her he was researching a case, and needed to visit the local university. She was easy. She had no reason to question him.

The scenery began to blend together. He couldn't figure out what in the hell had drawn her to such a place. It was mostly open spaces with a house scattered here and there. There was nothing to look at but green grass and an occasional cow. Clearly this was a place where there was nothing to do.

He pulled into a gas station, relieved himself, and peered at the map before heading out on the road again. He dialed Catherine's number. She answered rather weakly, sounding like she'd been asleep.

"Catherine, Hi. It's Roger. Listen, sweetie, I've got a case that requires me to do some research at the university there. I rented a car and I'm on the road headed toward you."

Catherine was surprised and also irritated by his unwelcome visit.

"Roger, I'm not in very good shape for company."

"I know, darling, but I need to see you and make sure you are all right."

She felt entrapped. "Okay. Just call when you get closer and I'll give you directions."

"I think I'll be there in about an hour. Bye, baby."

She hated him calling her anything, let alone "baby." She sat up, dangled her legs over the side of the bed, and thought about how disgusting he made her feel. She just didn't like him. She wanted to pull up the covers again; instead, she slowly walked into the closet to get dressed.

She stood in front of the mirror in the bathroom, looking at herself. She still looked pale and her clothes hung on her. She couldn't believe she was so thin.

Roger was one of those people who are mushy. Whenever he hugged her—something she truly tried to avoid—he felt like he was made of dough. His skin was pale and pastey looking. She felt like she would stick to him if she touched him. His hair was almost always stuck to his forehead. The first time she shook his hand, it was clammy and wet. There wasn't anything much to like about him, not even his voice. She couldn't describe it, but it wasn't pleasant. He seemed sleazy, untrustworthy. The worst was all the pet names he called her now that James was gone. He carried himself with such arrogance that it made her nauseated.

Catherine had been so distraught when James died she hadn't thought about Roger stepping in as James' representative and her legal counsel. Recently, when Hamilton's attorney friend, Preston, checked into her situation, he discovered that Roger had unscrupulously helped himself to a large chunk of her money. Roger had no idea that she was on to his indiscretions. She had also recently learned that very few people had anything favorable to say about him. Whenever she was near him, she instinctively wanted to back away. She felt an undercurrent like she was about to be sucked into something. She dreaded talking to him now, especially face to face. She didn't want him pulling up all the emotions she was trying to avoid.

~~~

Zane watched the navy blue Cadillac Escalade come
~~~

down the drive. He hurried to call the dogs onto the porch and closed the door just as Roger stepped out of the car. Zane knew instantly who he was. His photos were in the file Buck had given him. They had suspected him early in the investigation. So far, they didn't have the hard evidence they needed to nail him for James' death, but there was definitely a lot of finger pointing. The persistent problem was how to prove Roger was the one who had invaded James' computer and set up the meeting that killed him. Zane's hair stood up on the back of his neck as he walked toward Roger.

Roger and Zane eyeballed each other like two fighting cocks about to spur each other to death. You could cut the tension between them.

Zane spoke first. "May I help you with something?" He planned to keep Roger off guard by acting like he didn't know the bastard.

"I'm Roger Halvesord, Catherine's attorney and friend. I've come to see about her."

See about her my ass. Zane could feel his blood begin to boil.

"Wait here and I'll tell her." He left Roger standing in the yard. The dogs were making a horrible ruckus at the door, so Zane let them out.

Zane was startled when he heard Catherine's voice from the living room as he almost bolted up the stairs.

"So I guess he's arrived," she said softly. She was sitting in her armchair in the living room, dressed in a pale pink fuzzy sweater, jeans, and with her hair pulled back. She was holding a teacup. She had even put on a little makeup.

Zane said, "Wow. You're all dressed up and downstairs. Are you sure you're up to this?"

Catherine frowned. "Not really, but do I have a

choice? Let's see what he wants."

"I'll be close by if you need me."

As soon as Zane let the dogs out, they immediately surrounded Roger, barking and jumping at him. Even Scuz got involved in the mayhem. Roger was spinning around, trying to keep his eyes on all of them. He was yelling "Get away from me. Get. Get."

Zane made no attempt to stop them as he told Roger, "Catherine is in the living room. She will see you now." He watched Roger make his way through the dogs and up the back steps.

It took a minute for Roger's eyes to adjust to the dim light, and then he heard Catherine say, "I'm in here."

~~~

Catherine never understood James' friendship with Roger. They were at completely different ends of the spectrum. Whatever James was, Roger wasn't. She could never figure out what bound those two together. She knew they spoke on the phone, text messaged, and sent each other e-mails. They always introduced each other as "my college roommate" or "my college friend." Now, here was Roger still trying to be involved with James even after his death. He had always given her the creeps, but James had defended him anytime she was negative about him. Eventually, she learned not to say anything. She silently played dialogues in her head whenever she was forced to be around him.

"Hello, Roger. What is this about?"

She stayed seated in her chair as he hurried to her side. "My God, Catherine, what happened to you? You are so incredibly thin."

It was so typically Roger. He didn't have a clue what
~~~

was appropriate to say.

"I've been sick. Remember? I told you."

"Yes, I know. I was worried, but I would have been just scared to death if I'd actually seen how bad you look. And then you've had this complete stranger living with you."

Catherine cut him off. "He's not living with me. I wasn't even here. He was managing my farm."

Roger was irritating. He sat down on the couch near her chair and reached to pat her arm.

"Catherine, I wish I could stay and take care of you, but I can't. Let me hire you a nurse, a housekeeper. Maybe you should get this guy out of here."

She could read him. He wanted Zane out of the picture so he could continue to control her and James' affairs.

"What do you know about this guy anyway, Cath? What if he's been snooping around in your things?"

She was somewhat amused by his sudden concern over "her things."

She chose her words carefully. "Zane has been nothing but a perfect gentleman. I have complete confidence in him. He wouldn't do that."

"You don't know that. You know nothing about him." Roger's tone was becoming argumentative.

"I know what I've seen. He stepped right in at a moment's notice and did an outstanding job taking care of the farm and all my animals. Then, he stepped right up again to take care of me. I don't know what would have happened if he hadn't been here. No one else cared about me."

She was right and she knew he knew it.

"I think that you need...."

Catherine cut him off sharply, slightly projecting

her voice. "What do you know about what I need? What I need is to get my life back in order. I need to move away from the past and the things I can't do anything about." He was completely annoying her.

"Catherine, let me...."

"Listen to me, Roger. Zane can stay here as long as he likes, and I don't need you or your opinion about it."

The back door suddenly opened and Zane came in with his arms full of firewood.

"I thought I would freshen up the fire for you two so it would be all cozy while you talked." He winked at Catherine.

~~~

Roger could feel the blood creeping up into his already red face.

"Zane, that's so thoughtful of you. Thank you."

He was angry. He had promised James he would take care of Catherine, and she needed him to take care of her now more than ever. Instead, she was pushing him away. He didn't like it, and he didn't like the way she and Zane were acting. He saw Zane wink at her. He couldn't believe Catherine would allow this type of man into her house. It wasn't like her at all.

"Catherine, I need to discuss some personal matters with you. Is there some place where we can be alone?"

Zane finished at the fireplace, walked into the kitchen, and poured himself a cup of coffee. Roger watched him through the open doorway as he sat down at the table.

Zane called to Catherine, "Do you want me to let the dogs in?"
~~~

She tried not to laugh. "No, let them stay out until Roger leaves."

Roger was growing impatient. "Catherine, we really need to talk."

"Everything is fine, Roger. Zane is going to stay until I'm well."

"I don't like this one bit, Catherine, and I don't think James would like it either." He sounded rather aggressive.

Catherine straightened in her chair and stuck her chin out. "What did you say to me?"

"I said I don't think James would like this." He was glaring at her.

Roger was shocked at how fast she moved when Catherine jumped out of her chair and launched toward him. Before he could react, she was standing over him, right there where he sat. She put her hands on the armrests on either side of him and bent forward into his face.

"Roger, you need to be careful. You are about to overstep your bounds. As painful as this is for me, James isn't here anymore. I have to make some hard decisions. What I decide about Zane is none of your business."

Roger tried to lean back as she leaned a little farther into his face, glaring into his eyes; then she straightened up, turned, and walked into the kitchen. As she walked past Zane, she let her hand slide over his shoulders. She stood at the kitchen window, looking out toward the barn.

~ ~ ~

Catherine heard Roger sigh and get up. He walked to the back door and announced, "I'm leaving. I'll call you so we can speak privately. I understand that you aren't feeling well enough to talk right now. I'll give you a few days."

She didn't say a word in response as Roger looked at Zane, who gave him a cold solid look. Roger turned and went out the door. Catherine tried hard not to laugh as she watched him make his way through her dogs to his car.

"Zane, thank you. Thank you for making a difficult situation rather amusing."

Zane was smiling his wonderful smile. "You are welcome." She sat down at the table across from him.

"Now," she said, "quit the bullshit and tell me how you and Roger know each other?"

Her question was direct. He sat quietly for a minute then finally said, "Would you like to go see your horses? You haven't been outside in a long time, and you certainly are all dressed up with nowhere to go."

He was stalling. There was something nagging at her about them. She didn't like the way they had danced around each other. She had to get at the truth one way or another.

"Okay, it's pretty obvious that I'll have to postpone the inquiry, but it's only temporary."

"Grab a coat and your gloves, and I'll take you in my truck. I'll be back in a minute."

Catherine was happy when she found her gloves in her coat pocket. It was a convenient little trick her grandmother had taught her. It made her feel like she was near. *"Oh, Nanny, how I wish you were here with your good sense to help unravel my life."*

She was standing on the back steps when he pulled his truck around. He walked around his truck, just picked her up, and lifted her easily onto the seat and shut the door. At the barn, he gently stood her right on the concrete inside the doors.

"Your dogs sure are full of themselves today. They were cavorting around like a bunch of puppies. I nearly cracked up watching your friend." He slid the barn door shut behind them to keep them from coming in and knocking her down.

"He's not my friend and you know it. He was James' roommate, his best man, and attorney. That's all. He really means nothing to me."

"You enjoy looking at your babies while I throw them some more hay."

The barn was warm and smelled of fresh pine bedding. Everything was immaculate. The horses had their blankets on. She peeked in at Pearl. All four of her legs were wrapped.

"My gosh, the barn smells wonderful. How in the world do you manage?"

"All I have is time, ma'am." If he had been closer, she would have hit him. She really had to make him stop calling her that.

Catherine opened the tack room door and was startled to hear a soft "Meow!" A furry gray thing scurried to her and began rubbing on her leg. "What is this?" she asked, not expecting anyone to answer.

"I have to take her over to Buck and let him find her a home. The dogs had her cornered in the woodpile. She was tiny. I thought it was a possum. I didn't plan to keep her this long, but she sort of...." Catherine was rubbing the little kitten's face on its cheek.

"What's her name?"

"Oh, I didn't really name her since I didn't expect her to be here that long."

"Okay, then, what do you call her?"

He hesitated. "Sweetie. I've been calling her Sweetie. Silly, isn't it?"

"No, it isn't silly. I think you are the sweetie for saving her. And Trouble. You saved him too! You are really quite remarkable. Think of all you've done for us."

He reached over to pet the kitten and smiled at Catherine. "It was really no big deal."

"You are nothing but a little fluff, that's all." The kitten was purring as Catherine tucked her up inside her jacket.

Zane smiled. He couldn't help himself as he said, "There are two sweeties in the barn now."

CHAPTER 31

Zane was glad Catherine had finally emerged from her cocoon. He swore she'd gotten better as a result of letting out her anger at Roger Halvesord. Since then, he had watched her grow stronger every day. The rhythm of the farm was easy for them. Zane had everything organized for every day, and with the break in the weather, the old fences had been mended and new fences were in place. They began a new training schedule for several of the horses. He wanted her finally to focus on her breeding program, decide what bloodlines she wanted to secure, and determine the type of Arabians she wanted to produce. In the evenings, he watched her pour over magazines and books, learning everything she could in order to begin her new endeavor.

She tried to get Zane's opinion, but he watched her from a distance, trying hard to stay in neutral. After all, this was not any of his business. Tonight he intended to tell her he was leaving. He insisted on hiring help for the fence work, and he had handpicked two men through Buck. They would be competent to step in and help Catherine after he was gone.

He would talk to her after dinner and leave next Monday in the evening because there would be less traffic. Once he got out of Florida, he was never coming back. Telling her tonight would give her a week in case she had anything she wanted him to get done before he took off.

Even though she seemed much better, she hadn't said one word to him about James, her uncle, nothing, not even a whisper about Roger. It was as if she were dancing around her real life while trying to create a whole new one. He kept telling himself, *"Stay in neutral, old boy! Not yours to deal with. Stay in neutral."*

~~~

Catherine made sure all of her phone calls and personal business were handled when Zane was out of the house or late at night when he was asleep. She talked to her stepfather, and then contacted his attorney friend, Preston Rutledge, who wrote a polite but formal dismissal letter to Roger. Fortunately, his irate phone call came when Zane was in town. She'd already rehearsed what to say to him, but on her second attempt, he was involved in such a screaming tirade that she simply told him, "Please do not call here again" and hung up the phone.

His letter to her was long and handwritten as if it would have made a difference. He went on and on about how mistaken she was about him and how James must be "rolling over in his grave." He wrote in large red letters, "DO NOT TRUST, ZANE!"

The letter was followed by another phone call that included more yelling.

"You are an idiot to get involved with someone you don't even know. He murdered people in cold blood, for God's sake. There you are sleeping with him. He's a federal agent for Christ's sakes! He worked with the CIA."

She admirably held her ground.

"Listen, Roger, who do you think you are calling an idiot? Things aren't always what they seem. You of all people should know that with your own history. He's a
~~~

federal agent? He's killed people. God bless him for that."

If she'd had half a brain, she would have thrown his letter in the fire without reading it, but now at the very least, she had more information about Zane. So, he was a federal agent with the CIA! Did she really care? Should she care? Hadn't her whole life been spent on expectations? She had expected James to tell her the truth. She had expected James to be a part of her life forever. Those expectations disappeared like sand trickling through her fingers? Her life had become full of unexpected lies.

The back door opened and there was Zane with those blue eyes looking at her. He took off his hat and placed it on the hook by the back door, hung his flannel over the back of a kitchen chair, and ran his fingers through his hair.

"The house smells really good. What are you cooking?" he asked.

"It's a pot roast. After dinner, let's sit and talk. Will you fix a fire? Dinner is almost ready. Do you want to get cleaned up first? You have time."

"Sure, I can do that."

~~~

He swore sometimes she could read his mind. He needed to talk to her. He wanted to tell her he was leaving.

He finished with the fire and headed upstairs. He paid attention to his shaving, splashed on a little aftershave, dressed in his purple long-sleeved shirt and best pair of jeans. He even put on his good boots. He sat on the bed for a bit, looking out the window. It would be very hard to leave, harder still to tell her, but there was no point in lingering any longer. He would just do it. He needed to get on with it. There was no point in wishing
~~~

things could be different.

He had a knot in his stomach as he headed for the kitchen. This was not going to be easy.

~~~

As quietly as she could, she hurried upstairs and took a quick shower. She slipped into her purple dress that had been tucked in the far corner of her closet. The bodice was covered with delicate beadwork. It reminded her of her uncle. She even put on her boots, let her hair down, and placed a feather on the right side with a small barrette. She felt a little silly as she rushed back down the stairs.

When she heard him coming, she turned so she would be facing him. As they saw each other, they burst out laughing. Neither of them had expected this. Then, there was nothing but silence. He couldn't say a word because the lump in his throat made it impossible to speak. They stood for a moment still looking at each other.

"You sure do clean up good," she teased him.

"You're not too bad yourself. You look really nice tonight, Catherine."

"So, okay, then," she said as her face flushed, "let's eat. You light the candles."

She handed him matches and pointed toward the table. She placed the platter with the pot roast in the middle. The meat was surrounded with carrots and potatoes. She had made two nice salads in individual bowls. There were biscuits. He pulled out her chair for her, and when she was settled, he sat down. They were two people eating dinner, talking about nothing in particular, but inside, they were both dying with the anticipation of what they were about to say. They were
~~~

desperately trying to read each other, but neither one realized it.

~~~

Zane was hoping Catherine would be okay enough for him to leave. She looked radiant in the candlelight. Her features were beautiful with the pale light on her face. He loved her deep, dark gorgeous eyes, her soft lips. Her dark hair lay in curls around her neck. He thought she looked lovely in her purple dress. He couldn't stop looking at her.

~~~

Catherine searched Zane's face for any hint of what he was thinking. She hoped it would be easy when she asked him. Would he feel too pressured? Could he say yes?

~~~

It seemed like they ate forever. It seemed like it was over in a moment.

Catherine poured them each a cup of coffee and suggested they move into the living room. The dogs were settled and quiet. The fire had burned down and the light was perfect. Zane sat on the couch and she sat right next to him. She usually sat in her chair closer to the fire with her feet up on the stool. She placed her cup carefully on the table and turned to look straight into his eyes.

They both spoke at exactly the same time.

"I've decided I'm leaving next Monday."

"Will you stay here with me for a while?"

It felt like you could split the depth of the long silence. Everything stood deafeningly still.

She couldn't believe what she had heard. Her heart
~~~

was beating too fast. *He's leaving. He wants to go.*

He couldn't breathe. His chest felt like something heavy was sitting right in the middle of it. *My God, she wants me to—she wants me. She actually wants me to stay.*

She couldn't stand another moment of it. She just leaned toward him and tenderly kissed him. She heard him drop the coffee cup. She didn't care. Neither did he. He wrapped himself around her and kissed her long and hard.

~~~

Catherine awoke on the floor in front of the fire. The down comforter underneath her and the soft pillows behind her head felt like a cozy nest. A blanket was over her and he was beside her. They were both fully clothed. She was afraid to move. She didn't want to wake him. It didn't matter. He opened his eyes, reached up, touched her cheek, and softly kissed her.

Like two school kids, exploring each other, they couldn't stop kissing. They played with each other's fingers. He pulled off her boots and rubbed her feet. He played with her hair, blew in her ear. They melted slowly and comfortably into each other.

In the midst of it all, he whispered softly to her, "I want to savor every moment of this. I want to slow it down and let us find each other. For me, it began the morning my truck broke down and you came to pick up Trouble and walked out of the mist. I want to enjoy every step through this dream."

"It happened for me the moment you grinned at me, and I saw those big blue eyes. I guess I had to be sick so long, so you wouldn't leave me."
~~~

"You were completely delirious." He was grinning.

"You can call it whatever you want, but even in my delirium, I knew I should keep you."

"Hell of a way to get a man, by nearly dying."

She kissed him again and again. "Thank you for taking such good care of us. And thank you for staying."

"Now wait just a minute here! I never said I would stay. You kissed me before I could say a word."

CHAPTER 32

Roger was so furious his face was blood red. He threw a book across the room just as his secretary knocked and started to open the door. She heard something slam into the wood and peeked inside.

"Okay if I come in?" she asked sheepishly.

Roger motioned for her to come in. She bent over, picked up the book, and began folding down some of the crumpled pages.

"Are we having a bad day?" she asked.

"I'm not even going to tell you," he said. He didn't even look at her.

~~~

He was certainly not going to tell his secretary anything. He'd been in a foul mood ever since Catherine's new attorney had "fired" him. He knew the entire office was walking on eggshells all week because of his attitude. Yes, he had taken a nice portion of Catherine's settlement. That's how he had bought the fancy new car he'd been sporting around in. He'd given his staff a small raise to thank them for their work. Now, he had been dismissed. He had gone berserk. A lot more was going on than money; that's why he had been ranting for days. Just moments before his secretary entered, he had been on the phone.

"Who the hell does he think he is?" he had shouted
~~~

into the phone. "This could get messy. If she finds out about James, this could really blow up on us."

He had heard the secretary coming and quickly said, "I'll call you back" and hung up the phone, but not without throwing the book at the door.

"Don't mind me. I'll be fine. It's a little setback. We will get new clients, new cases. They always present themselves. It's usually slow this time of year anyway." He didn't know if he were lying to her or himself.

He glanced up at her, "Okay, back to work we go. What's my agenda for today?"

She handed him the book she was holding.

"Except for an eleven o'clock conference, you are all clear." That was not what he wanted to hear.

"Here's the drill. Go through the files for the last six months and make me a list. Give me names, phone numbers, the type of case. I'll make some calls. Oh, and write down the opposing attorney's name and phone number too."

He watched as she turned and walked out.

"Close my door, please."

He knew they were in trouble. They had never had to peruse their files and try to drum up business. His last partner had pulled out after the first year and things had been steadily going downhill until Catherine's settlement had saved them. But he'd gone crazy with the money— trips, the car, expensive girlfriends. Still, he wasn't going to go down like a sinking ship. He would figure out a way to salvage this.

Roger beat his fists on the desk. "I'll show these stupid bastards."

CHAPTER 33

Zane was glad Catherine was finally enjoying herself. He couldn't remember ever laughing this much. Three weeks ago today, they had admitted they had feelings for each other. Now it felt like they were steadily moving toward each other.

He was glad she had accepted his idea to keep it slow, just in case, but he knew they were both hungry for the intimacy. He found himself spending a lot of time imagining what it was going to be like when they finally had that moment together.

He had decided it was best to be cautious because at some point soon he would have to tell her about James' death and also what he knew about Roger's involvement. Zane hoped she wouldn't feel like he had betrayed her. Whatever her reaction, he was prepared to deal with it. His goal was to manage the information in such a way that she would understand his position. That was one of the reasons he had decided to slow everything down. If they moved into an intimate relationship, it might get complicated. What if she turned on him because of the truth about James? She would never forgive herself for allowing him to do that to her. On the other hand, if she understood his situation and accepted what he told her and still cared about him, it would make it that much sweeter when they took it to the next level. It sounded logical in his head, but when he was kissing her, when he was lying next to her, it was nearly impossible to stop. He had to shake himself back to reality on more than one occasion. It was getting harder to control. That was why he had to bite the bullet and tell her soon. He was spending entirely too much time fantasizing about her. He wanted to stop thinking about her and be with her.

He had driven to town to talk to Buck. Their friendship was strained because of the tiff they'd had, but Buck had finally conceded. "I guess if I have to give up all hopes of getting that girl, I would rather lose to you." He had punched Zane on the shoulder and said, "So, okay, you win!" He never said a word about his situation with Deb Albom.

Zane said, "I may end up the loser too if it doesn't go well when I tell her."

"She's an intelligent lady. I wonder if she doesn't already suspect more than you think. You know, it may be the ostrich syndrome. If you don't look, you won't see! Good luck, man!"

They shook hands and gave each other a half-hearted hug.

"Buck, this woman means a lot to me. I have never felt this way in my entire life."

"I know," Buck said. "I can see it in you. Now go and get her."

Zane climbed into his truck, tipped his gray felt hat to his friend, and backed out.

"God, please let him get his lady," Buck whispered to himself. He did a little dance with a couple of thrusts at the end. "Whooppeeee! Ride her cowboy!" he shouted, then quickly glanced around, hoping no one had seen him.

~~~
~~~

Catherine was reading on the porch when Zane drove into the driveway. The dogs barked happily as they vigorously wagged their tails to greet him.

"It was so nice I decided to sit outdoors," she said.

He sat in the rocker next to her, silently gathering his courage.

"Catherine, I don't know when will be a good time to tell you this, but I need to explain some things to you. I might as well go for broke right now."

She saw the deep look in his eye and the furrow in his brow. Her heart picked up its pace and her face felt flushed. She wanted to be brave.

"What is it? Have you decided to leave after all?"

He reached over and took her hand, "No, no. I don't want to leave you, not ever, but after you hear what I am about to tell you, you may not want me here."

She was scared and she felt her heart skip a beat.

"Tell me. Please, just tell me." She was searching his face.

"I swear, I am not telling you this to hurt you. I have given this a lot of thought. I've rehearsed this conversation with you for a long time. I've been just dreading it. I feel like I'm in a no-win situation." He took a deep breath. Her eyes were looking at him questioningly and right back into his eyes. He loved her face, her eyebrows, the twinkle in her eyes. He swallowed hard.

"Catherine, James was murdered. He was already dead when they shoved the car over the ravine. Roger knew about it but chose to keep it from you."

He searched her face for a clue of what she was feeling. She didn't say a word. He continued.

"James was involved in a specific project; when he said he had stumbled onto something, it was a lie. It was a way to divert attention away from what he was really working on. The corporate meltdown that involved a lot of CEO's had been somewhat of a decoy and had nothing to do with James' death. He was actually working on a specific drug. It was a lethal drug. Someone got access to his computer, all of his classified files—someone very close to him. The night he died, someone had called him and set him up. We are confident that it was Roger. Catherine, I know this is terrible for you, but I swear, it's the truth."

"Who is 'we'? You said 'we.' You said 'we are very confident that it was Roger.'"

"Buck and me." That was all she needed to hear. She didn't need to know there was a bigger network of people involved.

"How do you know all this? I mean Roger's letter said you were working with the government. Is that true?"

This was the first time he was hearing anything about a letter from Roger. He wondered what else she knew.

"We were. You know Buck and I were partners. Buck was contacted to check on you. I sort of stumbled into it when I decided to come here to say goodbye to him. I had no intention of coming here, but I did and that's when my truck broke down. You know the rest of the story."

He conveniently omitted the part about Buck and her computer. He didn't feel the need to disclose that Buck had been inside her house. He wasn't about to tell her that they thought she had been in danger. Not now.

"I know this is hard for you, but I wanted you to know before things between us went any further. I am trying to do this right. There were indictments, but that wasn't the real problem. The government covered up the leak and diverted the attention to keep the press off of James' death. I'm sure if you asked Roger, he'd have some contorted answer, but he had a significant role in this. I'm telling you because there is still an ongoing internal investigation. I didn't want you to learn this from someone else.

"Catherine, I'm so sorry. I've been thinking about this for a while now. It's why I wanted to slow things down. I didn't want you to hate me when this came out. If things had gone farther, I didn't want you to feel like you had been sleeping with someone you couldn't trust."

~~~

Catherine was attempting to process it all. She pulled her hand away from him and ran her fingers through her hair, pushing it back behind her ears away from her face. She just wasn't able to wrap her mind around it. She was afraid that if she started to speak, she would lose control. She stared out into the pasture and rocked.

She stopped rocking and stood up. Without a word she walked into her house, climbed the stairs, and went into her bedroom, closing the door behind her. She sat on the bed, rubbing her forehead.

She didn't feel mad at Zane. What had he done? She needed, wanted to be mad at Roger. She needed to be mad at James for not telling her what was really going on. Had she been that naïve? How had he gotten into this mess? He had told her he was a salesman for a pharmaceutical company. She had never doubted him. What had he been doing working on some lethal drug? Why hadn't the police questioned her? Why hadn't the government come to her? Roger, the snake, had known everything all along. He'd been the one who brought her the settlement checks and supposedly took care of
~~~

"everything" for her.

She wondered whether Zane knew more and just wasn't telling her. Right now, she really needed to talk to someone. Her family had surrounded her when James had died, but they had soon left and returned to their lives. The last calls she had made to her mother and Kiki were right before she had left her Uncle Walton's. No one had called her since she had returned to the farm. She was very much alone. She let herself fall back on the bed and beat her fists into it as she silently screamed. *This can't be happening. This just can't be happening.* Catherine couldn't hold back the tears.

CHAPTER 34

Celia was sitting at the kitchen table in her house, staring out the window at nothing at all. She couldn't get Catherine out of her mind. In fact, ever since her grandmother had told her they were half-sisters, Celia had spent quite a bit of time thinking about Catherine. Would Catherine accept her as her sister? Celia's grandmother tried to prepare her.

"Honey, not all people want to face these things. Some people don't like the complication of people they consider outsiders. It may be she just won't want that in her life."

Celia understood what Mimi was saying. After all, she and Catherine lived entirely different lives. Even so, Celia felt very connected to her newfound sister. Today, Celia had her on her mind more than ever.

~~~

Catherine was upstairs in her bedroom, fumbling through her purse, looking through her wallet. She knew the card was somewhere, but where?

"Dear Saint Anthony, please come around. Something is lost and cannot be found."

She was muttering. She unzipped the little pocket on the inside of her purse and felt inside. Relief! She had found the card. There was no reason she should call. There was no reason she shouldn't call either. After all,
~~~

hadn't she said, "I wrote my home number on the back, just in case." Catherine slowly dialed the number.

Celia jumped when the phone rang. Catherine was so focused on trying to pull herself together that Celia had already said, "Hello" twice. Catherine finally spoke.

"Hello. Oh, hello. I don't know if you'll remember me, but this is Catherine DeLong. You know, I visited the school."

"Catherine. Oh, Catherine. Hello. Of course, I know who you are. I've had you on my mind all day. Is something wrong?"

Catherine's heart was racing and she felt sick to her stomach. Why in the world had she dialed the number of this practically complete stranger?

"Catherine, are you there? Is something wrong?"

Catherine slowed her breathing a little as she tried to regain her composure. Then she lied.

"No, nothing is wrong. Everything is fine here. I had you on my mind all day, and then I came across your card."

"I'm so glad to hear from you. I'm glad everything is good," Celia said, knowing all the while something was terribly wrong.

"Yes, everything was remarkably fine on the farm when I got home."

"Did you need me for something? Did you want to talk?" Celia asked.

Catherine wanted to blurt everything out.

"Yes, yes, just talk. It's good to hear a woman's voice."

"Now, since you've called me," Celia said, trying to hold back her excitement, "I have something I'd like to tell you, if you have a little time."

"Yes, right now is a good time." Catherine sat down

on the bed and placed the card on the nightstand.

Celia drew in a good long breath, crossed herself, and sat down on the stool at the corner of the kitchen counter.

"Catherine, the day you came into the Center in Jensen, the day before you were leaving to go back to your farm, you told me your name. Before that we had been bumping into each other and I had even talked to my grandmother about it. First, we saw each other at the turnpike plaza, then the grocery store, and then the Environmental Center. At some point, you mentioned your Uncle Walton's name, and I was amazed because he had given so many things for our displays. I felt like we had a connection through him. It turns out we do, and it is far beyond the chance meetings and the connectedness I had felt. I'm taking a big risk here right now, but we have a lot more in common than you might think. Boy, this is harder to say than I thought. Catherine, it seems that you and I have the same father. According to my grandmother, Mimi, you and I are half-sisters. Our father is John, your Uncle Walton's brother."

Celia wasn't sure whether Catherine was still there until she heard her take a breath and thought she heard her crying. Celia felt a little breathless herself and her eyes were tearing up.

~~~

Catherine didn't know what to say. Today was one thing after another. Her brain was on overload. First, Zane had told her about James and Roger, and now she had just been told that she had another sister. She closed her eyes and waited for the spinning to stop.

"Celia, I don't know what to think about this,
~~~

really." Her brain was remembering scenes, and things she had said, and the day at the Center.

Catherine tried to breathe. "I'm at a loss for words right now. It's really pretty amazing news."

They sat in silence for too long, and then Catherine spoke.

"I guess that means that my little sister, Kiki, is your sister too. You know, she lives right in Jensen too." Catherine's mind was attempting to put it all together. Her life had certainly just become more complicated.

"It's okay, Catherine. Why don't you take a while to digest all this; then call me whenever you'd like."

~~~

Catherine jumped. She was dreaming. Her arms were reaching up into the air and she heard herself saying, "I've got you. I've got you." She was disoriented at first, but then she realized she was in her bedroom on the farm. The dream was puzzling. In it, she was with a chestnut horse and the horse was floating through the air falling. She tried to catch it. That's when she awoke with her arms trying to reach around the horse's neck and the words coming out of her mouth. She shook her head.

Catherine had no idea how long she'd been asleep. Zane had let her sleep. He was never invasive, not at all. She swore sometimes he read her mind. He stayed away when she needed some space, and he was right there when she, well, when she needed him. It was too bad she hadn't been more intuitive. Then she wouldn't have been shocked when she learned the truth about James. She wished that she had been more clued in about Celia, too. She didn't quite know what to do about her newfound half-sister and that situation. Her horseshoer, Phil, had
~~~

joked with her about his psychic friend. He had told Catherine, "If they are so psychic, why do they send out notices about their meetings? Why don't they all show up?" She admitted to him sometimes she felt very intuitive, but she was definitely not psychic. She suddenly wished she had been able to read James' mind? *Where was that crystal ball when you needed it?*

Catherine walked into the bathroom, washed her face, and stared into the mirror. *"God, Catherine, what do you do now?"* She wished the mirror would answer her, because at this particular moment, she didn't have a clue. She felt unsure and even a little unsafe. Had she been sleeping with the enemy? She hoped not. She wanted him to be different. She wanted desperately to be right about him.

She brushed her hair and headed downstairs. The house was eerily quiet and dark except for the kitchen nightlight and the sound of the clock ticking. She peered out the back door into the almost dark yard. The light over the barn illuminated the barn doors, but little else. She wondered whether Zane was even out there. She didn't know what to do. It was true. None of this was really his fault. Like he had said, he had fallen into the situation. At least that's what he had told her. Catherine wanted to believe him.

There was no evidence he had eaten anything. Surely he would come up to the house soon. She was standing at the stove with the kettle in her hand when the back door suddenly opened and the entourage of dogs piled in. Neither of them said a word. Zane walked past her, opened the refrigerator door, and stood looking inside. She couldn't stand the silence.

"Are you hungry?" she asked.

"Not really. I just need something in my stomach."

"I know what you mean." She had an ache in the pit of her stomach and around her heart.

"How does French toast sound?" He didn't answer, but she busied herself preparing things anyway. In no time, the griddle was warm and the French toast cooking. They were standing on a cliff neither of them was brave enough to plunge off.

~~~

The half-hearted dinner and idle conversation was difficult. She cleared the table. He rinsed the dishes and put them in the dishwasher. She watched him scrub the griddle, dry it and put it back in the cupboard. He was so easy to be with. She quickly turned and hurried up the stairs to her bedroom. She felt drained, empty and cold.

Catherine lay on her stomach on her bed and pulled her journal from the nightstand drawer. She hadn't written anything in it for a long time. She allowed the pages to flip open and she read where her eyes landed:

In the morning, I will be leaving to check on my uncle. I have to go, but I am in total turmoil over it. I am forced into a situation I have absolutely no control over. I have to depend on a total stranger to take care of my animals and live in my house. I am terrified. I have no other options. My uncle is ill and he needs me. I have to go.

Catherine wasn't sure she had any more control over her life now than she had then. A lot had happened since she had written those words. She walked into the hall and headed toward his room. His door was open. Zane was methodically folding his clothes and putting them into a green duffel bag.

"What are you doing?" She felt panicked.
~~~

"I can't complicate your life like this. You have enough to deal with."

"I don't understand."

"I understand," he said, taking hold of her arms and pulling her straight in front of him. "I understand that you have been through a lot. I understand that you need time to figure it all out. I don't want you making decisions while you are so distressed. Not decisions about us. You will be better off without my interference for a while. Trouble and I can stay at Buck's until I'm ready to head out."

She couldn't believe what she was hearing.

"You don't get it at all." She pulled her arms away from him. "Don't you see? I've fallen in love with you. I'm not in love with who I think you are or who you used to be. I'm in love with you, right here, right now, in this moment. I don't care what happened to me yesterday. I don't care what happened in your past. I only know that we're supposed to be together."

She stood away from him, wanting so badly to be in his arms. She didn't want to have to fight with him in order for him to stay. She wanted him to want to stay—to want to be with her.

"I love you," she said, looking deep into his eyes, hoping.

He looked away, staring at his hands, his feet, looking at the floor. It was a long time before he looked up. He stood there, looking at her without saying a thing.

"Zane, admit it. We are supposed to be together. Let me get through this. You said that you would be behind me or beside me, but either way, you would hold me up."

He was looking at her beautiful dark brown hair, her brown eyes. She had tears sitting on the bottom of her lids, ready to fall down her cheek with the next blink. He knew what he was about to lose. He reached up and touched her hair as she moved into his arms. She felt him slowly wrap his arms around her. She felt his skin against her cheek, his chest fill up with air. He breathed out slowly, warm across the top of her head. He slowly rubbed her back and then just kept holding her.

"Please let me love you. Don't shut me out, not now." She kissed his cheek, his neck, fumbled for the buttons on his shirt. She continued kissing him, from his chest up to his neck until she found his mouth so hungry for her. He couldn't restrain himself any more. His tongue found hers as she pulled him down onto his bed.

"Zane. Zane. It's okay. Let me love you."

It was slow and easy, each of them savoring every movement. They embraced everything they felt for each other and allowed it to happen. They lay holding each other as she watched a tear form at the corner of his eye and slide down his face. There would never be another moment in their lives like this one.

CHAPTER 35

They settled in, finding the daily chores easy and fulfilling. Now that everything was out in the open, they could explore each other. She hoped there would be no more secrets. They were both at a place in their lives where they really knew what they wanted. She was willing to let him protect her, but she was independent enough to make her own way. Still, she couldn't imagine her life without him.

They rode early in the morning down the dirt road that ran to the south of the farm. It led into a pine forest apparently planted long ago by someone who intended to cut the trees for profit. She hoped that would never happen. The towering canopy gave a peaceful, serene feeling. The trees were in straight rows as far as she could see.

Zane rode Trouble. She was on her gelding, Sundy. She didn't even know why she had bought him, except that he was well-trained and had a certain look in his eye. He was kind. He had a nice full body, and he wasn't a deadhead. He was fairly sensible, and she had learned to sit deep and expect his occasionally silly spook.

They made a nice contrast—the black stallion and the flea-bitten gray. They were as opposite in color as she and Zane were in their lives. The two of them rode silently, enjoying the woods and the day.

When they stopped their horses, she rode up

alongside him. "Are you having fun?" he asked. Before she could answer, he reached over and grabbed the back of her neck and pulled her closer and kissed her. When he let go of her, she swore she was seeing stars and the earth was spinning.

These two horses got along so well that Zane had started putting them out together. It was nice that Trouble had a companion, and Sundy seemed to love his newfound friend. They would often stand watching them as they grazed nose to nose in the pasture.

"We were meant to be together and so were they," she said, smiling that "I told you so" kind of smile.

"I'm only going to admit this once, and if you say I said it, I will adamantly deny it, but I was scared. That's not a word I allow in my vocabulary. I'm not afraid of anything. Nothing. But I was afraid I would mess this up and lose you."

"You're not going to lose me, unless you can't keep up," she shouted as she closed her legs on Sundy and took off in a quick, ground-covering canter. Zane and Trouble followed as they suddenly came out of the trees and into a beautiful sunlit hayfield. They knew it couldn't get any better than this.

~~~

Catherine sat at her desk in her office, making a half-hearted attempt at organizing her papers and sifting through bills. It felt as if she were replacing one stack for another as she shuffled through the mess. None of it seemed to be going anywhere. She let out a loud sigh and looked out the window. Perched in the tree right in front of her was a gray squirrel flipping his tail as if to get her attention. She hadn't really noticed him until now.
~~~

Suddenly, she remembered the Animal Wisdom Cards. She thought they might still be in one of her totes.

After rummaging around for about ten minutes, she found the right tote on the floor in the closet. She pulled the box out, took out the little book, and flipped to the index. She began reading softly out loud.

Squirrels bring us blessings for our journey in life. They are in constant motion reminding us that good things come from honest labor. They are also playful, friendly, and sociable. The lesson here may be to slow down, seek silence, or speak more slowly and distinctly. Squirrels are both skittish and trusting. This quality teaches us to trust each other in personal relationships, but to trust the Creator in all things. Squirrel energy reminds us to gather our energies for all the important tasks in life and prepare for the changes of the future.

She whispered softly, "*Good grief, Catherine. Like you could stand any more change.*" She continued to read:

Take no more than you need. Society is under the impression that everything is available for the taking. Lighten your load—get rid of thoughts, worries, pressures, stresses.

It all sounded very good. Maybe you had to practice it into perfection! The one thing that struck her the most was, "In moving too fast, have you taken on the erratic nature of Squirrel?"

She had to confess that not having an agenda presented its own set of problems. Recently, she had felt like nothing was getting done. Her life had been so out of control, unorganized, and, oh yes, she wasn't focused. Well, yes she was, maybe focused on Zane, and wasn't it okay to relax and enjoy yourself for a while?

The squirrel was gone when she looked up, but a black bird flew onto a branch near the feeder. He looked more like a crow than a raven. She flipped back to the index. Catherine didn't like what she read at first, that is, until she got to the part that said, "Crow is an omen of change. Crow lives in the void and is the power of the unknown. Do not try to figure out Crow. Something special is about to happen. Crow brings about newness and dispels disease or illness."

That pretty well summed up the last few months of her life. Catherine wanted more than anything to figure out some sort of balance. It felt like the puzzle was almost finished, but some of the pieces were missing, and a few just didn't fit.

The crow silently flew off the limb. She tucked the book back into the box, stuck the box back in the tote, and closed it in the closet again. *"One door closes and another...."*

~~~

Zane walked into the house with the mail. He placed it on the kitchen table and called out to Catherine, who was sitting in the living room. "There's a notice here about a certified package. You have to pick it up in town at the post office."

"I wonder what that could be."

"I would pick it up for you, but you have to sign for it." Certified mail always preceded a problem in his life. Maybe Catherine would be lucky.

"Well, I guess we can swing into town and pick it up," she said. "Let me get my purse."

They drove silently toward town. Catherine enjoyed
~~~

the countryside, the rolling hills, the tall trees just beginning to fill out with beautiful young green leaves. She was hoping for good news, but she had a sinking feeling.

The clerk at the counter was courteous, required her identification, handed the slip to her to sign, and then the envelope. She cringed as she recognized the return address. It was from her ex-attorney, Roger. She slowly walked back to Zane's truck. He looked at her, questioningly. She slumped into the front seat, wrinkled up her face, and said, "Yes, it's from Roger." She flipped the envelope onto the backseat. "I'll deal with it at the house. I'm not sure I want to open it."

Zane studied her. "I think you have to open it. You know, if only for curiosity's sake. I want to know what's in there. Don't you?"

"No, I don't. What if we end up with even more questions? It can't be good. Not coming from Roger. You know it's something about James. I just don't want to deal with that anymore. Not now."

"Here's the way I see it. Wouldn't it be better to know what it says? I think it's harder to face what you don't know sometimes than it is just to face what you need to know."

He was right. Catherine knew he was right. Not opening it would be worse. Still, she hated to ruin a perfectly good day.

<div style="text-align: center;">~~~</div>

She could have sworn she heard a rooster crow. She carefully snuck out of bed, hesitating for a moment to look at Zane as he slept. She crept down the stairs, quietly motioning to the dogs to stay as she headed to her office. She really wanted everything to be okay between them—no secrets, but she'd put off opening the envelope last night, waiting for an opportunity to be alone. She made herself a glass of warm milk and then slid the sharp edge of the scissors down the end of the package and pulled out the pages. She settled into the green cozy chair. Three and a half hours later, she got up from the chair and threw the papers on her desk. It was almost nine in the morning.

Whatever Roger had expected to accomplish wasn't going to happen. She looked out the kitchen window as Zane strolled from the barn toward the house. The dogs were happily following him.

"Good morning!" she said as Zane took off his hat and hung it on a hook by the door.

"Good morning, yourself!" he said back to her. Catherine walked over to meet him as the dogs surrounded her. She petted a few eager heads and then picked up Friskie, who began vigorously licking her face. She held him in her arm and leaned forward to kiss Zane.

"I've been up since five o'clock, reading Roger's papers, musing over the report."

"I know. That's why I left you alone."

"Thank you. I didn't really know what to expect."

"And?" he asked.

"There's nothing I didn't already know or suspect. James was murdered because of what he knew. They thought they had to kill him before the wrong people got his information, but they were too late. The report said he notified the appropriate people about his concerns, and then they used him for collateral damage. They could have saved him, protected him, but instead, they let them kill him."

"It must be very upsetting to you. I'm so sorry." He was running his fingers up and down the back of her arm.

"I'm trying hard not to let it upset me. I can't

change what happened. He made his choices. He had to know the extent of the danger. What hurts the most is he lied and he didn't trust me."

"Catherine, maybe he didn't want you to know in order to protect you."

"But it seems like he didn't care about anyone. It wasn't just about me. A lot of people were arrested. Dear God, it just never occurred to me how many people he involved. When did I become so naïve?"

Zane took her into his arms again. "You're not. How could you possibly know? People like James are very good at what they do. They play a very deceitful game. As far as the people arrested, the government wanted those people out of the way. You can't know. They may have had another agenda."

"What else do you know about all this?" she asked.

"I know that they wanted to protect you from any danger. That's it. There isn't anything else to know." He chose his words carefully and lied. "If I thought there was anything else you should know, don't you think I would tell you? It's okay now."

Catherine was ready for it to be over. Tears began to stream down her face.

"It is over, isn't it?" she asked.

"It's as over as it's going to be." He wanted it to be true for her sake. He kissed her tenderly, then reached up and wiped a tear from her cheek.

"I want to enjoy the farm and you. I don't want to think about anything else. Not James and certainly not Roger. When I bought this place, I thought it would be special. I knew that something would happen here. I didn't think it would get so complicated."

"It won't be anymore. I promise." If only it would be that easy.

Catherine walked over to look out the kitchen window at the land, her land. Buying this place had been a good decision, even if it had come from terrible circumstances. She smiled as she moved across the room and back into Zane's arms.

To be continued....

About <u>Linda Kendall McLendon</u>

Linda Kendall McLendon is well qualified to write a dynamic story with extensive experience in the medical/legal world and 40 years in the equestrian business and service-oriented community outreach. As Founder and Executive Director of a therapeutic riding program, she developed grant writing skills as a means to fund the programs. Featured in numerous newspaper articles and television newscasts, including a segment on Good Life TV of New York, Linda was awarded American Riding Instructor Certification Program 1998 Instructor of the Year and later the horse, Black Willie Moon, was Horse of the Year.

Nominated by Soroptimist International of Stuart for the 22nd annual "Women of Distinction" award, Past President of Twin Rivers Saddle Club, former leader of the local 4-H Horsemanship Program, she has been a member of the North American Riding for the Handicapped Association, the American Hippotherapy Association, the Equine Facilitated Mental Health Association, and the American Riding Instructors Association. Linda, an almost life-long resident of South Florida, enjoys her small ranch, numerous horses and critters, and a life-style that is far removed from the beatin' path.

REVIEW

Unintended Lies
Linda Kendall McLendon

Author, Linda McLendon does an excellent job of creating likeable, believable characters, showing us their fears and flaws, as well as their resilience, while allowing us to join them every step of the way as they discover new aspects of themselves. I couldn't help but like Buck despite his somewhat sexist way of thinking, and I admired how Zane would stand up for Catherine whenever Buck crossed the line. Zane is a true gentleman and the kind of protector every lady would wish for when sick or vulnerable. Even the deathbed scenes with Catherine's uncle left me unwilling to put the book down because I identified with and liked her so much that I was willing to accompany her even when her journey was painful. "Unintended Lies" is a true page-turner of a novel, and if I'd had time, I would have read it all in one sitting.

Secrets, and Romance Make for a True Page-Turner
 Tyler R. Tichelaar, Ph.D. and author of the award-winning *Narrow Lives*